PRAISE FOR

WICKED HOUR

"Elisa is a fierce and endearing heroine readers will root for. This urban fantasy is a treat." —*Publishers Weekly*

"Readers of the original Chicagoland Vampires series will enjoy Elisa, and fans of Faith Hunter's Jane Yellowrock series will appreciate the struggle between Elisa and the monster hidden within her." —*Booklist*

"Fans introduced to the new generation of Chicagoland vampires will find even more excitement, supernatural politics, and colorful characters in the second in the series." —*Library Journal*

"Chloe Neill delivers yet another phenomenal urban fantasy tale. . . . A must-read author for urban fantasy fans."
—Fresh Fiction

PRAISE FOR

WILD HUNGER

"*Wild Hunger* is a great start to this spin-off series, with plenty of action, political intrigue, [and] chemistry between the main characters, and I already can't wait for more."
—Booklovers for Life

"Neill's storytelling takes you along for a wonderful ride full of great characters, effortless description, and imaginative magic."
—*Galaxy's Edge*

"It's a great spin-off for Neill, and promises a long story arc . . . and some serious romance for the future."
—Kings River Life Magazine

SHADOWED STEEL

An Heirs of Chicagoland Novel

CHLOE NEILL

BERKLEY
New York

BERKLEY

An imprint of Penguin Random House LLC

penguinrandomhouse.com

Library of Congress Cataloging-in-Publication Data

Names: Neill, Chloe, author.
Title: Shadowed steel / Chloe Neill.
Description: First edition. | New York: Berkley, 2021. |
Series: An heirs of Chicagoland novel; 3
Identifiers: LCCN 2020052772 (print) | LCCN 2020052773 (ebook) |
ISBN 9780593102626 (trade paperback) | ISBN 9780593102633 (ebook)
Subjects: GSAFD: Horror fiction. | Suspense fiction.
Classification: LCC PS3614.E4432 S53 2021 (print) |
LCC PS3614.E4432 (ebook) | DDC 813/.6—dc23
LC record available at https://lccn.loc.gov/2020052772
LC ebook record available at https://lccn.loc.gov/2020052773

First Edition: May 2021

Printed in the United States of America

1st Printing

"*Kindness can be very hard. We are vulnerable when we are kind, when we believe the best of others and offer them the best of ourselves in return. But that vulnerability makes kindness wonderful. It makes kindness brave.*"
—ETHAN SULLIVAN

"*It was still my crayon.*"
—ELISA SULLIVAN, AGE 7

"*You're still a brat.*"
—CONNOR KEENE, AGE 10

SHADOWED STEEL

ONE

An ill wind moves through Chicago," Lulu said, sniffing the air.

"It's not an ill wind," I said. But I stared down at the mal-formed lump of sickly gray dough currently spreading across the sheet pan and admitted to myself I didn't have much room to argue.

"It worked in Paris," I muttered, frowning as I mentally re-traced my steps. Measure the ingredients. Add the sourdough starter. Knead, rise, shape, proof.

Lulu Bell, the thoroughly anti-magic daughter of two sorcerers and my best friend, moved into the kitchen area of the Near North loft she was letting me share, and looked down at the lump.

"But not in Chicago." She patted my shoulder. "Maybe you could try something else."

By "something else," she meant hobbies—fun, stress-relieving activities meant to give me an outlet other than coffee, katanas, and, since I'd returned to Chicago from my stint in France, su-pernatural politics. The latter was partly the fault of my temp job at the city's supernatural Ombudsman's office, the OMB, and partly because I was a vampire. We were dramatic sorts.

And maybe because of that, the Great Hobby Search had not been a success. Baking bread was only my latest and not-greatest attempt. We had a half dozen succulents on the window ledge that had gone either mushy or crispy, a pyramid of tangled yarn, and an array of glass vials and jars, sellers of which had promised me the best coffee experience of my life. Lulu now used them to store paintbrushes, and I continued to buy cups from Leo's, which slung the best coffee in Chicago.

"We have an hour before everyone gets here. We can call someone and ask them to pick up bread. Maybe Connor can bring something from NAC."

Connor Keene was the crown prince of the North American Central Pack of shapeshifters, which had a lucrative restaurant business.

"The only NAC goods Connor will bring is Alexei. And I'm not begging at the Pack's table."

Lulu ignored my mentioning Alexei Breckenridge. She found Connor's Packmate irritating; he had a crush on her, which made for interesting watching. "I'll bet it's not the first time you've begged a member of the Pack," she said with a wily grin.

In addition to being my occasional supplier of barbecue, Connor was also my boyfriend. Tall, built, with dark hair and blue eyes that usually carried a wolfish gleam. I'd seen him as a human and as a wolf. Both were impressive.

"Why do you need bread anyway?"

I walked to the trash can, dumped the bowl's contents inside. "I'm making sourdough crostini with burrata, arugula, and tomato jam. Or I was."

She just looked at me.

"What?" I put the bowl in the sink. "A potluck was your idea. 'Let's have people over,' you said. 'Just make your favorite food,' you said."

Lulu rolled her eyes. She opened the refrigerator, pointed to the shelves inside the door, where bottles of blood and caffè mocha were chilling. (In separate containers. Because mocha-flavored blood was a crime against vampirity.) "Your favorite food is not crostini or burrata or arugula or tomato jam. It's coffee and blood, in that order."

"I like other things," I protested. "And your favorite food is not deviled eggs, but that doesn't explain why there are three dozen percolating in the refrigerator." I wrinkled my nose in disgust. The person who'd decided the best way to eat boiled eggs was to mix the innards with relish and mayo should be drawn and quartered.

She plucked one from the tray before closing the door again. "They're just an experiment," she said, then looked at it with narrowed eyes, as if inspecting it.

I didn't believe her. But I watched her for a full minute, and she didn't so much as twitch. Fortunately, I only had to wait a little for the truth. "When the party starts, all will be revealed," I predicted, spreading my hands in a rainbow for dramatic effect.

"And speaking of deviled things," I murmured, as Eleanor of Aquitaine, Lulu's cat of sleek black fur and prickly attitude, sauntered toward us. She looked up at Lulu with tolerance, and at me with unconcealed disdain.

"Hello, devil cat."

"If you call her things like that, she'll pee in your shoes."

"Again."

"Again," Lulu acknowledged.

I'd tried being nice to her. I bought her catnip, made salmon for her dinner, read from a book of poetry I'd brought home from Paris, showed her the only legitimate version of *Pride and Prejudice* that Lulu and I acknowledged. (Sure, fans loved Harry Styles as Darcy, but that was just for the novelty. Colin Firth was the One and Only, thank you very much.) But she would have none of it. I was the third wheel. Maybe cats didn't like vampires. Or maybe she'd seen what so many others hadn't. That I wasn't just a vampire, or just the only vampire born instead of made.

Whatever the reason, she'd decided we were enemies.

I leaned down to look her in the eyes, smiled. "I'm going to dress you up like a cowgirl while you sleep. Then I'm going to take pictures and send them to the *Tribune*."

If her dirty looks were stakes, I'd have been deceased. But she hissed and ran away, conceding the ground. I called that a win.

"Peeing in your shoes will only be the beginning," Lulu said and popped the deviled egg into her mouth.

Boxed brownies substituted when bread failed. While they cooled on the stove, I pulled my wavy blond hair into a low braid and paired a flowy black sleeveless tank with dark, shimmery leggings and boots. I added dark mascara over green eyes and brilliant crimson lipstick to shine against my pale skin.

An hour later, the loft was full of chatter and humans and the bowls, pans, and bags of food brought by guests. Eleanor of Aquitaine lounged under the dining room table, hoping for scraps. Connor hadn't yet made an appearance, but the apparent winner of the deviled eggs sat on the ledge that fronted the wall of windows, each covered with plastic in a different color so they made a rainbow of light.

Mateo, Lulu's newish beau, was a glassblower who worked on big, expensive art pieces. He was muscled in the lean way of a person who rarely stopped moving, and had a tan complexion and a shorn head. His eyes were dark and deeply set beneath heavy brows, his lips generous, his jaw square. He chatted with some of his artsy friends—they were all angular clothes and hair—and Petra, another OMB friend. She was petite, with tan skin and dark hair and eyes, and was an aeromancer in her own right.

"Your glassblower seems cool," I said. Lulu and Mateo had been seeing each other for a few weeks, since we'd returned from a short trip to Minnesota. She'd traveled in an RV with my OMB colleagues to help deal with a Pack crisis. I wasn't sure if it was the trip, the company, or the magic, but she'd seemed sadder after returning, at least until she'd connected with Mateo.

"Yeah. He is. His friends are cool, too. Very . . . edgy."

"I haven't talked to them yet. But if you like them, I like them."

And since they were all human, I could break them like a twig if they hurt her. So that was a nice benefit.

The conversation in the loft quieted, and I instinctively glanced up to find the source of the change.

The source was a shifter. *My* shifter.

He'd emerged from the long hallway that led to the loft door, his body tough and strong. He wore jeans and a heathered NAC Industries henley that hugged muscle, and he carried a bottle of wine. His dark hair waved around a chiseled face punctuated by brilliant blue eyes and a mouth that was usually arranged into a self-assured grin. He had the bearing of a prince, the body of a god, and the ego to match both, all of it matched by his integrity, wit, and concern for his Pack.

And his eyes were fixed on me.

His mouth curved, and more than one human around me made little sounds of appreciation and lust. The prince, allowing the commoners to take a look.

"People look at him like he's a properly made baguette," Lulu whispered. "Ready to be devoured."

They did, and I couldn't blame them, given that my thoughts ran along the same lines. Minus the implicit insult to my bread-making skills.

"And then he looks at you," she continued, "like he's the big, bad wolf and you're the grandmother."

"That is a very disturbing analogy."

She held up her hands. "You're right. It was, and I take it back. I tried something out, it wasn't the right direction. I made a mistake."

Connor's best friend, Alexei, stepped in behind him. Alexei was just as tall and built, with dark blond hair and hazel eyes that scanned the room with suspicion. Alexei was the quiet and loyal sort. Unless he was harassing Lulu.

"Oh, good," Lulu said. "Alexei's here." There was conviction in the sarcasm, but joined by a spark in her eyes that I was glad to see.

I liked Alexei, and not just because he was loyal to Connor and the Pack. He and Lulu bickered like children, and he was pretty creative with the teasing. Never, I thought, crossing the line into inappropriate—not when she seemed to enjoy their sparring as much as he did. Still.

"You want me to tell him to knock it off?" I knew she could take care of herself, and usually had no qualms about telling off bullies. But, again, still . . .

"Please," she said and waved me off. "I can handle one puppy."

"He's not a wolf," I said. "He's a very big cat."

She just stared at me. "What?"

"The Breckenridges aren't wolves. They're panthers." I cocked my head at her. "I thought you knew that."

"I did not."

"Does it matter?"

"I don't know."

"Good evening," Connor said when they reached us, kissing me softly. Just a brush of his lips against mine. A hint and a promise. "Sorry we're late."

"You're right on time."

Literally and figuratively, I thought, still marveling that this boy I'd thought was conceited and obnoxious had grown into . . . well, still conceited. But much less obnoxious. As if he understood the line of my thoughts, he smiled widely. "We were both right on time."

Maybe a little obnoxious. But in the best possible way.

"Lulu," Connor said with a smile. "Thanks for having us over." He offered up the wine. "Hostess gift."

"Thank you," she said, taking it.

"A friend of mine has a vineyard near the Wisconsin border. It's supposed to be pretty good."

"How does it pair with deviled eggs?"

He blinked. "I have no idea and don't want one."

Lulu turned her gaze to Alexei. "I see you brought the tabby."

She'd made that switch quickly enough. Alexei just looked at her, and the challenge in his eyes was clear. *I'll take you on. In every possible way.*

Pink rose on her cheeks. "Go climb a tree."

"Go suck on a paintbrush."

"Weak," Lulu said, then strode off toward Mateo. He smiled as she approached, waved her closer, then added her to the conversation with Petra.

"Suck on a paintbrush?" I asked, looking back at Alexei with obvious pity.

"I haven't been able to come up with many artist-specific insults." And he was considerate enough not to use her magic—or decision not to practice it—against her. "Who's the human?"

"Date," I said.

Alexei snorted dubiously and wandered off toward the food. With, I belatedly realized, a bottle of vodka in hand. His hostess gift, I assumed.

"Was that disdain for Mateo, or the idea of her dating him?" I wondered.

"I think it was for the concept of her dating, generally. He knows she's not interested, but I think that's actually made it worse. The thrill of the chase, and all."

I gave him a speculative look. "Maybe I should have made you chase me harder. Or further."

His smile went feral, and I could actually hear girls sighing on

the other side of the room. "Try it," he said, a dare in his brilliantly blue eyes.

"You think you could catch me?"

This time, the kiss was possessive and consuming, and as arrogant as the dare had been.

"Elisa Sullivan," he said, smiling against my lips. "I'll always
catch you."

A throat was cleared. We turned our gazes, found Theo smiling
at us, raising a crusty loaf of bread in a paper envelope in greeting.
"I'm interrupting," he said with amused and unapologetic eyes.

Theo was a former cop who'd become my partner at the OMB.
He had dark brown skin and dark hair in short whirls, and hazel
eyes above a generous mouth.

"It's a party," Connor said. "Interruption is impossible."

But I narrowed my gaze at him. "Why did you bring bread?"

Theo blinked. "Because I like bread? And it's a party? And
Lulu said to bring something?"

"But did she specifically say to bring bread?"

Theo looked at Connor for help, but Connor just shrugged.

"I got nothing, man." He put an arm around my waist, kissed
my temple. "Why are you interrogating your partner over bread?"

I grunted. "It's a long story." A long, smelly story.

"Is it related to deviled eggs?" Connor asked.

"I feel like I've stepped into some kind of alternate universe,"
Theo said. "Are 'bread' and 'deviled eggs' code words for state
enemies or secret missions or anything else that would actually
make sense?"

"They are not," Connor said. "I think we're literally talking
about bread and deviled eggs. And it looks like those aren't the
only two options, so I'm going to take the bread"—he plucked it
from Theo's hand—"and put it with the rest of the food, and grab
myself something to eat, and you can discuss important Ombudsman things."

I'd taken the night off yesterday to help Lulu clean and prep the loft, so it was possible I'd missed drama. "Do you have any important Ombudsman things to discuss?"

He frowned, considered. "River nymphs fighting over the Chicago River boardwalk again."

"Old news," I said. "Pass."

He smirked. "Bank robbery by two of Claudia's fairies?"

Claudia was the queen of Chicago's band of rather mercenary fairies, including those who'd tried to magically shift Chicago into a facsimile of their green homeland.

"Getting warmer," I said. "How much did they take?"

"They tried for about two hundred pounds of gold bullion because, you know, they like the shiny. But with the weight, they didn't make it very far."

"Arrogant of them," I said. "What did Claudia have to say?"

"She said it was a 'noble effort.'"

I snorted. That sounded just like her. Like the other fairies, she had a great love of gems and jewelry.

"Bread has been delivered," Connor said, returning with three glasses of wine. "Meatballs have been devoured, and wine has been uncorked."

"He's handy," Theo said, taking a sip. "I'm not much of a wine drinker, but this isn't bad."

"He is," I agreed, and sipped. It wasn't bad. Dry, but bright. A good drink on a late summer day, as we all waited for fall to cool off the city.

"A toast," Theo said, raising his glass. "To friendships."

"You're such a dillhole," Lulu said to Alexei nearby.

"And to whatever that is," I said, and drank.

We talked and ate until midnight, then—because of a promise I'd made to our grouchy downstairs neighbor—did all that, but quieter. She lived two floors down and couldn't possibly have heard anything we did in the loft. But that had never stopped her from complaining.

When the calendar turned, the noise dropped, and so did the humans. They left first, with take-out containers of deviled eggs Lulu had managed to shove into their arms on the way out.

When I heard the knock on the door, I sighed in resignation.

"I swear, Mrs. Prohaska," I called out, as I strode toward it. "We're done. Everyone's gone." Well, most of them. The core group was still here—me and Lulu, Connor and Alexei, Theo and Petra. Mostly supernaturals. All friends and partners.

I opened the door, fully expecting to see the tiny woman and her dark, beady eyes. But it wasn't Mrs. Prohaska. There were three of them. Taller, stronger, and undoubtedly older.

Vampires, all in black. Two men and one woman, all of them pale skinned. None that I recognized.

I stood a little straighter, wished I was wearing my sword. And adjusted my body to block the doorway, just in case they made a move.

"Yes?" I asked, the word and my expression as mild as I could manage.

"Elisa Sullivan," said the one in the front.

I just looked at him, waited.

"We're from the Assembly of American Masters. It's time for you to answer for your crime."

TWO

My eyes silvered immediately, fury like a heated poison through my veins. The AAM was the ruling body of American vampires . . . and they weren't here for a friendly visit.

"I have committed no crime," I said, and each word was bitter.

But I knew why they were here, the violation they believed I'd committed.

I'd changed a human named Carlie into a vampire without authority or consent—the AAM's or hers—during that trip to Minnesota. But I'd done it to save her. Carlie was still in Minnesota, now living with the local vampire coven; that was the best place for her, but knowing that didn't ease the thorn of guilt lodged beneath my heart.

"We'd like to come in to discuss this matter."

"No," I said, not even bothering to consider the request. "You are not invited in."

Magic wouldn't keep them out; that was one of the vampire myths that wasn't true. It was a courtesy, and most were fastidious enough about rules to adhere to it. As if a second line of defense, I felt them move in behind me—my army of friends. Lulu and Connor took point.

"Is there a problem?" Connor asked. That the heir apparent of the North American Central Pack stood before them didn't seem to faze them at all. They'd probably researched me, uncovered the basics. But not everything.

A monster lived inside me. It was, or so I thought, a fragment of the singular magic that had allowed my mother to conceive me, as I was the first and only vampire to be born. My conception had been unexpected, facilitated by bonding magic Lulu's mother had created to trap a creature ravaging Chicago. I wasn't just uniquely born, but uniquely fused to a consciousness not my own—and one that only Connor knew about.

"There's no problem," I said, with more calm than I actually felt, and pushed down the monster's sudden perk of interest. "These vampires are going to say their piece and leave."

The vampire's eyes flashed silver, a sure sign of his flaring anger. But he could get in line behind me.

"Then I suppose we'll do this in the hallway," the vampire said with obvious disdain. "I'm Blake. This is Sloan, and Levi," he said, introducing the vampires beside him. "We are representatives of the Assembly's Compliance Bureau."

By tradition, vampires that weren't Masters used only their first names. Blake was the one talking. Sloan was the dark-haired female behind him on his right, Levi the blond-haired male behind and on his left. They all wore the same dark and fitted suits, although each with a different flourish. Sloan had a string of pearls; Levi had a rose tucked into his lapel. Blake wore a pendant on a leather thong. They looked official and posh in the way of vampires, who knew how to use fashion to intimidate.

"This will formally advise you that you have breached vampiric *Canon*, laws and regulations, by making a vampire without authority to do so and without the human's prior agreement," Blake said. "Your activities risked the exposure of the local coven, harm to the human, and danger to all vampires. You are summoned to appear before Bureau representatives at midnight tomorrow for adjudication. Grant Park."

"She saved someone's life," Lulu said.

"Carlie," I said, because the AAM knew her name by now. "Her name is Carlie, and she didn't deserve to die in someone else's fight."

Blake's expression stayed bland. "You broke the rules."

"Not the rules that matter," Lulu said.

Blake turned his chilly gaze to Lulu. "She broke *our* rules. She is a vampire, sorceress. You are not."

I shifted, putting myself between them. Sorceress was the path Lulu had purposefully not chosen, and she didn't like the reminder. Bickering wasn't going to help. Most important, I didn't want their anger directed at her.

"Who told you about Carlie?" I asked.

Blake's lips thinned. "A confidential informant."

More than a few candidates for that position, I thought ruefully, including the Minnesota Pack members still angry at our interference in their dysfunctional little community and the head of the vampire coven now sheltering Carlie, who hadn't been happy I'd made a vampire.

"I'm entitled to know their name."

"You aren't," Blake said with a smirk. "That's why it's confidential, particularly since they were doing a service to American vampires. You, of all people, should know better."

"Blake," Sloan said. "That's enough." She looked at me with what I thought was sympathy. But given who and what she was, I doubted her sincerity.

"At the meeting, you'll be able to tell your side of the story," she promised.

Also doubtful, I thought. "You've delivered your message," was all I said.

"Please formally acknowledge receipt of the summons."

I didn't like the way that sounded; vampires liked rules and bargains, and a formal acknowledgment sounded like something that would snap an obligation into place, magical or otherwise.

"I acknowledge you have attempted to issue a summons," I said, "but I do not agree to your terms. Grant Park is too public." And too large, and too difficult to secure, I added silently.

"What location do you propose?" Blake asked after a moment.

"I'll let you know."

Blake nodded, glanced at Sloan, who tapped her screen—the sleek devices that kept us connected to the world.

I felt a sudden pinch at my clavicle and looked down to find a small but glowing X across the bone. "You *marked* me." I scratched at the X, which did nothing.

"Magically tagged summons," Blake said, and he slid a glance to Lulu. "We have our own magical resources."

"When will it disappear?" I asked.

"After midnight tomorrow," Blake said. "When you show up at a mutually agreed location."

I cursed silently. "How do I contact you?"

They looked at me for a moment before my screen beeped. "Instructions," said Blake, and all three of them turned on their heels and left.

I closed the door. And locked it tight.

We all moved to the long windows and watched the street in silence, waiting until the three vampires had climbed into a black vehicle with tinted windows and driven away.

"Compliance Bureau?" Theo asked.

I shook my head. "I don't know anything about it. I've heard Nicole Heart is a stickler for rules and committees, so I guess this is one of them."

Heart, Master of Atlanta's Heart House, had been one of the Assembly's founders and was its leader. The AAM had replaced the Greenwich Presidium, Europe's controlling vampire body, when vampires in Chicago—led by Cadogan House, of which my father was Master—had pushed back against its dictatorial ways.

She'd barely beaten out my father in the vote to lead the organization; there'd been animosity between them in those early days, but time had faded those wounds. Or so I thought.

I regretted I hadn't given more attention to the details of their authority when I was at Cadogan House. But I'd had the privilege of being a child in a time of relative supernatural peace. The Assembly had been quiet in those years. But then fairies had attacked Chicago, and vampires had been at the forefront of the fight against them. That thrust us back—at arrow point—into the spotlight. Of course the Assembly's ears would have perked up. And I should have expected it. I should have planned for it.

I looked up, found Connor's gaze on mine. Strong, but seeking. "What are you thinking?" he asked.

"That I should have known this was going to happen. I knew there was a possibility after Minnesota. But it's been weeks. I thought they'd decided not to act on it."

There was a loud *crunch* across the room. We all looked up to find Alexei snapping into a celery stick. "Your parents are gone," he said and bit again.

"What?" I asked, trying to ignore that it sounded like he was crunching bones.

"They're in India, right?" Petra asked. "Visiting Amit Patel. I doubt it's a coincidence the Assembly showed up to accuse you of crimes against vampire when they're several continents away."

"I mean, your parents could just fly home," Lulu said. "They're not on a space station."

"Yeah," I said, "but we're talking about vampires. The AAM would see a strategic advantage, even if a temporary one, to their being out of Chicago. And they'd take it." The truth of it settled into my bones.

Alexei went into the kitchen, grabbed his gifted bottle of vodka and a shot glass. He brought them both to me, filled the cup, offered it. "Drink," he said. "You need this."

"I don't know about need," I said, but I downed it, winced. He hadn't splurged on the good stuff. But I said thanks and handed him back the glass.

"I'll take one of those," Lulu said and downed a shot. "Not often I find vampires in suits at the door."

"I'm sorry," I said.

"Not your fault." She coughed. "God, this is awful." She thrust the glass back at Alexei. "Next time, bring better."

"No," Alexei said with a grin, and took the bottle and glass to the couch.

We were a strange assemblage, but a bonded one. We'd fought fairies and feral monsters, suffered arrows and sword wounds and magically shifting landscapes and fireside battles. And we'd come through it as friends—the kind you could rely on for crappy vodka and excellent planning.

"Why did they come all this way?" Theo asked. "Surely the AAM doesn't have to approve every new vampire made."

"No. But 'regular' vampires aren't supposed to make them. And that's the kind of thing that threatens the ones in charge. They'll want to punish me."

"How?" Connor asked, voice grim.

"I'm honestly not sure. Give me demerits?"

"Are you taking this seriously?" Lulu asked, concern pulling down her brows.

"I am. And I'll deal with them." I looked down at my collarbone. "It doesn't look like I have much of a choice."

"It's a pretty simple spell," Lulu said.

We all looked at her, given she'd generally avoided any and all discussion of magic or its details, with surprise. "I knew a little about some basic spells, before . . ."

Before she turned away from magic completely, she meant. Before she learned her mother had, at least for a little while, been seduced by dark magic and become an enemy to Chicago.

"Do you know if they're right?" I asked. "About it disappearing?"

"If the spell was done correctly, yeah. Think of it as a little contract. You fulfill the terms, and the deal is done."

"And if she doesn't?" Connor asked. "What happens?"

"Depends on the sorcerer they had on speed dial. But it probably wouldn't feel very good."

"So she can't ghost the vampires, ha ha," Petra said.

"No. But I'd have to deal with them eventually. They aren't just going to walk away from this; admitting defeat is not something vampires do easily."

"Yes, we're aware of the stubbornness of the fanged," Connor said, managing to work a little exhaustion into his voice.

"So I'll meet them tomorrow night. And since they're vampires, I'll handle them the vampire way."

"With fancy clothes and arrogance and posturing?" Petra asked. There was no insult in the words, because she was absolutely right.

"Pretty much," I said.

"In that case, you're right about the location—it's best if you don't meet them in Grant Park," Theo said, leaning back against the refrigerator. "It's in the middle of the Loop and full of tourists. We don't want humans caught in the cross fire."

"Or cops watching us fight back," Alexei said with a smile.

"Preferably no fighting, wherever the location," I said. "But a place I choose."

"A place *we* choose," Theo said. "Some of your family members may be out of town. But not all of us."

"Hear, hear," Connor said. I squeezed his hand, had to fight back tears as I looked at them, my weird little family.

"Thanks," I said. "The floor is open for location suggestions."

"I'm on that," Petra said. She'd pulled out her screen and was scrolling. "I'll get back to you."

"Appreciate it."

"I'll advise the Pack," Connor said.

I frowned. "I don't want them in the middle of this."

He ignored that, typed something into his screen. And when he glanced up at me, his eyes were steady. "We're already in the middle of this; the Pack helped create this problem."

"Saving her was a decision I made," I insisted. "It was a choice, and I'd make the same one again."

"I know you would," Connor said, voice softer. "But that doesn't mean the Pack won't help as it can. If all else fails, we'll leave Chicago. Go to Memphis and enjoy blues and barbecue."

Memphis was the Pack's ancestral home. While I wouldn't have minded the blues or barbecue, I hoped it wouldn't come to that—when running away was my only viable option.

"I'll tell Yuen," Theo said and turned his attention to his screen. Roger Yuen was the actual Ombudsman, and our boss. "He'll want the CPD there in case things go south. But he'll coordinate with them to give you some room."

I nodded.

All but Lulu had pulled out screens now, all sending messages to protect, to rally, to defend. A strange assemblage, I thought again. But I was so lucky to have found them. "Thank you."

They all looked up at me.

"You're welcome," Theo said, understanding in his kind smile. "But I'm pretty sure you still owe me twenty for coffee."

We finished cleaning up the party and said goodbye to everyone but Connor.

Lulu gave me a hug. "We'll figure out a way through this. Maybe you aren't measuring the flour correctly."

"Funny." I pulled back, looked at her. "You have to be careful. I don't think they'll approach you, but I didn't think they'd show up at my door, either."

"I'll be careful. And it's my turn to add to the community collective mural, so I'll be around people all week."

Lulu was part of a volunteer group that painted murals in urban areas that needed care and brilliant colors. Even though she didn't live as a Sup, she kept supernatural hours. That meant even outdoor murals were painted at night, usually under the glow of work lights she'd picked up secondhand. She liked working at night, being awake in the relative quiet of sleeping Chicago. And she especially liked working through to dawn, when the colors began to shift and change as the sunlight rose and spread.

"Okay. If anything weird happens, let me know."

"You'll be the first I call." She went to her room, Eleanor of Aquitaine trotting behind, head and tail high.

When her door closed, Connor pulled me into his arms. I wrapped around him, breathed in sunshine and cologne and Pack. And breathed deeply for the first time in hours.

"Are you all right?" he asked.

"I'm fine. This is going to be a mess."

"It won't be the first one you've handled. But if I find out someone in Minnesota reported you, we're going to have some words."

I put a hand on his chest, felt his heart thud beneath my palm. "Don't take it out on the Pack. It was probably Ronan. He was furious when he discovered what I'd done." I thought we'd worked through some of that anger before I left Minnesota, when he realized I hadn't changed a human because I was spoiled and out of control. But it had only been a few weeks ago. Maybe something had festered, or gone wrong? It had been a few days since I'd checked on Carlie. I made a note to send her a message.

"So we assume the AAM didn't tell your parents what they're doing. Are you going to tell them?"

"No," I decided. "Not yet. I don't want them feeling like they have to fly to my rescue. And their being here would . . . complicate things."

"Would it?" Connor asked.

"I don't know exactly what the Compliance Bureau will want," I said, "but I'm guessing they want me in a House, under the authority of a Master. They'll want me to swear an oath."

"And your parents will want it to be Cadogan House," Connor finished.

I nodded. "They took it hard when I told them I didn't consider myself a Novitiate and didn't want to be. And if the AAM is pressuring me, that puts pressure on them, on Cadogan House." I blew out a breath. "I know they can't avoid all the blowback, but maybe the heat on them stays lower if they stay where they are."

"They can't be used against you," Connor said, and I felt the immediate relief that came from being understood.

"Yeah," I said. "Exactly. I understand why the AAM has rules," I continued. "I understand the need to protect against vampires who'd build their own armies. Humans would annihilate us all if it came to that."

"But that's not what this is," Connor said. "And if the rules can't be flexible in situations like this, they're bad rules." He paused. "And there's no way you'd consider taking an oath?"

I stepped back, putting space between us.

His eyes flashed. "A question," he said. "Not an accusation."

"I don't want to be owned by a House. This is pretty good evidence that it involves obeying rules I don't agree with."

"I've always said vampires are trouble."

"And yet, here you are."

"And yet," Connor said, lowering his mouth to mine. His kiss was warm and comforting, a reminder that I didn't stand alone. But its edges were sharp—desire and anger, both dangerously honed. Both reminders of what could be. What would be.

"I guess this means we'll be missing dinner tomorrow," he said.

"Dinner?" I asked, tilting my head at him. "What dinner?"

His expression went flat. "I was going to bring over Italian food. Chianti."

I winced. "I'm sorry. I totally forgot."

"That might be the first time a woman has forgotten about a rendezvous with me."

"You know what I like most about you? Your quiet and humble nature."

He gave me his cockiest smile—all self-assured confidence. "Also the first time anyone has said that."

"I bet. And again, I'm sorry. It would have been nice." And that was putting it mildly. Eating a microwaved burrito in a convenience store parking lot would have been nice with Connor. But meatballs and sauce and excellent wine? Delectable.

He put a hand at the back of my head, leaned in to kiss my forehead. "There will be other times, other meals. And as for my ego?" He leaned in, whispered, "I earned it."

And left me with a grin—and my pulse humming in my ears.

I closed the door, locked it, leaned against it. Flirting was an underrated art. Four years in Paris had taught me plenty, but I had nothing on the prince of wolves.

Now alone, I sat down on the hallway floor, stretched out my legs, closed my eyes. I let the monster stretch, unfurl the dark wings of its anger. It didn't exactly consider me a friend, but I was at least an ally. And it didn't care for its vehicle being threatened by outsiders.

When it had burned away some of the rage, I rose again, steadying myself with a hand against the wall. Its retreat was a vacuum, and it left me light-headed. And I'd have sworn I'd felt its pitying humor.

"Hilarious," I muttered. "You try controlling two consciousnesses in a single body and see how well you do."

Maybe I imagined it. But I'd have sworn its answer was *Let me try.*

I wasn't yet tired—exhausted, but not tired—so I drank a bottle of blood, tidied up the rest of the loft, and flipped through the mail that had arrived earlier that day. And found a square envelope with my name printed on it in tidy block letters. No return address. Wedding invitation, I guessed, because why else would someone send something by hand when screens could transmit messages immediately.

I slipped a thumb under the seal, pulled out the folded paper, and read.

Elisa:

I was so glad you decided to stay in Chicago instead of returning to Paris; let the European vampires deal with their own problems. You are beautiful and strong and an example of what vampires should be. I know we'll meet in the future and have so much to talk about.

Until then, I am,

—A friend

That was it. Just those words written in tidy letters in the middle of a sheet of white paper.

It wasn't the first weird note I'd received and wouldn't be the last. Humans wrote me because they wanted to become vampires—or date one. Vampires wrote me because they wanted connections to my parents. Or, apparently, they came to my door and demanded my obedience.

We'd see who'd win.

THREE

Sleep. Blood. Yoga. I needed all three before my date with destiny.

I'd accomplished the first, and could thank the sun and resulting unconsciousness for that. Yoga I would manage on a mat I'd squeezed into my bedroom, as it was the only way I'd found to keep Eleanor of Aquitaine from intentionally trying to knock me over.

I'd done yoga for years, not just because I liked the results, but because the practice was the healthiest coping mechanism I'd managed to find for the monster. I hadn't planned on sharing my body, but I'd accepted the necessity of accepting it.

I'd started katana training again, something I hadn't done since my Paris graduation, partly to stay in shape for my Ombudsman work, and partly because the monster needed the outlet. But katana training didn't soothe it, and tequila, while delicious in small doses, wasn't nearly as effective at slowing my mind, or cooling its temper. Yoga had done wonders. And as long as the monster had an outlet for its energy and rather impressive rage, it let me stay in control.

It didn't look through me with crimson eyes.

That was the other reason I kept the monster hidden. Because it wouldn't be a nightmare just for my mother, but for everyone else, as well. A demon's red eyes. A leviathan's power.

I defied explanation. I was *other*.

"All right," I said quietly, closing my eyes as I settled on the mat. "Your turn."

It shifted within me, the movement still vaguely unsettling. It didn't care as much for yoga as I did, but viewed it, I think, the way I viewed sword training—as a necessity for our survival. In the quiet of dusk, we worked through a dozen poses, each more challenging than the last. And with each movement, each stretch, each slow and steady and deep breath, I could feel its tension ease, like tight restraints loosened.

With each stretch, I became more aware of its consciousness. And because of that, a little less aware of my own, as if its thoughts replaced mine. This was tricky territory, as I had no idea if I might accidentally let it go too far and permanently give up control. I didn't want that. This was still my body; I'd been here first. But I was getting to know it as a creature with its own awareness and emotions. Which felt very strange to say, and even stranger to feel. And it was a creature of *power*. Of strength and speed that would hurt or help me, depending on its mood.

And right now, its mood was feisty.

Yoga had apparently not been enough, probably because my own adrenaline was up in anticipation of our midnight rendezvous. It wanted more action. But this wasn't the time or place to show the AAM how unusual we were, how I carried some sort of second spirit along with my own. Whatever punishment they'd designed for my "crimes" would pale next to those sanctions. Letting it loose in front of the AAM could get both of us killed.

It may have agreed, but that didn't ease its gnawing hunger. Not for food, but for fight.

"A compromise," I murmured, aware I was murmuring to myself while alone in my room. "I'll let you train with the dagger, and you can move all you want here. But tonight is just for me. I like staying alive, and you'll frighten them."

It seemed excited by that, and I couldn't fault the sentiment. But still.

"Dagger," I said. "Or nothing."

It relented, was angry for a moment, but by the time I'd taken my dagger from its sheath and opened the bedroom door, the anger had dissolved into excitement. The loft was still quiet, Lulu's bedroom door still closed. So I padded into the main room, the only light the glow of streetlights outside, filtered into a smear of rainbow through the filter-covered windows. It was a big space, with plenty of room to move.

I glanced back at the hallway, waiting in silence for a moment to ensure I was alone, and felt the stab of guilt—not the first—that I was hiding this from Lulu. But she already put up with me, a vampire, in her Sup-free space, and was trying to avoid the worst of the supernatural drama. I still wasn't sure what the monster was, or why it existed, and dragging her into that mystery seemed unfair. Not that denial was a great foundation for a friendship. But it was all I could manage right now.

I stepped into the middle of the space, pulled my hair into a knot, and closed my eyes.

"All right," I whispered. "Go."

It didn't hesitate. The monster stretched, seemed to fill my limbs with its own shadows, and began to play. It flipped the dagger in the air, caught it so the point faced downward, and struck out in a neat curve around my body. Then into a crouch, one leg extended, before bouncing back to its feet again.

"Nicely done," I whispered, felt its acknowledgment, its pride. Then we were moving again.

A flip of the dagger, then forward slashes. Left, right, up would have done plenty of damage to an opponent. Then, much to my surprise, we were turning a side handspring, dagger tucked in, and landed in a classic fighting position. Body angled to prevent full frontal strikes, muscles warming, heart beating faster with the movement—and the thrill of it. The monster's origin was un-known, but I was decidedly vampire. And vampires loved to fight.

How had it learned these moves? I'd probably seen someone practice them—my four years at Maison Dumas had involved hand-to-hand and weapons training—but I couldn't remember having executed them before. Not like this—like katas in a martial arts practice.

"What were you?" I asked it, half-afraid of its answer—and the revelations or obligations that would follow it. But it dismissed the question, flipped the dagger into its left hand, and struck out again. Dagger strike, high kick. Dagger strike, crescent kick. Dagger strike, side kick. All good moves. Moves I might need to try.

The shadow of emotion I sensed from it was mostly condescension. Because, I was slow to realize, that was exactly the point. It wasn't just stretching or exercising, or working out anger. It was trying to remind me, like flipping back through those lessons I'd learned in Paris. Because I had foes to face tonight. We both had foes. And the monster knew that if I was gone, it was gone, too.

"Okay," I whispered, pausing for a moment to open my eyes, to watch and listen for movement. And when I was sure the loft was still dark, still quiet, I closed my eyes again. And instead of trying to *watch* what the monster was doing, I tried to just feel it.

Sweep down with the dagger into a spin, bring the dagger up again. Block an invisible strike with the forearm, sweep left with the dagger. Pivot, crouch to avoid a high strike, back kick.

The movements began to blend, each strike flowing into the next. It was like flying, total freedom from gravity, from limitations. A dance of magic and strength and speed. And with the two of us together, a finesse I didn't think I'd had before.

And then a side kick, and glass exploded, and the noise was tremendous. I rushed back to the surface of my mind like a swimmer who'd been down too long, gulping in air, and looked around.

I'd knocked over the damned recycling.

I'd gotten too close to the island and kicked over a small bin I'd filled the night before with empty bottles. Glass, still sticky with the dregs of beer, lay scattered on the floor like a mosaic.

There was running down the hall. *Go,* I urged it, and looked down at my bare feet. I was trapped in a circle of my own making.

Lulu ran into the room, still in her pajama bottoms and tank. "What the hell happened?"

Back, I ordered silently, because I could still feel it pacing. It had enjoyed the fight and didn't want to go back now. But we had no choice.

Back, I demanded, putting every ounce of power and glamour I could manage into the command. *Before you get us both kicked out.*

Finally, it receded.

"I'm sorry," I said. "I was practicing some katas for tonight, but I screwed up my aim on a kick and knocked over the damn bin."

Lulu surveyed the room like a cop reviewing a crime scene, and I all but held my breath while she did it. But then she sighed and walked to the kitchen, righted the bin, and began putting glass chunks into it. "You're barefoot," she said. "Stay where you are. I'll get this. Kicking is for the gym, not the loft."

"I know. I'm sorry."

"Last thing you need is stitches before you go to the principal's office."

I snorted, because she was right. That was exactly how it felt. "Is that what we're calling it?"

"So I don't freak out about it, yes."

I looked back at her, saw the worry in her eyes. And felt immediately guilty that I'd missed that last night—and had been entertaining a monster of indeterminate supernatural origin in the meantime.

"It's going to be fine," I said.

"You can't promise that," she said. "And they aren't here to take your word for it that you'll be a good little vampire. Misogynist pricks. They're going to pick a fight with you."

"I know. I promise I won't take any unnecessary risks, and I won't be going out there alone. Arrogant as they may be, there's only so much they can do." Or so I hoped. I looked back at her. "Where are you going tonight?"

"To hang with Mateo at the furnace. Why?"

"Stay with him, stay away from the loft, until you hear from me. Just in case."

"Okay," she said after a moment. "I'd thought about staying the night over there."

I lifted my brows. "Staying at Mateo's?"

"It was an idea," she said slyly. "If the mood strikes."

"Good for you," I said with a smile.

Lulu chucked a big piece of glass into the bin, then used a wet paper towel to clean up the rest of the mess I'd made. And I didn't care for that metaphor.

Across the room, my screen rang.

Lulu glanced at it. "Are you in for Petra?"

"Sure," I said, and she tossed over my screen. I managed to catch it, avoiding another round of spilling things across the floor.

"Elisa," I said, answering it. Her face popped on-screen, her dark hair pulled into a tail. "And you're on speaker, so be clever enough for a crowd."

"How about the Grove?" she asked.

Lulu's brows lifted, then she looked at me with speculation. "The place in the burbs that does outdoor weddings?"

"Yeah. My cousin was married there," Petra said. "She had eighteen bridesmaids."

"Who needs eighteen bridesmaids?" I asked. "That's horrifying."

"A woman who wants a three-hour wedding ceremony." Petra sighed hugely. "She organized them like a chorus and made them sing a song for her."

"No way that happened."

"Would you like to see the evidence? I can send you pictures. It was a beautiful ceremony . . . until the lightning storm." Her voice was mild and pleasant, belied by the glimmer in her eyes.

"You ruined your cousin's wedding with a lightning storm?" Lulu asked, and even she looked a little impressed.

"I didn't ruin it," said the aeromancer. "I just made it shorter."

"What does the Grove look like?" I asked.

"There's a pergola for outdoor weddings, a building where receptions are held, and a meadow behind, where brides take pictures with boots on or whatever. It's atmospheric."

"Not unlike your cousin's wedding," I said.

She grinned. "Yup. The place is yours if you want it. There's nothing scheduled tonight, and the owner said she owed me one for getting my cousin's people out of their building. They were ready to clean up and go home after the wedding."

"Cost?"

"Free," she said. "Due to that favor. I mean, if you trash the place, you have to clean it up. But otherwise free."

I seriously hoped "trashing the place" wasn't on the menu. The AAM couldn't expect to come to Chicago and pull a stunt like that without consequences.

"I'll have to get the AAM's okay," I said. "But if they're good with it, it's fine by me. It's out of town, there's open space, and it's free. Thanks for doing the legwork."

"You're welcome," Petra said. "Now, let's discuss your entrance music."

Cool as it might have been to walk in to my own theme song, we were trying to avoid attention, not attract it. And while I wasn't going to kowtow to the AAM, I also wasn't trying to provoke them further.

When Connor and Alexei gave me the thumbs-up for the

Grove, I told the AAM. They agreed. They'd arrive at midnight; we'd arrive at eleven, an hour early.

Lulu came out as I put my screen away, tote bag over her shoulder. "I'm out like skinny jeans."

"You're wearing skinny jeans," I pointed out.

"I'm wearing them ironically." Petite as she was, she leaned up on tiptoes to kiss my cheek. "Be careful."

"I will. Hey, before you leave, do you by chance have a cloak?"

Sighing woefully, she walked to the door. "You aren't wearing a cloak."

"I could pull it off."

"You'd pull off nineties vampire princess goth. And that's not a compliment."

But the worry seemed to have drained from the hard set of her shoulders, which was what I'd wanted. I'd nudged too closely to the supernatural boundary she'd drawn, and that wasn't fair to her.

It was time for vampires to learn some boundaries, too.

Vampires being vampires, how I presented myself at the meeting was essential. There must be black, there must be leather, there must be blades, and there must be ferocity.

Fortunately, I was well stocked.

I considered and discarded a trim suit, leggings and a military-style jacket, and a leather fighting ensemble. I couldn't go in looking like a warrior, a fighter. They'd assume I'd already given up the argument and was ready to fight.

No, I needed to show authority. Power. I wasn't a Master, but I was someone to be reckoned with.

I opted for an ensemble I'd never worn, one I'd purchased in Paris to wear for a night at the clubs. And hadn't gotten there before coming home again. It was a fitted black jumpsuit that smoothed down the body from neck to ankles in the front, the back open in a deep vee. No sleeves, but a cape of pleated panels of black organza that fell from the shoulders. It was a little red carpet, a little military, and very badass. Part of me was irritated by the superficiality; part of me was very psyched about the look.

There was a chance I'd have to fight, so I opted for kitten-heeled leather boots rather than the stilettos the jumpsuit demanded—and despite the fact that they'd have made excellent weapons of their own.

A dagger went into my boot, and I'd belt on my katana on-site. I slicked back my hair into a low bun and pushed diamond studs into my ears. Wealth also impressed vampires. Not to the same degree as fairies, who were like magpies when gold and silver glinted, but it mattered.

Eyes and lips were accented, cheekbones highlighted, so that when I was done I looked fierce, fashionable, intimidating.

"Good," I said and snapped off the light. It was time for some intimidation.

Connor was waiting outside, already on Thelma—his low, matte-black motorcycle. He was in head-to-toe black leather, from boots to sleek jacket, his dark hair waving in the breeze. He looked up at the sound of my footsteps, his smile widening as he watched me move toward him. I could feel his magic stretch out, caress, and beckon.

I kept my gaze on him as I walked, practicing my bravado, and liked seeing the desire that clouded his eyes.

"Elisa Sullivan," he said, voice deep. "You are a picture."

I tipped up his chin with a finger, pressed a kiss to his lips, giving the same teasing caress that he usually offered to me.

His hand found my hip, squeezed. "If we didn't have business right now . . ." he began, but we both knew this was unavoidable.

"Let's hope they're as intimidated as you are impressed."

"How are you feeling?"

"Unsettled," I decided, and he nodded.

"That sounds about right. Let's head out."

I picked up the helmet already waiting for me on the second seat, slung a leg over the bike.

Connor was teaching me to ride solo, but had insisted on taking the lead tonight. I considered arguing, but riding across Chicago with my arms around his waist, curled into him as he bobbed and weaved through traffic, wasn't exactly a hardship.

Forty minutes later, we drove down the tallgrass-lined gravel road that led to the Grove. The reception hall, low and organic, with lots of tall wooden beams and rocks, sat at the end of the drive to the right, just behind a large parking lot. To the right was a pavilion, an open cathedral of wood and glass. Behind them, according to the maps I'd checked online, was the meadow where we'd meet.

Theo and Petra were already waiting, leaning against Theo's car. Alexei zoomed up on his motorcycle, brilliantly red compared to Thelma's darkness, and parked beside us. We climbed off, unfastened helmets, and stowed them on the bike.

"What do you know?" Connor asked, striding toward them.

"Not as much as we'd like," Theo said. "The Compliance Bureau is a relatively new part of the AAM. Established two months ago."

"That seems convenient," Connor said, brows raised.

I shook my head. "We've had relative peace. At least until the fairies. Vampires hate negative publicity about Sups."

Theo nodded. "The Bureau is led by a vampire named Clive, formerly of Cabot House in New York. He was a guard before joining the AAM."

"He also has a brother, made at the same time, who's in the Bureau. Name's Levi."

"Levi was one of the vamps who came to my door. Levi, Sloan, Blake. Clive didn't bother with the meet-and-greet."

"Have they done this before?" Connor asked. "Made these demands?"

"I don't know," Theo said. "We don't have access to their records."

"We searched even the darkest corners of the Internet," Petra said, "and haven't found anything that suggests they've taken this kind of enforcement action."

"So I'm special," I said, but I didn't want any part of that designation. Not from them.

Connor reached out, squeezed my hand. "We'll handle this tonight, and finish it."

I gave him a smile, even as I knew that was a lie. But appreciated it all the same.

Crushed stone paths led around the main building and branched off to other parts of the property. We walked toward the actual grove, my hand firmly on my katana, and the monster watching and waiting.

We have a deal, I reminded it, and was pretty sure it metaphorically flipped me off.

The path split again around a wide, round meadow, grass carefully shorn and scenting the quiet air. There was a rise at the far end, and a hill covered in trees that made a dark silhouette against the stars. For a moment, I stared at those trees, and thought of that forest where monsters and fire had raged and blood had been spilled. My heart beat hard against my ribs, each thump like the pounding of paws—malformed and full of rage—pacing through darkness.

Connor slipped his hand into mine, squeezed. I looked at him, found comfort in his steady gaze. "Even then, you were victori-

ous. And will be again." He leaned down, his dark curls brushing
my cheek. "No mere vampire can stop you, Lis."

"And a wolf?" I asked, smiling as he'd meant me to.

His grin was wide, possessive, intoxicating. "I'll only stop you
if you run. But you aren't a coward."

"No," I said, to him and myself. "I'm not."

Theo, who'd walked into the middle of the meadow, looked
around, put his hands on his hips. "If one is obliged to have a
vampire showdown, this looks like as good a place as any."

"The weather is garbage," Petra said, looking gloomily up at
the star-scattered sky. "I can't do anything with this."

"It's a gorgeous night," Alexei said.

"Exactly." She held up her hand and scrunched up her face—
and three little sparks hissed in her palm before disappearing
again. "Garbage," she said again.

Alexei just looked at her. "You're weird."

With a curl of her lip, she snapped her fingers, and Alexei's eyes
widened at the blue spark in her palm. She might have wanted
storms, but she didn't need them to work her magic.

"Am I?" she asked.

"Yes," he said. "That wasn't an insult."

She huffed, but snapped again, and the spark disappeared.
Then she pulled white gloves from her pocket, slid them on.

"With friends like these," Connor asked, "who needs enemies?"

"Vampires, evidently." I looked around. "Does everybody understand their roles?"

"Standing by and not exacerbating the situation?" Petra asked.

"Yes," Theo said and looked at me. "Officially, we're here as
observers, to intervene only if necessary. To protect the public,
and our Sups." His smile was thin. "We'll also keep a line to
Roger. The CPD's Sup liaison has a couple of cars about two miles

down the road. Close enough to intervene if necessary. Not so close as to be visible."

"Good," I said. "Thanks for arranging it."

"You're welcome."

We all went quiet, preparing to wait for the stroke of midnight. And when the hour struck, two dozen black-clad vamps, looking stern and severe and thoroughly righteous, moved through the verge in silence, with nary a whisper of grass to mark their arrival. There were no trim and tailored suits for tonight's event. Just dark fatigues and katanas in lacquered scabbards. Vampire workwear. Work intended to be bloody. Were they intimidated by me, or just afraid I'd slip their net? The gear made me worry the five of us wouldn't be enough—and that I'd put my friends in harm's way.

Their magic slunk forward like fog, glamour intended to soften, to soothe. And to lure me into submission, I assumed. It wasn't subtle, which made it easy to counter. I used my own glamour as a shield, wrapped around me like a cloak. I schooled my features into bland and arrogant dismissal, and the fog dissipated. They'd made their first move, and I wasn't impressed.

I recognized the three vamps who'd come to my door, but not the man who led them, who'd positioned himself at the front of a tidy triangle. (Seriously—did they practice formations?) This must be Clive—the Bureau's head. He was thickly built, more like a defensive tackle than a katana-swinging vampire, despite the black and gold scabbard gleaming at his waist. His skin was pale, his hair short, dark, and tidy, and he had high, round cheekbones and deep-set eyes. He was older than me in vampire terms, at least fifty or sixty, judging by the weight of his magic, but his face looked considerably younger. He'd been in his twenties when he'd been turned, I guessed.

Time to play my part, I thought, and lifted my chin, hands at my sides. A hand on my katana would have comforted, but it also threatened—and signaled I was worried, on the defensive.

"Clive," I said, getting in the first word. "I'm Elisa Sullivan. I have, at your request, agreed to meet you to discuss the AAM's concerns about my saving Carlie's life." I gestured to the X on my clavicle. "As I have arrived as promised, please remove this."

He didn't appear to appreciate my opening demand, however politely phrased, and looked at a vampire behind him, nodded. The vampire entered something into a small screen. After a moment, I felt a bright pinch and the mark disappeared.

I inclined my head. "Thank you."

Clive looked perturbed by my taking the lead, then glanced at Connor and the others. "I'm not sure why you felt it necessary to bring Pack with you. I see no need to involve them in vampire affairs."

"I see a need," Connor said. "The incident happened in Pack territory, and Elisa saved a friend of the Pack."

"Given you've brought twenty vampires," I said, "you can hardly complain about the five of us."

"Your tone does you no credit." Temper crossed his face then, hot and sharp. He wasn't just enforcing rules; he was actively angry at me. Because of Carlie?

"Being accused of vampiric treason tends to make me irritable. Now, please get to the point. What do you want?"

Clive gritted his teeth, but maintained his control. "Elisa Sullivan. You are accused of making a vampire without the authority to do so, either by permission or position. You had no legal right to so act."

"She was going to die."

"Not relevant. There are rules for a reason, and you violated those rules. You threaten all of us by your recklessness."

"*She was going to die,*" I repeated.

"Then she would have been one of many humans. All mortals die; it is their nature. Is her life worth all of ours?"

I narrowed my gaze. "Has your life been threatened in any way because Carlie is alive? Because I saved her? And do you show up at the home of every Rogue vampire who makes a new one without your permission?"

Rogues were vampires who were unHoused, who eschewed Houses but had banded together under a common name and leader. Carlie lived with a coven of vampires in Minnesota who were technically Rogues; they'd affiliated with one another. That defeated the point of being "Rogue," to my mind, but to each his own. Whatever the reason, the rules were different.

"Rogues are rarely strong enough to make vampires, and rarely do so. Regardless, the AAM has no information suggesting you've deemed yourself a Rogue vampire, or affiliated with Chicago's Rogues. Have you done so?"

"No," I said after a moment.

"And you've refused to commit even to your parents' House. Interesting."

How did the AAM know I didn't consider myself a member of Cadogan House? Had my parents told Nicole? Didn't matter, I told myself. I could deal with that later, talk to my parents. Right now, I had to stay focused, because his anger kept growing, pushing hot and prickling magic toward us.

"And what," Clive continued, "of the next human you change? Or the next human changed—successfully or not—by someone else who believed it was allowed?"

For this first time, it occurred to me that maybe this wasn't just about me having changed Carlie. Something bigger was going on here. Something more. What did they think I was going to do?

"Since this apparently needs to be said aloud," I offered, "I have no interest in building a coven or a vampire army, nor do I plan to make any more vampires."

"Your word is worth little."

"My word is all I have," I said, keeping my voice calm. "Word and intention. I've told you my intention. So what's yours, Clive?"

"You are a risk, and you are unrepentant, so you will be dealt with accordingly. Elisa Sullivan," he said, voice booming across the darkness, "you will agree to be Commended into a recognized House. You will submit to the authority of its Master. And you will undertake formal Testing of your Strengths. If you fail to agree to these demands, your freedom is forfeit."

FOUR

My blood went cold, ice slipping through my veins.

Testing was the process would-be Masters went through to ensure they were physically and mentally strong enough for the position. It was a measurement of the Strengths vampires valued: physical prowess, psychic ability, and strategic thinking.

There was no way in hell I'd agree to that. I didn't want to be a Master, and I wouldn't be able to hide the monster during that kind of ordeal. They'd see. They'd know. And if they wanted to control me now, wait until they found the monster.

I couldn't see Connor, but I felt a wave of magic, the flash of his concern. It was a reminder that I wasn't here alone, that I had the support to handle whatever the AAM threw at me—vampire to vampire.

"Are you afraid of me, Clive?" I kept my eyes hard, my voice cold. "Because I can't think of any other reason you'd demand Testing of a vampire who doesn't want to be a Master."

"You cannot flout our rules, our law, with impunity."

"I saved a human from a monster. I made vampires look like heroes." I cocked my head at him, forced arrogance into my eyes. "Does Nicole know that you're here? That you've threatened me?"

His face was a study in raw fury, his eyes swirling quicksilver with hatred, his knuckles white as he gripped his katana in its scabbard. "We act with the authority of the AAM," he said, which sounded like evasion, but I had no basis to counter it.

"Your parents should have controlled you," he continued. "Should have taught you how to behave. How to obey. But they didn't, did they? They allowed you to run wild, to ignore the rules because of the manner of your making."

"You don't know how wrong you are."

"You made your choice," he said, ignoring that. "You'll pay the consequences." His eyes fired again, and his hand crept toward his katana.

"I would be very careful," I said, "what you do with that sword."

"Is that a threat?"

"No. It's a reminder that I have witnesses."

"He takes one step forward," Connor said, voice low and threatening, "and he is *mine*."

I heard rustling, impatient and ready. But I kept my eyes on Clive.

"A fight won't benefit any of us," I said. "That's the kind of behavior that humans don't like to see. And as for Carlie, I will break whatever rules are necessary to save an innocent life."

"You will obey," Clive said. "Or you will be taken into custody and placed into seclusion until you submit to the AAM's demands."

"No," I said, simply. "I don't agree to your demands, and I won't go with you. So I suggest you leave Chicago, report back to Nicole, and tell her what I've just told you. And if she has questions, she can talk to me directly."

"Wrong answer," Clive said. His eyes had gone diamond-bright with magic and satisfaction at my refusal. Unsurprisingly, this meeting had nothing to do with telling my story; the outcome was preordained. And so, I guessed, was what came next.

Something whistled through the air above us—something sleek

and fast. Knife or arrow or shuriken, but not just that. It was a first shot from the AAM. It was a dare.

It was provocation.

"Hold!" I called out, but an instant too late. Another missile moving, even before the last had landed. I looked back, saw Alexei's hand extended . . . and heard the pop of flesh.

I looked back, found a knife buried in Clive's thigh.

"First blood," Clive said, through gritted teeth, "has been spilled."

"Only because you missed," I muttered.

Jaw hard, Clive pulled the blade from his leg, tossed it away. "You've now attacked a member of the AAM undertaking his sworn duty. That will not stand."

That was the next signal, the order to attack. AAM vampires rushed forward, katanas raised. All except Clive, who let the others flow around him, a rock in a stream, as they rushed us.

I unsheathed my blade with my right hand, pulled my dagger with my left, and prepared to defend.

A man came at me, katana raised overhead. I met his strike with my own, jabbed forward with my dagger. He pivoted, spun his katana, and knocked my dagger hand away. I went low, kicked at his shins. He staggered back, and I jumped forward, slashing again. He blocked, and I spun, slashed, caught his arms. He screamed in fury, put a hand over the wound to stanch it, and looked at me with loathing in his eyes.

"You came at me first," I pointed out. Then balanced, pivoted, and gave him a side kick that had him stumbling. But he maintained, roared forward again.

Something whistled overhead again, and this time I managed to duck—and watched as metal buried itself in the man's chest. He hit the ground. It wouldn't be a fatal injury—not to a vampire—but it would keep him occupied.

I turned, looked at Alexei, who smiled at me.

"I had him," I said.

"I finished him," Alexei said with a smile, and lunged toward another one.

I heard footsteps behind me, snapped back to look, found a woman, petite but grinning, running forward with katana parallel in front of her, fangs extended and ready to fight.

"I'll bite," I said with a grin, and bounced once, centered myself.

She swung and I met her sword against mine, sparks flying as steel burned against steel. We both pushed back, reset, swung forward again. She came high again. I went low, spun to avoid her blade. But she caught one of the floating cap sleeves, ripped it clean away.

Damn it. I'd *liked* this jumpsuit. But I sighed and ripped away the other one, tossed it down. At least I'd be symmetrical.

By the time I pivoted she was on the attack again. We met each other blow for blow, the shriek of meeting metal searing my ears each time we made contact. I was taller, so I used my height to my advantage, brought the katana down overhand. She blocked it, then again, but I had better leverage coming in high, and her arms began to shake from the effort of holding off the blows.

I could have used the monster. I was strong and I was fast, but holding it back took energy I didn't need to waste. Energy I could have better directed at this short and angry vampire in front of me.

One more blow, I thought, and I pushed as much power and magic into it as I could. A groan escaped her, and she fell to her knees, arms shaking. I plucked her katana from her hands. "Go," I said, and she rose, ran toward the edge of the meadow.

Now with two katanas, I spun toward the next attacker. He was one of the vampires from the night before—the one with the pendant that now gleamed against his dark fatigues.

"Blake, right?" I asked pleasantly and, when he blinked, sunk into a low crescent, swept his legs. He jumped to avoid it and, by the time I made the full circle, spun his arm backward, so the butt of his katana handle struck me in the chest.

I felt nothing break, but hit the ground hard. I landed on my shoulder and felt the instant tear and, in the split second before pain struck, knew it was going to be bad.

It was worse.

It was a wave of red heat, sending pain through my arm so fiercely I dropped the female vampire's katana. I nearly vomited, but breathed quickly through pursed lips, refusing to give in to the searing agony. I was immortal, and it was going to take more than that to stop me.

He realized the same and advanced, aimed a kick at my ribs. I rolled to dodge it, pain screaming in my shoulder as it took my weight, and climbed back to my feet, my left arm all but useless. I raised my katana again, still firmly in my good hand.

Blake's smile was thin. "You're going down."

"Went down," I reminded him. "Just got back up again. I think there's a song about that." But I was out of time for fighting, as sirens filled the air.

There was a pause in the fight, a long inhalation, and AAM vampires began to scatter like seeds in the wind, drifting back into the shadows from which they'd emerged. Clive still stood apart, watching the battlefield.

I faced him, refusing to yield.

"We aren't done," Clive said. "You'll submit to the AAM's authority one way or the other. The only difference is how many people will die before it's done."

I saw the truth in his eyes. That I was his quarry, and he didn't care who else he had to run down to bring me in. To bring me down.

I met his gaze squarely. "You're in Chicago now, Clive. You so much as threaten a human in my town, and I'll bury you."

His eyes gleamed with hatred, with purpose. And then he followed the others into darkness.

"You're injured," Connor said, finding me as cruiser lights cast blue and red upon the ground. He put a hand on my cheek, checked my eyes.

"Left shoulder," I said. "I think I tore something." Vampires healed quickly, and I could feel the dull ache as tendon worked to stitch itself back together. "But I'll be fine," I said, to settle the worry in his eyes. "You okay?"

"Nothing major."

"Alexei?"

"He's fine."

"Good," I said and accepted the bottle of water Theo handed me, drank thirstily.

"Maybe it's because we're in the Midwest," Theo said, "but I think Chicago's vampires are much friendlier."

"They're certainly smarter," Connor said dryly, finishing the bottle I handed him.

A woman came toward us. She had medium brown skin and wide brown eyes, her black hair pulled into a sleek bun. Her dark burgundy suit was just as sleek, and a gleaming detective's shield was pinned to her narrow waist.

"Detective," Theo said with a nod. "This is Elisa Sullivan. Elisa, Detective Gwen Robinson. She's the CPD's new liaison for supernatural issues."

"Elisa," the woman said. "Trouble here tonight?"

"Unfortunately," I said. "Did Roger give you the basics?"

"He told me the vamps came to Chicago to cause trouble for you," she said, then glanced around. "They disappeared quickly."

"They didn't get what they want, and they need to be free for round two."

"So you think they'll be back?"

"Not here, and not tonight. But after me? Yes."

She looked around. "You had permission to be here."

"We did. Express, from the owners."

"Any injuries?"

"A few. None major." My shoulder was the worst, as far as I knew, and giving her the details on that wasn't going to help.

"Do you want to press charges?"

"No. Why would I?"

She just sighed. "Vampires."

"They are *a lot*," Theo said with a smirk.

"With all due respect, Detective, arresting him would cost the taxpayers money, and it won't change anything. I don't want you or Theo to waste your time."

She looked like she approved of the reasoning, if not of the answer. "All right." She looked back at Alexei. "I'd like to speak with him, too."

"Good luck," I said, and she made her way toward him.

"Trustworthy?" Connor asked Theo when we were alone again.

"Yeah. We worked together before I transferred to OMB. She's good people."

"Okay," I said, and made myself relax. Odds were high I'd be seeing more of Detective Robinson before this was all done.

We found a hot dog stand on the way downtown, ate Chicago dogs standing beside the bikes. I shouldn't have had an appetite. Not after the threats, the fight, my absolute confidence that something very ugly had started tonight. Something that had begun with Carlie, but was going to have to end with me.

But I'd fought, wielded my sword, and my body needed the recharge. I managed two dogs, and Alexei ate three before he rubbed his belly in satisfaction.

"That's the sixth one he's had this week," Connor said, smiling as he licked mustard from his thumb. "It's a miracle he can walk."

"Sport peppers aid the digestion," Alexei said.

"No," Connor said. "They don't."

Alexei shrugged, wiped his mouth with a napkin, tossed it neatly into a waiting trash can. Unparalleled aim, I thought. Which raised a question.

"Why did you throw the knife?"

Alexei looked at me, brows raised. "Because someone threw one at you."

As simple as that, I thought, and I looked at Connor, who nodded. There was a reason they were friends. Loyalty was part of it.

Alexei reached into his pocket, pulled out the thin stiletto blade. The handle was bare metal stamped with a sideways figure eight. Leave it to a vampire, I thought, to scribe the symbol of immortality into one of his weapons.

"Nice," Connor said, looking it over. "You keeping it?"

"Of course. Nearly makes up for the trouble. Vampires don't know how to fight."

"Some vampires do," Connor said, his gaze warm on mine.

"She's not bad with a blade," Alexei allowed.

"Damned by faint praise," I said. "They lured us into striking first."

"Oh, absolutely," Connor said. "That was the only bit of strategy that actually impressed me."

"They'll milk it for everything they can," I said. "Claim they were merely trying to enforce AAM rules, and I attacked them without provocation."

"Sorry," Alexei said.

"Not your fault. I appreciate your helping tonight."

"I'm still hungry," Alexei said.

I pulled out my screen, sent him a message. He glanced at it, raised his brows.

"What?" Connor asked. "What did you send him?" His eyes narrowed. "It better not have been lascivious."

"It's money for more dogs," Alexei said.

"I pay my debts," I said and tossed my cup into the trash can. "You boys ready to ride?"

"Always," Connor said and leaned over to press a kiss to my temple. "Good work, brat."

"Thank you, puppy."

Shifters may have been old-fashioned, but their corporate headquarters were uniquely modern. Lots of steel and glass and, thanks to Lulu, a gorgeous mural featuring an abstracted and diverse array of women. The building included a bar and restaurant, the industrial kitchens where they created their meaty fare, and the offices where, one assumed, business was conducted. The entire building had a faint tingle of magic, as if it had suffused the structure, collected in the pores of concrete.

I followed Connor inside, and we were immediately set upon by the scents of smoke and meat and the magic they made together.

A woman in a motorized scooter met us a few steps inside. "Come," she said, narrowing the eyes that looked at us from beneath a wave of bleached hair. "There is work."

"Good to see you, too, Aunt Berna," Connor said, but we followed her down the hallway and into the kitchen, where shifters worked at long stainless steel tables, scooping food into containers or covering disposable pans with foil. But all movement stopped at our appearance in the doorway.

There were nods of acknowledgment for Connor, mostly curious glances at me. A couple of women in the corner lifted their chins defiantly, and I wasn't sure if that's because I was a vampire, or because I'd nabbed the prince they'd wanted.

Berna pulled aprons, gloves, and hairnets from a table, shoved them at us. "Put on," she said dourly. She wasn't really the convivial sort, but I usually got more than orders from her. And she adored Connor.

Connor watched her for a moment. "Why?" There was no sarcasm in the comment, just an honest inquiry.

"You fight on screen," she said, looking from Connor to me, then back again. "Vampires make trouble; you join trouble." She threw up her hands. "And then entire city in trouble. Father says you work."

"Alexei was there, too," Connor said.

Berna made a dismissive sound. "Alexei is not nephew," she said and puttered away.

"Were you able to translate that?" he asked.

"Your father saw video of you fighting the Bureau, and now you're being grounded. With what smells like brisket."

Sighing, he looked around. "Yeah, that pretty much sums it up."

"Who got the video?" I wondered. "I didn't see anyone with a screen or a camera. Did you?"

"No. Maybe the Grove's owners?"

"Maybe," I said, but that didn't seem to fit with what Petra had told us.

And if shifters had seen the video, it would almost certainly have made its way to vampires. Including my parents. I pulled out my screen, found two messages waiting—one from Lulu, and one from Mom and Dad. There was a world of distance between them, but they'd all seen the fight.

"Damn it," I muttered. I assured Lulu I was fine and sent my parents a similar message: I'M SAFE AND HANDLING. WILL CALL LATER. LOVE YOU.

"Everything okay?" Connor asked.

"Parents," I said, sliding the screen into my pocket again. "What's going on here?"

Connor moved to a rack on a stainless wall where clipboards hung from two dozen hooks. He glanced over them, flipped through the papers on one, then looked back at the tables as if to confirm.

"Big order," he said. "Delivery's at dawn for a big conference tomorrow in the Loop. They must have gotten behind." He rolled his neck, slid me a glance. "You can go. I don't think even Berna, formidable though she is, has the power to punish you."

"And your father?" I asked.

He frowned. "That depends on some things. But I'm still thinking it through."

The kitchen door swung open, and a female shifter walked in. Light brown skin scattered with freckles, dark curls that framed her dark eyes, thick brows. Miranda Mitchell was beautiful, but had an enormous chip on her shoulder about vampires and unrequited feelings for Connor. Those were only two of the apparently myriad reasons she didn't like me. I couldn't fault her loyalty to the Pack, but I didn't usually care for the way she tried to protect it.

"Well, well," she said, striding toward us. "Look who's slumming it today," she said, her dark eyes filled with loathing as she took in what remained of my jumpsuit, jewelry. "Manual labor's quite a change for you, isn't it?"

"Miranda," Connor said pleasantly as he pulled on gloves. "How about you help instead of complaining?"

"I have other things to do," she said. "She's got you doing her dirty work, too? I saw video of the fight."

Had they broadcast the damn thing in the bar? I wondered, but knew I needed to deal with this myself.

"Then you'll know what I'm capable of," I said. I turned to face her, getting close enough that she took a step back. "Help, or get out of the way."

There was clapping across the room that silenced quickly when Miranda turned her gaze toward it.

When she looked back at me, mouth open, whatever she saw in Connor's eyes had her quieting down. "Get to the things you have to do," he said, the words a warning.

"Okay," I said when she stomped out of the room; I pulled on my gloves. "Let's get to work."

FIVE

We worked for two hours, scooping baked beans into containers, preparing pans of corn bread for transport to the conference hotel, and moving the entire feast into the Pack's delivery van. Aluminum pans weren't stable in the best of times, and full of barbecue and beans, they were even harder to deal with. And burning hot.

There was a rack in the back of the van with slots the pans should slide into to keep, one presumed, sauce from splattering the walls of the van during transport. But even with vampiric strength, maneuvering hot, full, and bendable trays wasn't the easiest endeavor.

"I'm going to end up wearing it," I muttered, trying again to match the edges of pan to rack.

"Let me help you with that," said a voice behind me.

I glanced back, found a man with light brown skin and straight, dark hair that fell to his shoulders. His eyes were brown below dark, straight brows, and above sculpted cheekbones. His grin was wide.

"Thanks," I said, as he gripped the other end of the tray.

"I know you can take the weight," he said, as we lifted and slid the tray home. "But it's awkward."

"It is."

He locked the tray in place, shifting so the fall of dark hair slid across his face, then pushing it away again.

"I'm Daniel Liu." He offered a hand.

"Elisa Sullivan," I said, and we shook. His hand was strong, his nails carefully manicured, and elegant as his dark gray trousers and black shirt.

"You manage a sword very well," he said.

They'd absolutely shown the video in the bar. "Thank you. I was well trained."

"So I saw." He slid his hands into his pockets. "Do you think the AAM will continue to trouble you?"

This man was obviously Pack—the magic was undeniable—but I didn't know which members, other than Alexei and his relatives, Connor considered trustworthy, or how much information he wanted them to have.

I settled on, "Probably. They didn't come all this way to be turned down."

Connor appeared around the vehicle's corner. "Daniel. You're just the man I wanted to see."

Daniel's smile widened. "Prince. I was just making Elisa's acquaintance."

"Good," Connor said, closing the van door. "Daniel just joined us from Memphis. And you don't have to call me 'prince.'"

"Prince," Daniel agreed pleasantly. Connor just rolled his eyes.

"Welcome to Chicago," I said. "What brings you north?"

Daniel slid a look at Connor. "He does. Memphis has an interest in the Pack's future, its leadership. And we support the Keene family. Since much of the Pack is still in Alaska, I was nominated to ride up and . . . help."

"He means he lost a bet," Connor translated, leaning back against the van. "So instead of running the Tongass or enjoying some Delta blues, he gets to work security and endure lake effect snow."

Daniel's brows lifted. "What's lake effect snow?"

"Newbies are so adorable," I said and elbowed Connor. "Make sure he buys a good coat."

A shifter came out of the building, clipboard in hand. "Get off my van, loafers." This was Eli, one of Connor's uncles.

Connor pushed off the van, nodded at him. "Uncle."

"Whelp." He looked at me, nodded. "Vampire."

"Wolf," I said, and he smirked.

"Everything loaded?"

"And ready," Connor said. "Strange thing—I didn't see you packing beans."

"I'm management," he said and opened the driver's side door.

"I believe that's my cue to find something else to do," Daniel said and glanced at me. "Good to meet you."

"And you. Thanks again for the help."

"You're welcome. Prince," Daniel said again and walked back to the building.

"He seems cool," I said, as we moved away from the van, lest Eli run us down to get the food on the road.

"Dan is good Pack," Connor said. He leaned toward me, so I caught the scene of his cologne, woodsy and warm. "And he's an incorrigible flirt."

"Is that a statement or a warning?"

"Yes."

I rolled my eyes. "He's fine. But, seriously, make sure he buys a good coat."

It would take a month, I guessed, before I'd be able to wash the smoke and paprika and molasses out of the jumpsuit.

"Come with me," Connor said when the van was gone.

"Only if you have a frosty margarita and a hot bath," I said, rolling my shoulder.

"How is it?" he asked.

"Healing, but slowly. I'm not sure if this extra workout will keep it from stiffening up, or make it worse."

"Then I'll make it up to you. I don't have baths or margaritas. But how about barbecue and a hot shifter?"

"I could probably manage that."

"Good." He took my hand, led me through the loading bay and into a quiet hallway lit by the glow of the tea light candles used to warm chafing dishes. Two disposable plates of food flanked the candles, their compartments filled with meats and sides.

I looked up at him, eyes sparkling. "We're getting our romantic dinner after all."

"I wasn't sure how long two dogs would last you, and I didn't want you to start biting my relatives."

"Wrong species," I said. "I don't bite shifters."

"Oh, we'll see about that," he said with a grin. "Not as nice as I had planned for tonight, and none of the baguettes you were going to make from scratch." He paused, looked at me. "I forgot to ask—did you make them?"

"Let us never speak of it again. But do let us speak of dinner, because I'm starving."

The barbecue was, of course, delicious. We ate like hungry kids who'd snuck forbidden candy—stuffing in the food as quickly as possible, lest someone come to take it away, and grinning the entire time.

When we were done, we leaned back against the wall, legs stretched in front of us.

"You do know how to show a girl a good time."

"Just wait until January. You're going to love grilling burgers outside when it's twenty degrees below zero."

I slid him a glance. "Is that a dare?"

"You think you can handle it?"

"Recall that I had to shovel the Cadogan House sidewalk. Until I saved enough money to pay someone to do it."

"Always strategizing," he said and climbed to his feet.

"It's the vampire way."

He checked his watch. "About two hours until dawn," he said, then offered me a hand, pulled me up. "Now that we've done our penance and refueled, let's go see the boss."

"We already talked to Berna," I pointed out.

"Hilarious. And maybe don't mention that to the Apex."

We found him in the lounge behind the public bar, where the Pack's senior members handled shifter business or played cards, or both, depending on the business.

There were four shifters in the room now. Miranda, two men I didn't recognize, and last but never least, Gabriel Keene, the Apex of the North American Central Pack.

He sat at the head of a well-worn table, booted ankles crossed on the tabletop, arms folded. He seemed to take up more space in the room than he physically occupied. Power given substance. I wondered how much of that was being Apex, and how much was just *him*.

Gabriel's gaze was on a screen on the opposite wall. And on that screen, in brilliant color, Connor and I fought side by side against the AAM.

"Well," Gabriel said, without shifting his gaze. "You two certainly had an evening."

"Fucking vampires," Miranda muttered, smiling mirthlessly at me while she said it.

With a sigh, Gabriel dropped his feet to the floor, looked back at me and Connor. "I suppose we need to have a conversation."

"All right," Connor said, voice all smooth confidence.

"Give us the room," Gabriel said. The two men exchanged a

glance before slipping out. Miranda strode toward us with a well-practiced sneer. "Jumping into petty vampire squabbles doesn't help us," she said, then gave Connor a long look before following the men.

Connor closed the door, walked to the table, and touched a control that had the screen flicking to darkness. "We've done our chores," he said, turning back to his father.

"Chores?" Gabriel asked.

"Berna was waiting in the lobby. Put us to work on the McAlister order."

"Okay?"

Connor blinked. "She said you were pissed at me for making a scene and ordered us to help in the kitchens."

Gabriel's laugh was deep and generous. "I haven't spoken with her all night, and I didn't order you punished."

Connor looked at his father for a moment, then sighed. "Berna's still angry."

"And passive-aggressive."

Connor looked at me, humor and apology mixing in his eyes. "I guess you took my punishment for me."

At least it let me ignore the vampires for a while. "What did you do to deserve that?"

"I forgot her birthday."

"Dangerous," I said.

Gabriel clucked his tongue. "He's learned his lesson now. As for the incident, I assume it's about Carlie?"

"It is," Connor said, and he laid it out, from the late-night visit to the confrontation at the Grove.

"Showed up at your door," Gabriel said, linking his hands behind his head. "That takes guts or stupidity."

"Or both," Connor said. "The arrogance to try and the belief that what you're doing is necessary."

Gabriel glanced at me. "Nice sword work."

"Thanks. Practice."

"Good. Your parents still gone?"

"For now," I said. But I had a feeling it wouldn't be the case for long.

"That explains the AAM's timing." He frowned. "What do they want?"

"Testing and my agreement to join a House."

He looked at me for a very long time. Long enough that I began to wonder if he'd seen the monster lurking behind my eyes.

"I'd have fought back, too," Gabriel finally said, his voice utterly casual. "Did the vamps think you'd just go along with it?"

"I'm not sure," I decided. "The leader looked eager for a fight, and more than a little thrilled when I said no."

"So he could then use you as an example?"

"Maybe," I said. "I'm going to talk to my parents when I get home. They'll have contacted the AAM by now, and they might have more information."

I nodded, and Gabriel shifted his gaze to Connor.

"As for the fighting, while I absolutely encourage a good old-fashioned brawl, it's best to avoid political nonsense when we can. Vampire problems are not Pack problems. On the other hand," he added, before Connor could interject, "many vampires and members of the Pack are friends, and they help each other. And sometimes," he said, that knowing gaze landing on me, "helping results in consequences that seem unfair."

And what, I wondered, would have been a fair consequence? In its most technical sense, I had broken the AAM's rules, and the unspoken covenant with humans that we wouldn't treat them like prey or potentials—unless they asked nicely. Yes, I'd done it for good reason, but the rule had still been broken.

"I'd do the same thing again," I said.

"That's because you have honor," Gabriel said. "I'd have expected nothing less of a Sullivan kid."

"What about sanctuary?" Connor asked. "The Pack could give her protection until the AAM gives up. We've offered it before."

"And I'd decline if you offered it," I said.

Gabriel's brows lifted with interest; Connor's furrowed with obvious frustration.

"You'd decline it," he said, voice flat and suddenly angry.

"I can't refuse to join a vampire House—violently—and then turn around and accept protection from the Pack. It's hypocritical."

"It's practical."

"It's impossible." We both looked back at Gabriel. "We cannot offer sanctuary to non-shifters."

Connor stalked to the other side of the room, as if to burn off frustration. "That's ridiculous."

"That's Pack."

"She's in trouble because of us."

"And she doesn't want sanctuary," Gabriel said.

"She's also in the room," I said. "So stop talking about me like I'm not here. I'm in trouble because of something I did. I accept that, and I'll figure out a way to deal with it." I turned to Connor. "I appreciate the offer and the concern. But that's not the way to resolve this."

He growled, a low rumble of warning. If I'd been in a different place, and in the middle of a different discussion, I might have taken a step back. But I wasn't in the mood to be handled or growled at.

"Growl at me again," I said, taking a step closer.

"I'll growl in my own territory if I feel like growling."

"Children."

We both looked at his father.

"Might I suggest you both take a break? You've had a long night."

I couldn't argue with that, so we said our goodbyes and made for the door—but stopped short at the new chyron that practically screamed from the bottom of the screen: ATLANTA VAMPS CAUSING TROUBLE IN CHICAGO? Above it, blurry figures moved in grainy footage of the fight.

Really, the chyron was about the best we could hope for. And I'd take it.

My relief lasted only until my arrival at the loft.

Lulu was gone, presumably at Mateo's, and the apartment was dark and secure. Out of habit I turned on the wall screen when we went inside, to check the coverage again, and found the AAM had released its own statement. The précis: Chicago vampire breaks rules, refuses to accept due punishment. The statement was vague on details; they didn't go so far as to say what rules I'd broken, probably because they didn't want to kick up sympathy for me, or fear, given the reason for Carlie's change.

The AAM would be waging this war in the media and on the ground, it seemed.

"Assholes," Connor murmured.

"Yeah," I said. "They are." I was exhausted, and dawn was drawing ever closer. I wanted to sit down with him, sink into his arms, and let his nearness wash away the dregs of the night, of battle, of bloodshed. Of fighting a dozen vamps who'd flown across the country to detest me in person.

But I couldn't do that yet. Not when I still had a call to make.

"I'll be back," I said, screen in hand as I looked toward my bedroom.

"Your parents?"

I nodded.

"You can call them out here."

I put a hand on his chest, stretched up to kiss him. "Thank you.

But I think for this first volley, I'd better handle them myself. But could you stay until I'm done? I might need an emotional support wolf by then."

"Can I raid the fridge?"

"Only if you promise to eat the rest of the deviled eggs," I said and made my way down the hall.

SIX

Ipulled my hair into a knot, sat cross-legged on the bed, and turned on my screen.

Irony of ironies, I found four messages waiting. Three Houses had offered me membership, effective immediately. Chicago's Rogues made the same offer, ironically. I sent polite refusals to all of them. And then called the Master and Sentinel of Cadogan House.

They answered immediately. My mother, with pale skin and dark hair, wore a Cadogan T-shirt even while half a world away. My father, whose blond hair I'd inherited, wore a button-down white shirt, as he nearly always did.

"Elisa," said my mom. "Are you okay?"

"I'm fine," I said, and I gave them the entire story, from the AAM at my door to the fight at the Grove. And the promise of what was to come.

I left out no details, and would have sworn I could feel their furious magic through the connection. My mother's anger and concern were clear on her face. My father, who had four hundred years of vampirism on her, didn't let his emotions show as easily. But his eyes had gone quicksilver.

"You should have told us when they came to your door," he said sternly.

"If I'd told you, you'd have come here. That puts you both in the middle of it, and it pits you against the AAM. That's dangerous for you and for Cadogan."

"You're our daughter," he said, eyes blazing. "We'll get flights out as soon as we can."

"I can handle this myself."

"You don't have to handle it yourself," my mother said, taking his hand. "Not alone. And you won't. We know how to protect the House."

I wanted to argue more, but knew that would be a waste of time. They were my parents, and they were protective. And I'd come by my stubbornness honestly. "Okay."

"They waited until we were gone," my father said.

"That's the operative guess," I agreed. "What do you know about the Compliance Bureau? Theo says it's new." In vampire terms, at least.

"I'm now aware of its existence," Dad said. "Nicole created the Bureau, authorized it to investigate and deal with rule breaking. Now that we're in the public eye again, and contrary to the operations of the Greenwich Presidium, she wants to ensure rules are enforced without bias or favoritism."

I could all but feel part of the cage falling into place, and I didn't like the sensation.

"There are rules for a reason," he added after a moment, and with what sounded like regret. "We prohibit non-Masters from creating vampires because of the risks—to humans, because the vampires may not be strong enough to make them without injury. To vampires, because changing humans can attract human attention."

"I'm not the first person who's changed a vampire without being a Master. Or a Rogue," I added.

"No," Dad said. "You aren't. But you're strong, you're in Chicago . . . and you're our daughter."

"And that has benefits . . . and costs," I finished. My parents were physically strong and well-connected, and head of one of the most popular and powerful Houses in the country. I'd been fortunate enough to grow up in the midst of that privilege. But not all vampires trusted them, or the concentration of power. And then there was me—born without precedent. Another unknown.

"They demanded I join a House," I said. "Which means they know what we talked about—that I wasn't Initiated or Commended."

"You aren't in our registry," Dad said. A crease of worry appeared between his brows. "We provide information to the AAM regarding all Novitiates, Initiates. The AAM may have noticed your absence. Obviously you have an open invitation to join Cadogan House. Or you could join Washington House. Malik would offer you a position."

"I know."

"That would be an easy solution," Mom said, pushing her dark hair behind her ears. "All things considered. Fealty isn't so hard as it seems," she offered, her tone so gentle, so full of hope. "It wasn't how I imagined my life would go, but I adjusted." She slid my father a knowing glance. "Mostly."

"I can't swear fealty to someone, to a House, just to ease the minds of the AAM. They don't want me to join a House for the benefits. They want to know someone is watching me, or that someone can use me.

"It probably doesn't feel like it," I said, meeting their gazes, "but it's not personal. I'm glad I grew up in Cadogan, and I'm proud of what you did for its vampires. I just . . . need something different."

"Maybe the Pack—" my father said, and I shook my head.

"No fealty to the Pack, either," I said. "I wouldn't substitute one for the other. And the Pack can't offer sanctuary to a vampire."

My father's eyes narrowed, probably because I already knew the answer and he'd now begun wondering why.

"Fealty isn't the only thing they want," I said, changing the subject. "They also want me to be tested."

When my parents looked at each other—and something unspoken passed between them—my belly tightened.

"What?" I asked.

"Did they give any specifics?" my father asked.

"No. I assume they meant the usual Testing for would-be Masters. Why?"

My mother was the one to finally speak, and it took her a moment to meet my gaze. "This isn't the first time they've inquired about Testing."

I stared at her, and even the monster was concerned enough to sink down lower. "They asked you to let them test me? How? When?"

"It started when you were maybe eleven or twelve," Dad said. "The first time, they visited Cadogan House, asked our permission to test you. They said it was because you were unique. Because we'd been so fortunate to have you, and they wanted to understand how it had happened."

"But we'd already told them how," my mother said. "They knew about Mallory and the magic and the—biological component."

I held up a hand. "Skip the details of the biological component, please."

My mother didn't smile like I'd hoped, which made my fear heavier. "Then they changed their story. They said Testing would be for your protection, for ours . . . and for theirs. They wanted to know if you were stronger than other vampires. If you had unique talents."

I was something new, something not seen in the millennia of vampire history—and immortals didn't care for that kind of novelty. Or for the possibility, however small, that I would be different. Better.

"If I was a threat," I said, finishing her thought. "You said they came to the House?"

Now I wondered if I'd seen them. There had been plenty of vampires in and out of Cadogan, and I didn't know all of them. But I had a distinct memory of seeing my parents meet with a group of unfamiliar vampires, all of them dressed in formal black. There'd been something about this group—or maybe about the magic they'd triggered from my parents—that had stood out. That had made me think they weren't entirely friends of the House.

I'd been, like Dad had said, maybe twelve, and I'd finished with my classes for the day—the tutoring that served as my school. I'd been hungry, and I'd walked by my father's office on the way to the Cadogan kitchen. The door had been open, which wasn't unusual. The vampires were inside, their expressions cold. And when they'd seen me in the doorway, their eyes narrowed.

There'd been footsteps, and Dad had come to the doorway. He'd smiled at me. "We'll eat as soon as we're done in here," he'd said kindly, and closed the door.

I looked at my parents. "You told them no, obviously."

"We did," my mother said.

"Vehemently," Dad added.

"And they accepted that?"

"After the third or fourth time," Dad said. "Each time they asked, we told you you owed them nothing and they would not question you, examine you, or test you without your consent."

"He means he scared them," my mother said with a smile. "And they didn't ask again."

"They never contacted me," I said. I'd gone to college, made no waves, and had done nothing terribly interesting from a vampiric or magical standpoint. Maybe they'd decided I wasn't a threat.

But I'd interested them again, and I'd handed them a reason to pursue formal Testing this time. Not just because they were curious or afraid, but because they believed it was justified.

"You should have told me," I said, as kindly as I could manage. But even the monster was annoyed; I could feel the jagged edge of its betrayal. "I would have been better prepared for this."

"We're sorry," Mom said. "We thought it was over, that they'd been satisfied you were just . . . a vampire."

Oh, I was anything but that.

They promised their support, and to talk to Nicole again. I went back into the living room and found Connor on the couch, arms crossed and frowning as he stared at his screen.

"What now?"

He kicked down his legs and sat up, giving me his attention. "What?"

"You're glowering at whatever you're looking at there," I said and gestured toward the screen. "More bad news?"

"Oh, no. I was reading."

"Reading what?"

His expression was flat. "A book, brat."

"Shifters can read?"

He grunted. "I was reviewing a manual about the care and feeding of vampires."

I sat down beside him, put my head on his shoulder. "What did you learn?"

"Since I already knew they were high-maintenance, not much."

"Ha ha ha," I said, mimicking his flat tone.

"How did it go?" he asked.

"They want me to join a House. They're baffled I won't just join Cadogan. And that's not the only thing."

He drew me toward him, wrapped his arms around me. I let down the shields I hadn't realized I'd drawn around me, around the monster, and curled into him. And felt a knife-sharp pain in my shoulder. I winced, adjusted.

"Still hurts?"

"Only if I use it. Or touch it. Or think about it. I'll be fine by tomorrow." I hoped. Because I was over the ache.

"What's the other thing?" he asked.

"The AAM has apparently been curious about me for a long time. They came to Cadogan House when I was younger. They wanted to have me tested even then."

He stilled, as if his body was braced against his own rising fury. "When you were still in the House? You didn't tell me."

"I didn't know, or not the whole of it. Only that vampires had visited. Apparently they'd been trying to get my parents to agree to their examination."

He snorted, relaxed a little. "I imagine your dad had some choice words. And your mother showed them her sword. And it must have worked. The AAM hadn't contacted you directly after that?"

"No. Not until this."

Silence fell, and Connor stroked my back, up and down, up and down, and some of the tension I'd been holding melted away.

"You should think about telling your parents about the—your—monster," Connor said. "Not because you owe them," he added, noting my quick jerk, "but because there's nothing wrong with what you are."

"I'm not convinced they'd see it that way," I said. "And I'm not ready yet. I want to have—control's not the right word, but maybe more agreement with the monster before I do that."

That I felt its shimmering irritation at the notion that I controlled it just proved my point.

"Okay," he said. "But I want you to be prepared if they—if everyone—finds out before you're ready."

"Because of the AAM," I said quietly.

"Yeah. Maybe inadvertently, but yeah." He pressed a kiss to my forehead. "They're going to keep pushing you, because they want to either pressure you into giving up or provoke you into doing something. I've known plenty like Clive. He's the type who loves a fight. And if the fight doesn't come to him, he's happy to start one."

"And let others take the first swing."

"Absolutely. Bullies are usually cowards."

Silence fell across us, soft and comforting as a blanket.

"If you were me," I finally said, rustling that stillness, "what would you do?"

It took him a moment to answer, and I appreciated that he was actually considering the question. "I'm a shifter. I'd take freedom, always."

I exhaled, closed my eyes, felt well and truly *seen*. "Thank you."

"For?"

"For being you. And for letting me . . . be."

His strong arms were a wall against the world. "If you can't be who you are—if we can't be who we are—what's the point?"

"I don't disagree," I said, especially since he was the only one who knew the truth about me. The only one around whom I could lay down my armor.

He tipped up my chin, kissed me with a tenderness that surprised me. I curled my fingers into his hair and tugged him closer, felt the answering thud of his heart.

My heart became a drum, my blood a symphony of need. We hadn't had sex yet, and were again dancing on the precipice. We'd done plenty of flirting and a delicious amount of making out, but with supernatural drama nearly always intervening, we hadn't yet had the time or space to be physically vulnerable.

I nipped at his bottom lip, and his fingers drew lines up my back, pressing my body against his. I could feel Connor's own need, the tension of hard muscle as he wrestled desire against control.

And then he growled, and I heard regret in it. He pulled back.

I looked up at him. "What?"

"Not yet," he managed. "Not tonight. You're still wounded, and sex with shifters is usually . . . adventurous."

That didn't slow the racing of my heart. "I could use that kind of adventure."

Connor's smile was wide and satisfied. "And you'll get it. But for our first time, I don't want there to be pain. Only joy, only me and you. Not the AAM, not fear." He traced a fingertip across my lips. "Just us, Lis."

SEVEN

I slept poorly. Dreamed of being chained in old iron shackles, being led toward gallows where a vampire with a gleaming stake of oiled aspen waited to strike.

I didn't know what to do, what I could do. There was no precedent to follow, no procedures to take comfort in. Unless, of course, I swore fealty to a House or a band of Rogues. Swore an immortality's worth of service to a Master. Which wasn't, as far as I was concerned, an option.

I got dressed, returned to my room, eventually heard the shower running again. That meant Lulu had made it home either last night or this morning. And I was sure she'd tell me if Mateo's skills as an artist extended into . . . other areas.

Without a better idea, I decided to start with something uncomfortable. I should have done it yesterday, but there hadn't been time between vampires and shifters and dawn.

Ronan answered quickly. "Elisa. We just heard. Are you all right?"

I had to take a moment, because there was actual concern in his voice. I hadn't expected that from the man I assumed had ratted me out to the AAM.

"I'm—fine," I decided on. "You saw the video?"

"We did. You weren't injured?"

"Not seriously. Is everything okay there? Is Carlie okay?"

"She's fine. Do you think they'd harm her?" His voice had tightened, become deeper, as he donned the cloak of protector of his coven.

"I don't think so. They see her as a victim"—and undoubtedly she was, even if that's not all she was—"not a rule breaker. But it's possible they'd get in touch, or maybe visit. I don't know. Ronan—" I started, but he cut me off.

"I didn't tell them. I can hear the question in your voice, and I didn't tell them. I can't say that I'd have done what you did. But I wasn't there, and you had to make a decision. And Carlie is . . . special."

I was relieved to hear his honesty and to know that Carlie was appreciated.

"She is," I agreed. "Do you know who might have reported me?"

"No one here," he said. "What happened is Carlie's business. That is how we return her power. She has told no one how or why she was changed, and the coven has respected her silence."

If word hadn't come from Minnesota—vampire or shifter—then from who?

"Do you need protection?"

I winced, guilt now a warm wash across my skin. I'd underestimated Ronan, and badly. I'd demanded sympathy for my decision, and hadn't offered any when I'd brought trouble and a new vampire to his door and he'd reacted with suspicion.

"No, but the offer is appreciated. And I'll apologize for any difficulties I've caused you because of what happened."

Silence for a moment, then, "Thank you. That is appreciated. What will you do now that blood has been shed?"

"I don't know yet," I said, my honest answer. "We should tell her questions are being asked. I can do it, unless you prefer to do so."

He was quiet for so long I thought he'd disconnected me. "You should tell her. It will mean more coming from you."

"Okay."

"This likely feels complicated," Ronan said. "But in truth, it is not. You agree to their demands, or you don't. You must decide which consequences will be easier to live with. And Elisa?"

"Yes?"

"If you're searching for the person who reported you, you should probably look closer to home."

He left me with that, and I stared at the screen for a moment, and couldn't disagree with a word he'd said.

"Damn it," I said and rubbed my temples with my free hand. Too many knew about Minnesota, about Carlie. Anyone she or Ronan had told. Any Pack member in Minnesota who might have spread the word back here. Connor, Alexei, Gabriel, and whoever had learned it from them. My parents, and anyone in Cadogan House who might have overheard our conversation. Theo, Petra, Roger, and anyone else in the OMB.

It would have taken only a call, just that small and dangerous bait. And the AAM would have bitten immediately.

"Damn it," I said again and pulled up Carlie's number. I'd already insulted one person tonight; might as well give another bad news.

She answered immediately. "Elisa! How are you?" She always sounded cheery and charming, every time I called her.

"It's been a week," I admitted. "Are you okay? Is everything okay there?"

"We're great. I'm working night shifts at the doughnut shop, and I think they taste even better now."

"I'm glad to hear it." She'd worked at the doughnut shop before the change, and I was glad she'd been able to maintain that connection to her community.

"Listen, Carlie. There's something going on down here. The AAM, the vampire assembly, says I broke the rules when I changed you."

"I was *dying*." She sounded offended, which was exactly how I'd have taken it.

"They know. But they're technically right, and vampires like rules. They don't like exceptions. Has anyone tried to contact you? To talk to you about it?"

"No. I'd have told you or Ronan."

"Okay. That's what I thought. I just wanted to make sure. I don't want them harassing you or causing any trouble."

She snorted. "As if they'd come up to bumblefuck Minnesota for that. Chicago's much sexier."

I bit back a smile; I knew she was trying to make me laugh, but it felt too soon for that. Especially for her to be prodding at me, when this was all my doing.

I heard her shift, the tone of her voice change as if she'd sat suddenly upright. "Should I come down? Me and Ronan and the others? We would help you kick their uptight asses."

I'd barely known Carlie when she'd been attacked. But each time I talked to her, I became more convinced I'd done the right thing. Maybe that, too, had been why Ronan wanted me to talk to her.

"No," I said. "Let's hold on that for now. I wouldn't want to waste an army that talented on something as ridiculous as this."

"Good," she said, and she sounded relieved. "So it's no big?"

"It's no big," I lied. "But if they get in touch, let me know, so I can deal with that, too."

"Will do. Oh, I gotta go. Give Connor a big squeeze."

I promised I would and ended the call. Then I put my head on my knees, and breathed.

I dressed in a drapey emerald tank and fitted jeans, my summer uniform, and had just pulled on boots when there was a knock at the door.

I doubted the AAM would be so polite, and we hadn't made

nearly enough noise to irritate Mrs. Prohaska. I actually thought to check the security peep this time, and found Theo waiting, along with Roger Yuen and Detective Robinson.

Fear was a cold stone in my belly, but I opened the door. "What's wrong?"

"Elisa Sullivan," Robinson said, stepping forward. "You need to come with us."

"Why?"

"For questioning in the death of the vampire known as Blake."

I looked at her, battling confusion at the name, and relief that it wasn't someone I was close to. "From the Compliance Bureau?"

Yuen and Robinson exchanged a silent glance, then Robinson looked at me. "So you knew him."

She must have known this; Theo would have told her. "He was one of the vampires who came to my door, who gave me the summons." Fear was replaced by a sinking dread. "One of the AAM members is dead. And you think I did it."

I certainly hadn't killed him, and didn't even know how he'd died. Did the AAM have enemies in Chicago? Or was it still trying to make them?

"Lis?"

I looked back, found Lulu in a robe, hair damp from the shower, arms wrapped around her torso. "What's wrong?"

"Call Connor," I told her and grabbed my jacket. "Tell him I'm with the Ombuds, that a member of the AAM is dead."

It was all I had time to say before they hustled me down the hallway.

They put me in the back of a vehicle, drove me to the former brick factory that now housed the OMB office. No one spoke. Theo gave me a nod, but otherwise made no contact.

I wasn't angry, not yet. But the dread was heavy. I knew Theo and Yuen, trusted them both. I didn't know Robinson, and I didn't trust the AAM. I had trouble believing the AAM would sacrifice one of their own to frame me, but I didn't know of any other motive. If the AAM was behind this, they'd morphed from accusing me of breaking their rules to flat-out murder. What *wouldn't* they do to punish me?

We drove through the gate to the complex of brick buildings, fronted by a small parking lot for any humans or Sups who might find their way to the offices. The vehicle stopped in front. Detective Robinson helped me out of the car and kept a firm grip on my arm as she escorted me through the lobby, the receptionist wide-eyed, and into a narrow hallway to an interview room.

I'd been in the interview rooms before, had sat at the aluminum table with Theo to question Sups who'd been accused of causing trouble, or had accused someone else.

Other than the table, the two-way glass that led to the observation room, and the caged overhead lights, the room was empty. It was grim and functional, and not designed to put the interviewee at ease. It was effective that way.

I took the chair that perpetrators had occupied during my prior visits, tried to roll the tightness out of my shoulder; Gwen and Theo came in, took the chairs opposite me. Roger Yuen was apparently going to sit out the discussion. Maybe, I thought ruefully, because he was my employer.

Gwen was in the seat I usually filled, and that was another pinch around my heart. She'd brought in a file folder, dropped it onto the table.

Might as well get this started, I thought. "I don't need an attorney. And I'll answer any questions you like." And I was aware of the privilege that let me do that without further worry. "But I didn't kill Blake. I've only seen him twice—at my door two nights ago, and last night at the Grove. I don't know who killed him."

"Tell us about the night they came to your door," Gwen said.

"We'd had a party, and most everyone had left. Him, Levi, and . . ." I closed my eyes, trying to remember the name of the woman. "Sloan," I remembered. "Blake was an ass. Sloan tried to smooth it over. Or that was the role she played."

"Good cop," Gwen said.

I nodded.

"And after that?"

"At the Grove," I said again. I had a feeling I'd be saying lots of things twice. But I was still numb to my anger. For now there was only misery and disgust. "How was he killed?"

"Decapitated," Gwen said. And with a considering look at me, flipped open the folder and spread the photographs it contained on the table.

I drew one toward me with a fingertip, and studied death.

His body lay sprawled on a floor of gold-flecked stone, his arms and legs spread. As promised, his head had been removed and lay a few feet away, eyes open wide, as if shocked by the situation in which he'd found himself. Blood was everywhere, in great dark pools, in splatters across the floor and the stone wall. Some had been smeared, maybe by the killer, maybe by a crime scene investigator. There was a coldness to it—not just because of the gruesomeness. Blake had been murdered, dropped, and left there in the pool of his own blood. The killer had simply walked away.

I looked up, found both gazes on me. Watching. Considering. Evaluating my reaction. I'd seen death, had sent vampires into its bony hands, its wicked care. I didn't look for opportunities to kill, and regretted the need for it. I pitied his death, the insult of leaving him sprawled on the floor like garbage. But I didn't know him and found it hard to muster sympathy.

For me, for the city, for Carlie, I had plenty. My anger was growing now, sparked by the waste of life and the real possibility the AAM was bringing more trouble than they'd revealed to me. That made it imperative I help find who'd killed him, and keep them from hurting anyone else.

I pulled the other photographs nearer, the same bloody visual but from different angles, and frowned down at them. Something was missing. There was no visible katana, but he was dressed in jeans and a T-shirt. Casual clothing, so he may not have worn the scabbard anyway.

Something else.

I closed my eyes, thought of the night they'd come to the door in their matching suits, and last night in their matching fatigues. And the one feature they'd apparently been allowed to personalize.

I opened my eyes again. "His pendant is gone."

Gwen's eyes widened. "His what?"

I gestured to my neck. "He had a pendant necklace. Some kind of stone on a leather cord."

"You noticed he was wearing jewelry?" she asked.

"It was unusual," I said. "They all wear the same clothes—like uniforms. Suits the first night; combat gear the second. A few had on necklaces or pendants. They were noticeable against the sameness."

"That's good," Theo said and earned a sharp look from Gwen, who'd no doubt wanted him to maintain at least the pretense of objectivity.

"We'll look into it," Gwen said noncommittally. "Do you notice anything else?"

"The killer used a sword," I said. I knew what a katana could do.

"Based on the medical examiner's preliminary opinion, yes. Long, single-sided blade. And wielded by someone with skill. One cut, and no indication there'd been any second thought, any hesitation. The cut would have shown it."

Vampires liked bladed weapons, I thought. "Where was he killed?" I asked.

"Inside the Brass & Copper building."

It was one of the city's famous landmarks—a skyscraper of stone striped with brass and copper that stood on Michigan Avenue just south of the river. It had been built by an industrial magnate—Brass & Copper Amalgamated, natch—during the city's Gilded Age.

"In the shade, I assume, so the sun wouldn't disappear him." I looked up at her. "Someone wanted him to be found."

"You?"

"I didn't kill him, and I don't know why anyone would want him dead."

"He accused you of breaking AAM rules," Gwen said.

"The Bureau made the accusation; he's one of many. And I say there's an exception; the AAM disagrees."

"He and the others attacked you," Gwen said. "They want you in, what did they call it, seclusion."

"And I declined. Blake, as far as I can tell, was just the messenger. Clive is the one in charge."

Gwen ignored that. "Where were you last night?"

"The Grove, as you know. After that, NAC headquarters. We helped prepare a catering order, and there were at least two dozen shifters, including the Apex, who'd be happy to verify that. After that, we went home. It was nearly dawn when I went to bed."

"Alone?"

I looked up at Robinson, my eyes flat. "Yes. My bed empty, my apartment empty. Lulu was . . . gone." Presumably at Mateo's, but I hadn't even had time to ask her before they'd escorted me out.

"So you don't have an alibi for the time of the murder?"

Sneaky question. "I don't know when the murder occurred, so I don't know where I was."

"Six ten in the morning," Theo said.

I thought back. "I'd have been in bed and unconscious. The sun is so bad for the skin," I added dryly, then frowned as I began to think logically again. "That's, like, ten minutes before sunrise, and it's at least a twenty-minute drive from Brass & Copper to the loft, depending on traffic."

I paused, let them do the math. "You found me in the loft just after dawn. I had to be in the loft before the sun came up, or I'd have been burned." I pulled up my sleeves, showed the unmarred skin. "I wasn't."

"Armored car?" Gwen asked.

"I don't have a car, much less a sun-shielded one. Regardless, I was at the loft. The building has a security camera on the door. Lulu wanted to be sure she was in a secure building."

Gwen looked up at the window, nodded at someone on the other side, who, I guessed, was now in charge of obtaining a copy of the video.

She looked at me again. "So you ordered someone to do it."

I met her gaze, steadily. "Your first theory was that I killed a man I barely know in a building I've never been in for no apparent reason. That didn't pan out, so you think I have assassins on call, and I'd have them do my dirty work for me. I'm not sure which is more insulting," I said and heard the temper in my voice. Didn't mind it.

"If a vampire killed him," I continued, "he'd either have stayed in the building or had a sun-shielded car of his own. If it was a human, he could have walked away. Is the building secured?"

"Not the area where Blake was found," Gwen said. "There are public restaurants and shops in the lobby. He was found on that floor, albeit in a low-traffic area. You'd need a badge for the elevators to go up to the business floors."

"Residences?"

"No."

They might have pulled me in for questioning, but if they'd really believed I'd done it, they wouldn't be giving me so many details. So while I let myself relax, I didn't let my guard fully down.

"Why was Blake in the Brass & Copper building right before dawn?" I asked. "If there aren't any residences, there's nowhere to bed down if he misses the timing and the sun comes up. That's dangerous."

"Coffee," Theo said. "There's a coffee shop in the lobby, and it opens early. We have a surveillance shot of him buying a drink shortly before he was killed."

"Alone?"

"Alone," Theo said. "Doesn't mean he was alone when he went into the building or afterward."

"Perhaps you glamoured him," Gwen said. "Convinced him to do something risky. Maybe you hoped the sun would do the work for you."

Instinctively, I touched the spot on my thigh that still bore a pale scar, earned in Minnesota when a magic-crazed shifter had tried to rip the protective shielding off a window in the middle of the day. He'd managed only to damage it, but the thin bead of sunlight hurt worse than a blade. Had hurt badly enough to wake me from daytime unconsciousness.

"Glamour doesn't change minds," I said. "It lowers inhibitions. It's persuasive, but sunlight kills. You'd need something more than glamour to convince a vampire to risk it."

Coffee addiction or not—and I knew from coffee addiction— was a vampire going to risk death by scorching just to get a fix? "You'll need to check how he arrived—and how he intended to get out again. It's very risky behavior, especially for someone who isn't from Chicago and doesn't know their way around."

Gwen didn't look thrilled that I was giving her investigatory advice. Which I suppose seemed pretty cocky. "What do you have against the AAM?" she asked.

I understood that presumed motive was a fundamental part of her investigation. But it was becoming harder not to take the questions personally. "I have nothing against the AAM. As I said, we disagree about interpretation of the rules."

"And you're angry at them?"

"I'm angry that the organization gives so little value to the life of a human. Especially when that human was nearly killed in a supernatural feud that had nothing to do with her."

"Blake came to your home. Threatened you."

"He came to my home with two other vampires on behalf of the AAM. He didn't threaten me. He asked me to meet the Bureau in Grant Park."

"And you suggested the Grove." She looked up. "Why?"

"It's outside the city. Less populated, so there'd be less risk of human injury if things went awry. Which they did."

Her brows lifted. "You were expecting violence."

I knew she knew all this. Some she'd heard from me at the Grove; some she'd heard from Theo. But I kept playing along.

"The Bureau came to Chicago," I said with monumental patience, "to accuse me of breaking their rules by saving a human life. That doesn't scream 'reasonable' to me. So I expected more unreasonable behavior to follow. I was right."

"They claimed you drew first blood."

She had done her homework, so I nodded. "They claimed it, but they caused it. One of their vampires threw a knife at Alexei Breckenridge. He threw one back. Theirs missed; his didn't. They started the fight, but we technically drew first blood."

"You own a sword," Theo said.

I shifted my gaze to him. "I do. You've trained with it." We'd done a few rounds in the OMB gym.

"I know," he said, and there was regret and guilt in the words.

"Where is it?" Gwen asked, and added notes to her file.

"At the loft."

"Will you turn it over for forensic analysis?"

There were limits to everything. Including my cooperation.

"No," I said, and she stopped taking notes, looked up at me.

"You refuse?"

"If you have a duly executed warrant, you're welcome to take it. But since I didn't hurt Blake, I don't think you'll be able to get one. It's possible there's a trace of his blood on it; I don't know. The fight at the Grove was intense, and I'm not sure who the blade touched. But I didn't kill him." I looked at Theo. "I suggest you talk to Clive, find out who the Compliance Bureau has pissed off recently."

"Other than you?"

"Pissed off," I repeated, "and is willing to use murder as a tool of revenge. Because I'm not. Nor, for the record, are any of my friends."

"Killing Blake might slow down the AAM's prosecution of you," Theo said. "Divert their attention."

And killing Clive would have done that faster, I thought, but managed not to say that out loud. "I don't want to divert their attention," I said instead. "I want them to leave me alone. That's not going to happen now. Instead, they're probably going to draw the same conclusion you did. They're going to think I did it."

And they were going to come after me even harder.

Three more times. We went through it three more times, enough to have my temper flare and fall again. By the time we were done, it was midnight, and I was exhausted.

I hadn't killed Blake. But I didn't like the coincidence that he'd been killed here, during a trip to Chicago to investigate me, to confront me. And why Blake particularly?

"Theo," Gwen said, and the word snapped me out of my thoughts. "Would you give me and Ms. Sullivan a minute?"

Brows lifted, he looked between us, nodded. "I'll be right outside," he said and rose.

"And clear out the observation room," she said.

Another look of surprise, but after checking my face, he nodded at that, too, and left us alone.

I had no idea what to expect, or what she didn't think she could say in front of Theo. So I watched her. When the door closed with a decisive *click*, she rose, flicked a switch on the wall. The mirror went transparent, revealing the observation room on the other side. Empty and nearly as grim as this one was.

Our privacy confirmed, she leaned against the far wall, arms crossed. "It hurts him to interrogate you."

I hadn't expected that. "What?"

"He values your partnership and your friendship. He doesn't want to question you. But he also knows it's the right thing to do—for Chicago, and for you."

I considered that in silence. And she let me. "You and he are close?" I asked.

"We're just friends, if that's what you're asking." She pushed off from the wall, sat at the table again. "I knew him when he was with the CPD, and I was, frankly, disappointed when he moved to the OMB. It's those damn comic books."

Theo was a fan of graphic novels and comics, and told me he'd decided to join the Ombuds because he loved stories of superheroes, of supernaturally inclined crusaders who made a difference in the lives of humans. He thought the OMB was the best way to do that.

For the first time in hours, I smiled just a little. "Tell me about it," I said. "Connor shares the obsession."

"I know. Theo and I grab a beer every once in a while, and he tells me about the latest release or explains how number sixty-two is amazing or somebody I've never heard of is going to be at a comic con or whatever."

"It's a language I don't understand."

"Girl, same." She linked her hands on the table, gave me a level stare. "I know what you've done for Chicago, and what your parents have done. Your great-grandfather."

He'd been Chicago's first supernatural Ombudsman.

"But given what happened last night, there's a good chance this will get uglier before it gets better. For both of you."

I didn't know if she meant me and Theo, or me and Connor. Probably both. And I wasn't sure how much of this was earnest concern versus the questioning technique of a very skilled investigator. But Theo trusted her. So I decided I would, as well.

"I'm not angry at Theo." I scrubbed my hands over my face, giving myself a minute to collect, to gather my thoughts. Then pushed my hair back and sat up again, looked at Gwen.

"I don't know you, but I do know him. I like and respect him. He's smart, and he's savvy, and he's pretty funny, although I'd never admit that to his face. He's had my back, and I hope he'd say the same thing about me. As to the AAM, I probably wouldn't have any complaints about them if they hadn't decided to make an example of me."

I broke eye contact for a moment, deciding how much I should tell her. And, since she'd given me the space for it, opted for the truth.

"Carlie was dying," I said, glancing back. "We were in the woods, surrounded by monsters and too far away to get the help that she needed fast enough. I had to make a decision. And, honestly, I was scared shitless. I'd never made anyone before, and not everyone survives the transition. There was a very good chance I'd screw it up. But it was the only way I knew to save her. So I did, and she survived. I think that should be the end of it."

"She's in Minnesota?"

I nodded. "There's a small vampire coven near her home. The leader agreed to help her through the transition. That way, she could stay near her family and friends, the place she'd lived her entire life. I checked on her earlier. She's safe for now."

"The coven leader," Gwen said. "Is he still angry at you?"

"He says no," I said, and felt that clutch of guilt again.

"And the AAM has targeted you for this."

"Its Compliance Bureau, at any rate."

She nodded, shifted a little in her seat as she crossed one leg over the other. "From my discussions with them, I think most Masters would agree the AAM is necessary. Those in Chicago, certainly. And from what I've heard, Heart generally stays out of the way of Masters trying to do the best for their people." She frowned. "Is something else going on?"

Yes, and Testing was at least part of that something. But she hadn't raised that issue, and I certainly wasn't going to bring it up—or have the CPD wondering why I was so opposed to it. But there was another part.

"It's Clive, I think."

She looked at me. "Yeah?"

I thought back to the moments before the fighting had begun. "He had a lot to say, and a lot of it was personal. I get away with too much, I can't use my origin differences to break the rules, I'm a risk, et cetera. And it wasn't just the words. He had a look in his eyes."

"A look?"

"He was angry, and he was arrogant. But he was also . . . excited? Not like an officer carrying out a duty, but . . ."

"A believer," she said quietly, and I looked up at her.

"Yeah. That's it exactly. He had the glow of the righteous."

She blew out a breath through pursed lips. "That's going to make him—and all of this—difficult. More difficult than it is already."

"I don't want to make trouble for Chicago, for anyone. But I'm not going to give up my autonomy because he's on some kind of mission."

She nodded. "The press will be told you were interviewed, released. If the security footage confirms your whereabouts, they'll be told you were not near the scene when the incident occurred. And I would ask that you contact us, me or Theo, when the AAM makes contact again. I don't say 'if,' because you strike me as a logical person, and you can surmise as well as me that those who have the glow of the righteous, as you put it, won't stop."

I nodded. "I'll give you whatever information I can."

"Then I think we're done here." She rose, moved toward the door, opened it. "Thank you for your time. You're free to go, but don't leave the city for now."

I stepped into the hallway, found Theo waiting. And was unsure what I wanted to say to the man who'd been all but my partner a week ago . . . and felt the fury claw through the hallway like an angry tide.

Connor strode toward me with the bearing of a prince, blue eyes gleaming like a furious angel. His hair was furrowed, like he'd been running his fingers through it, and a lock fell over his eyes. Strong body, beautiful face, and hell in his eyes.

Furious angel indeed.

Then he reached me, and his hands were on my cheeks, strong and protective, as he searched my face with furrowed brows. "You're all right?"

"I'm fine," I said and put a hand on his, squeezed, and found tension had turned the muscle beneath to stone.

"A Compliance Bureau member was killed?" he asked.

"One of the guys who came to the loft. The one who did the talking. His name is Blake. Was Blake," I added grimly.

He nodded, pressed his lips to mine, the kiss as gentle as his anger was fierce. And then he turned that gaze on Theo and Gwen, who'd stepped out behind me.

He aimed that gaze at Theo, a weapon. "You know better. You know she wouldn't do this—wouldn't kill an innocent."

"And they know the AAM already believes we get special treatment," I said. "We can't give them an excuse for more violence."

He bared his teeth at them. "Are you taking their side?"

"No," I said and squeezed his hands again. "I'm taking my side. They know I didn't kill him. But they have to ask. That's the rule."

His gaze slipped back to mine. "Now we're following the rules?"

"We follow the rules we can; we break them if it's necessary to save others." Put that on a damn pennant, I thought, and fly it above the loft.

Connor looked at me for a long time, then nodded. One last stroke of his thumb across my cheek, and he stepped back.

"She's right," Theo said. "If we hadn't questioned her, the AAM would make this even uglier."

"Dropping down to the level of manipulators doesn't impress me," Connor said. "I take it you're satisfied she's innocent?"

Theo's dark eyes were hard. "There are details to confirm. But—in addition to her being a decent person who wouldn't kill out of spite—we expect to confirm she couldn't have been near the scene when the incident occurred."

"So who did it?" Connor asked.

"We can't provide details in an ongoing investigation," Gwen said, and she held up a hand when Connor opened his mouth to protest. "But you should both be careful. Perhaps this was a random killing, but I don't think it was. Whether this was aimed at the AAM, or the result of some AAM struggle, it's likely to touch you again."

"We're leaning toward AAM involvement," Theo said.

"Lean harder," Connor said, and we left them standing there.

EIGHT

I got the message on the way to the SUV he'd borrowed from the Pack. Simple, concise, and heartbreaking: I MUST SUSPEND YOU PENDING INVESTIGATION OF BLAKE'S MURDER. I'M SORRY—ROGER.

It wasn't a surprise. But that didn't make it any less painful. While my great-grandfather had been the first Ombudsman, I was the first one in the family to be fired from the office.

I had more than enough savings to cover rent; I rarely bought anything other than blood and coffee and fine leather pants. But the work kept me sharp, and I liked Roger and Theo and Petra, even if I wasn't thrilled about the current circumstances.

I stopped when we got to the vehicle, rested my head against the closed door.

Connor stopped, looked back at the dull *thump*. "That's not how you get in."

I grunted.

"Are you practicing a new vampire power, or taking a moment?"

I swiveled my head to look at him. "I got fired."

Temper flared in his eyes again. "They just said they believed you were innocent."

"The case is open," I said. "Having me continue to work for them while they investigate me looks like a cover-up."

"That's bullshit," he said, coming around to me. "And I'm sorry."

"Yeah." I lifted my head, looked at him. "I don't know how to feel."

"About Theo? Or Blake?"

"Yes."

"Come here," he said, and beckoned me forward. I went, and put my head against his chest with another dull *thump*.

"Your head is, and I'm not exaggerating, hard as a rock, Lis." He rubbed my arms. "How's your shoulder?"

"Better." The ache was slowly receding, a lowering tide.

"So what's wrong?" he asked.

"I can't get angry."

He chuckled. "If you want to be angry, I'm pretty sure I can make that happen."

"Shouldn't I be angry?" I lifted my head, looked at him. "Shouldn't I be pissed at Theo or Gwen, or Clive or whoever did this? Instead, I just feel numb. Someone is dead. Not because I killed him, but dead because the AAM had to come to Chicago and that precipitated it somehow."

"Lis," he said, concern furrowing his brow, "they want you unbalanced."

I frowned. "What?"

"The AAM comes to Chicago to threaten you. They make demands, and when you say no, they accuse you of starting a physical fight. Then a member of the entourage, one of the vampires that confronted you, is violently murdered. Maybe Blake's death has nothing to do with you. Maybe it was happenstance, or he was in the wrong place at the wrong time. But what are the odds? Maybe Blake's dead because the AAM wants to put more heat on you. Maybe they want you off your game."

"They have succeeded."

"Did you eat before they took you in?"

"No."

"Well, there's part of your problem." He scooted me toward the passenger door, opened it. "Get in. We're going to get you some food. And if you're a good little vampire, some coffee."

I wanted to pout—so deep in my feelings—but I couldn't muster the energy. "Fine," I said and climbed inside.

"It's ironic," I said, as Connor drove through the gate that surrounded the OMB compound, "that the AAM thinks I get away with everything. In reality, I'm the first one the CPD looked at."

He hadn't been privy to the interview, so I gave him all the details, or at least the ones I was aware of.

"A bad setup by the Bureau?" Connor asked. "Harsh to take out a member of your own unit."

"Especially with no obvious evidence that implicated me."

"They'd know you're smarter than that," Connor said. "Leaving evidence behind."

"Yeah," I said and stared out the window. The city was darker here on the outskirts, with fewer glowing houses and factories closed for the night. "What if it wasn't the AAM?"

"Who else would it be?"

"I don't know. But if Clive doesn't know who the actual perpetrator is, he's going to blame me. And he's not going to stop with a tussle at a wedding venue."

"You're worried."

"Concerned," I said. "And trying to think ahead. I don't think we should stay at the loft tonight. When Clive learns what happened, if he hasn't already, he'll come for me. Even if only to cover what he's done."

Connor was quiet for a moment. "I know a place you can stay."

"I'm not sleeping in the NAC building," I said. "I'll smell so much like meat, dogs will howl at me when I pass by."

He grinned. "Not the NAC building. But it's safe and secure, and there's room for both of you."

"Okay," I said. We could figure out the sleeping arrangements later. First, to get to Lulu. And as much as I hated to say it, to Eleanor of Aquitaine.

"We're going to have to bring the cat."

"That's fine," Connor said with a sly smile. "She likes me."

I sent Lulu a message, directing her to an address Connor gave me and offering to pick up things from the apartment. Including, because I was a generous soul, Eleanor of Aquitaine.

Lulu didn't argue about relocating and had some choice words for the AAM. She gave me a list of personal items to grab for her, but declined about the cat, assuring me Eleanor of Aquitaine could take care of herself for a few days—and apparently confident that I'd be able to handle the AAM before this dragged on too long. I hoped she was right, but didn't share her confidence. Not yet.

Connor stood at the windows, just out of view of the street, watching for any activity below.

I prepped a bag for Lulu, threw clothes into a duffel for me, and dropped them both by the door. Then I filled Eleanor of Aquitaine's food and water bowls. I found her on the radiator, tail swishing as she watched me.

"You'll be alone for a few days. I'm sure you'll be fine with that, but no wild parties, no drugs, and your curfew is midnight."

She met my gaze with obvious disdain.

"Good talk," I said. "We'll be back when we can. Don't pee in my shoes. Again."

I gave the mail a quick scan and found a thick envelope addressed to me with no return address. I opened it, pulled out the thick cardstock.

Elisa:

You deserve more, but this token of affection is all I can offer until we can be together.

—Your friend

Same handwriting, same cardstock, as the note I'd gotten the night of the party. Same anonymous "friend" who'd been creepy enough to send it.

I looked back in the envelope, wondering what "this" was, and my blood turned cold.

I pulled out a pendant on a leather thong. And it took only a moment for realization to strike. This was Blake's necklace—the one he'd worn at my door and the Grove.

Nausea rose, and I squeezed my eyes closed against the wave of it. *Someone had killed for me.* I dropped the pendant back into the envelope.

"What is it, Lis?" Connor must have felt my fear and magic from across the room, as he left his post by the windows and came closer.

I held the card out to him, fingers shaking with disgust, with violation, with fear.

Someone had killed for me.

Connor's expression darkened, and his eyes went dangerously flat. "'This'?"

"Blake wore a leather pendant," I said. "It's in the envelope."

"Who?"

"I don't know." I cursed, put the envelope down, the card on top of it. I didn't want to touch them more than I already had. "But I don't think it's the first time they've contacted me," I said. I pulled a clean kitchen towel from a drawer, used it to pick up the note I'd tossed aside after the party, brought it back to him.

He looked at it, then lifted his gaze to me. Anger percolated now. "You didn't tell me about this."

"It's not my first fan mail," I said. "I didn't even think about it. Do you tell me every time someone sends you underwear?"

Connor blinked, narrowed his gaze. "Do people send you underwear?"

"Only once," I said, then shook my head. "Not the point. The person who killed Blake says they did it for me."

"Or it has nothing to do with you, and they're trying again to drag you into it."

Either way, sickness and anger settled low in my belly. I didn't know Blake, didn't like the AAM. But I wouldn't wish death on any of them.

"He was killed—murdered—in my name."

"No," Connor said, voice firm. "He was murdered because someone wanted him dead. You didn't ask for it, and it wasn't for you in any possible way. This is about the killer."

I nodded, because I understood the words and the sentiment. But the killer had made it about me. And I didn't want that. I didn't want any of it.

"Whoever it is knows you didn't go to Paris," Connor said, looking over the first note. "They've been following your career."

"I was on-screen," I said. "Especially after Cardona's Master was killed."

"I remember. You got a lot of airtime."

"And he was watching." That thought put a line of sweat at the small of my back.

"There's no postmark. There is on the first envelope," Connor said, comparing them, "but not this one."

"So it was hand-delivered," I guessed.

"Yeah."

Creep factor increasing. "I have to tell Theo."

"Do you?" Connor's voice had gone tight again. He was still angry.

"You know I do," I said, softer than I might have under different circumstances. "Maybe he can use the building video to see who delivered it."

He growled, but relented. And returned to watch the street while I sent Theo pictures of the notes and Blake's necklace, then put them all into a plastic zip bag to be picked up by a CPD unit when we'd gotten somewhere safe.

I started when my screen buzzed, and I found Theo's concerned face. "Have you noticed anyone following you?" he asked.

"No," I said, squirming a little that someone might have been and I hadn't even noticed. So much for my training.

"When did you get the first one?"

"The night of the party."

"The night the AAM came to visit?"

"Yeah," I said, and didn't like that coincidence, either. I walked through the apartment, checking that the other windows were locked as discreetly as I could. No point in advertising to whoever might be watching that we were checking our security.

"No unusual calls? Contacts? Other emails? Or for Lulu?"

"I'll ask her, but I don't know of anything. She'd have mentioned it. We're going to stay somewhere else for a little while."

"That's a good idea," Theo said. "And I'm sorry. About all of this."

"I know, Theo. I'm sorry, too. Let me know if you have any leads—or if there's anyone I need to avoid."

"Let me know if the AAM contacts you, or if you get another note. And if the AAM tries to confront you, we'll step in." He paused. "We'll miss you over here."

I'd miss them, too. But even if I understood the choice they had to make, the impartiality they had to show, it was hard not to feel a little betrayed. "Yeah," was all I could manage.

"Be careful, Lis."

I said goodbye, and had just put my screen away, come back into the main living area, when Connor cursed.

"They're outside?" I asked.

"They are now."

Glad I'd lit only the small lamp, I joined him at the window. Two black SUVs—the supernatural's preferred vehicle—were parked across the street. Vampires emerged in dark clothes, drew swords as they looked up at our building.

"Damn," I said. We were here because of the possibility they'd show up, take me in. But I guess I hadn't actually thought they'd go so far. Be quite so bold. I'd been wrong, which I hated. So was it time to run, or time to fight?

At the steady knock on the door, we both looked back, then at each other. My blood began to speed, anticipating a fight.

"Wait," Connor said. "How'd they get up here so fast?"

He had a point. I cocked my head at the door. There was magic flowing in, but not animosity.

"I'm not sure it's them," I said and checked the peep. My relief was instantaneous.

I opened the door. "Uncle Malik," I said, grinning at the tall, dark-skinned man who stood in the doorway. "Come in."

I moved out of the way and, when he was inside, closed and locked the door behind us.

And when we were secure again, he held out his arms.

"Bring it in," he said, and I didn't hesitate, but let him wrap me in comfort. We weren't related by blood, but that didn't matter to me any more than it did to him. He was family, and always had been. And he felt the same about me even after he'd left the House to start his own. He'd been close to my parents, but had enough distance that he'd played neutral arbiter and advice giver dozens of times over the years, including about my decision to go to France.

"It's really good to see you."

"It's good to see you, too," he said, stepping back to get a good look. "You seem to be healthy and whole"—he cast an angry look toward the window—"contrary to the apparent wishes of those below. Compliance Bureau?"

I nodded. "You heard Blake was killed?"

"I did."

I offered him the plastic bag, watched his eyes go wide with horror, then anger, as he realized what it held.

"A stalker?" he asked.

I nodded. "Or made to look that way."

"You'll get this to the Ombuds?"

"We will. Why are you here?" I asked. "Is everything okay with the House? With Aunt Aaliyah?" Uncle Malik's wife was a writer, a profession that seemed to work well for night-bound vampires.

"She's fine. Worried about you, as we both were. I thought you might want to talk."

Without your parents, he meant. When you could be honest.

"Thank you," I said. "I'm sorry about the timing."

As if on cue, shouts echoed up from the street below.

"Elisa Sullivan." Clive's voice boomed through the night. "You have murdered a member of the AAM in cold blood. Surrender yourself now."

"Shut the fuck up," a human called out somewhere below us. "Or I'll surrender all of you to the CPD." Her accent was thickly Chicago, and I reminded myself to send her flowers when this was done.

Whatever Clive did—probably unsheathing his sword—had the window closing again beneath us. Flowers and cheesecake, I amended.

"We will have blood for blood!" Clive called out again. "You will answer for your crimes."

"How'd you make it past them?" Connor asked Malik, head tilted.

"I told them I was a member of the AAM and respected their work, and understood the necessity of rules and their consistent enforcement."

That might all be true—probably was true for a Master vampire in charge of his own House. But I didn't think he'd admit that to the vampires currently threatening his niece.

I smiled, understanding. "You glamoured them."

"Only a little," Uncle Malik admitted. "They were surprisingly willing to believe me."

"You're a Master," Connor said, "which puts you in a rarefied class. That probably helped."

"Possibly," Uncle Malik said, nodding, then glanced at me. "The glamour is already fading, and we need to get you out of here. Is there a back door?"

"I'd prefer a good brawl," I growled. "But there's a fire escape outside the window in Lulu's room. And there's an exit in the basement." Being a good vampire, I'd scoped out the egresses when I first moved in. "They've probably got vampires watching the fire escape, but they may not know about the basement door. It leads up stairs to the alley beside the building, and I think the well is covered by a grate."

"Which they probably wouldn't consider a viable exit," Malik said. "Could we remove the grate?"

"Probably? It was pretty rusty last time I checked."

"A little brute force does the body good," Connor said and glanced at the bags piled on the floor. "You have everything you need?"

Eleanor of Aquitaine made a sneering sound.

"Queen of the castle?" Uncle Malik asked.

"Or so she believes. And yes, I have everything I need." I gave the cat a thin smile. She began to wash.

"Then let's go," Malik said, pulling his sword. "I'll go first and offer them a bit more glamour."

I nodded, warned the monster to stay low. I'd give it a chance against Clive, but not tonight. Not when I'd need every bit of control I had.

Uncle Malik opened the door, checked the hallway.

"Left," I whispered, and we hurried outside, both of them guarding me while I closed and locked the apartment.

Voices and magic rose up from the stairs. "I want her tonight!" someone called out, anger tightening the words. My heart began to race.

"Fire stairs at the end of the hall," I whispered, and we ran down the hall and toward the open doorway. We made it inside. Carefully, I pulled up the doorstop and eased the door closed behind us, wincing at the click that echoed in the concrete stairway.

"All the way down," I said, and we began the trek, Malik in front.

Another door opened below us, magic slipping through. "I'm checking!" someone said and footsteps moved on a landing below us.

Connor pushed me back against the wall, out of their line of sight. We were close enough that I could feel his heartbeat, the thrumming of his blood.

Uncle Malik edged out of sight, pushed out a wave of glamour that seemed to warp the air.

"Anything?" another vampire called out.

If they looked up, they'd see us, and I'd have put both Connor and Uncle Malik in danger. This was an ever-expanding spiral of danger, wrapping more and more people that I loved into it. Guilt gripped me, nearly had me calling out, offering to go with the vampires to allow the others time to escape. But Connor put his lips against my ear. "We are here by choice. And they have glamour."

Of course they did, I thought, and hated that he'd had to remind me of it. Fear for Connor and Uncle Malik had made me susceptible. But knowing the weakness had me strengthening my defenses, and the guilt cleared away.

I met Connor's gaze, nodded once. Saw approval flash in his eyes.

"Nothing!" the vampire called out, the word just the slightest bit slurred. "It's empty. They must have taken the fire escape."

"Fuck," was the answer. "Let's get back out there."

We waited until the door slammed closed, the echo silenced. Then began to move downstairs again. BASEMENT was stenciled in black across the last door. We opened it, listened for noise, found none. And moved inside.

The lights were low here, spotlights that shone down on the cages that served as storage for those willing to pay the price for it. Some were empty, others piled high with extra furniture, sports equipment, cardboard boxes.

"This way," I said and took the lead, weaving through the pathway between them across the basement floor.

We'd made it halfway across when the door squeaked open behind us.

"I feel magic," someone said, and footsteps began to sound on the other end of the room.

"Elisa." Uncle Malik's voice was soft, but a warning all the same.

"There," I said and nodded toward the door on the far end of the basement. We ran toward it, more footsteps in our wake now, and reached the door. It was chained shut, the glass panel in the top painted over.

Malik pulled his dagger, brought the handle down once, twice, across the chain. It snapped; he pulled it through, tossed it into a nearby cardboard box to muffle the sound.

Uncle Malik pushed at the door, but it was all but sealed with grime and paint and years of disuse.

"Toward the back!" someone shouted behind us.

"Allow me," Connor said, and we moved out of his way, pulled our swords to face our pursuers.

He reared back and kicked at the door, and it squeaked open an inch. Once more, one more inch.

The sounds of running grew closer.

"Anytime now, puppy," I said quietly.

Beside me, Malik snorted, eyes gleaming. "It's been a long time since I've heard you say that."

Another kick, and metal dented, the door squealed open, revealing the leaf-strewn stairwell that rose to street level. And covered by a metal grate.

"This was the easy way?" Connor asked, glancing back with brow and mouth lifted.

"The other one would have been more fun, but much less politic."

Connor rolled his eyes, climbed halfway up the stairs, and looked over the grate. "Hinges are the weak spot," he diagnosed, as Uncle Malik and I shoved the door closed again.

"Allow me," I said this time, and we switched positions. I flipped the sword upside down, used the butt to push against the hinges, which groaned in protest. So did my shoulder.

"Outside!" came voices from the basement as I half stood, half crouched beneath the grate to slam the sword into the connection points. One hinge rolled, broke away.

"Brat," Connor said pleasantly, leaning against the door to block it. "Anytime now."

"Almost there," I said, and hit the other one, then again, until metal sheared with a rusty scream. "Got it," I said, and used the katana to lever the grate off.

"Pass the grate down," Connor said, feet planted as he and Uncle Malik pushed back against the door. I climbed up, maneuvered it into the stairwell.

Malik climbed up while Connor wedged it against the door.

"That'll work," I said and offered a hand to help him over it again.

We ran up to street level, and Malik gestured at a white SUV that rolled to a stop in front of us. He must have given someone a silent command to circle around and pick us up behind the building.

"Inside," he said, glancing over his shoulder. But the street was still clear.

We climbed in, drove away just as vampires emerged into the alley behind us.

It took all the strength I had not to stick out my tongue.

NINE

Malik's driver, a vampire I didn't know, was very skilled. He weaved rapidly through traffic, down side streets, until he was satisfied the AAM hadn't followed us.

I spent the ride sending Theo a report on the AAM's attempted attack.

DAMN, he responded. WE'LL FIND OUT WHERE THEY'RE STAYING, PUT A TAIL, AND WARN YOU IF THEY TRY AGAIN.

That would be a nice change, I thought, and put the screen away.

Chicago's four vampire Houses were located in central Chicago neighborhoods. Cadogan was in Hyde Park, home of the University of Chicago and the location of much of the 1837 World's Fair. Navarre was in Gold Coast, tree lined and stately, with its view of the lake. Grey House was in Wrigleyville, not far from the stadium.

Malik had placed Washington House just south of downtown in Dearborn Park. The house itself was a mansion of red brick and sculpted terra-cotta tiles, built in the 1880s by a gambler who hadn't managed to hold it for long. The building had been empty for decades, until Malik—with the assistance of a century's worth of compound interest—had restored it.

The SUV pulled under the portico, and we climbed out.

"Put the vehicle in the garage," he said to the driver. "Just in case."

"Liege," the driver agreed, and pulled away as we followed Malik inside.

The floors were wide and gleaming tiles of black and white, the walls paneled in wood that gleamed beneath gas lanterns. The hallway led to a great room with more tile and vampires relaxed on couches or reading in wingback chairs. They looked comfortable and at their ease, and smiled politely—or with curiosity—as we followed their Master across the room and into a hallway that echoed the first.

Uncle Malik's office wasn't unlike the room outside. Cozy and comfortable, with leather chairs and watercolors in vibrant shades.

"Sit," he said, and we both obeyed. He walked to a small refrigerator, pulled out a carafe of water, and poured a glass. Then he held it up, an offering.

I shook my head. "I'm fine."

He drank deeply, then put the glass and carafe away, turned back to us. "That was certainly more excitement than I've had in several years. Unless arguing with my wife about curtains counts."

I smiled. "Aunt Aaliyah is formidable."

"That she is. Much like you and your companion." He sat down on the edge of a chair, hands folded, and looked at us both in turn.

"I know what you're going to say," I threw out.

"Do you?"

"That I should pick a House and save myself and the city a lot of trouble."

"It's sound advice. Reasonable advice," he said, and I opened my mouth to argue, but he simply lifted a finger. "But not my advice."

"I'm listening," I said, brows lifted in surprise.

"You are their daughter. They love you beyond measure, beyond fear, and want to protect you. Their suggestion is practical, but it requires a certain . . . dishonesty to self."

Relief had my shoulders slumping. "Thank you for saying that. I was beginning to wonder if I was the only one who got it."

He nodded. "I care greatly for your parents, and for you, and for Cadogan House. I owe much of who I am now to the life I led there. But I do not have the same allegiance to it that your parents do. I'm simply not built that way. It served me, and I'm grateful. But when the opportunity arose to do something different—" He gestured at the room to finish the thought.

"You said goodbye to that chapter," Connor said quietly.

Uncle Malik looked at him, nodded. "You've grown quite a bit since your, shall we say, oat-sowing."

"We shall say," Connor said. His grin, I thought, still held some of his wicked teenage spirit, but his eyes were more solemn. They'd seen darker things now.

"I agree with you that they—this Clive and his people—won't stop until they are stopped. And, in the event it needs to be said, you have an open invitation to Commendation in Washington House. We don't do things exactly like Cadogan. We are more collaborative. We make good works the central mission of our immortality. But I believe you'd find a comfortable place here."

"Thank you," I said and hoped he could see the sincerity in my eyes. "But I have to decline." This was, notably, the only offer I'd received tonight. Word of Blake's death, and my suspicion in it, must have traveled. I'd become vampira non grata.

He nodded, smiled a little. "I expected you'd say that, and take no insult from the declination, but wanted to be clear that the offer was open." He crossed his arms. "To my way of thinking, you have two options other than joining a House. You confront them with arms, or you confront them with brains."

"Fight them or outwit them?"

"Exactly. Offer to fight them head-on, or make them stop by other means—because the AAM calls them back, or because you make your case in the press."

"Is there a possibility the AAM would call them back?" Connor asked, looking between us.

"Not now," I predicted. "Not until they're satisfied I didn't kill Blake." And even if they believed me, they might still see me as the symbol of wanton Chicago . . . and they were eager to exact punishment.

"We need to think," Connor said, reaching out across the space between our chairs to squeeze my hand. "Come up with a strategy to outwit them."

"Grown quite a bit," Malik said approvingly, then glanced at me. "You've chosen wisely."

I glanced at Connor, watched his grin spread, but couldn't disagree. "I know," I said, then looked back at him. "And I appreciate your advice. I know you love them, and it's probably not easy to give me advice you know they'll disagree with."

"They'll disagree for now," Uncle Malik said. "That's the fear. But understanding has a way of beating back that fear. It's one of the strongest weapons we have. They believe in you, and they trust you; they just need time."

I nodded. "Thank you."

"As much as I've enjoyed having you here," Malik said, "the AAM will likely realize soon enough that this was your destination. You're welcome to stay, of course, but I know that's not what you want. So you should go now while your exit is easy."

I nodded my agreement, rose, and gave him a hug. "I love you."

"I love you, too, Lis. Be careful. But be yourself."

* * *

I had no idea when I'd last eaten. Since the AAM hadn't followed us from Washington House, I requested food before we turned in for the night—wherever that turned out to be.

Connor called an Auto, requested an address in what I guessed was the Humboldt Park neighborhood. I didn't know the place, but since I was too hungry to make a suggestion, I had to trust him.

The building was low-slung and stubby, with a gravel lot filled with cars. The few windows had neon beer signs, and above the door was a blinking neon sign in brilliant pink and blue. Of a hot dog trying to jump out of a taco.

"Why is there a hot dog in the taco?"

"No one knows," Connor said. "Looks like they beat us here."

Lulu stood outside the building, sketching in a tiny notebook. Alexei sat on the steps a dozen feet away, watching her with an undecipherable expression. An intense one, though.

"She's working very hard to ignore him," Connor said.

"She's probably in the zone," I said. And knew that both were probably true.

When they saw us approach, Alexei stood, and Lulu slipped the book into the back pocket of her jeans.

"Light enough to draw?" Connor asked.

"Streetlight," she said and came to me. "You okay?"

"I am. You have any trouble?"

"No. You?"

I'd texted her at Washington House, let her know what had happened at the loft. "No. They either didn't guess we'd gone there, or weren't fast enough to follow us here."

"Where is 'here' exactly?" Lulu asked.

"An experience," Connor said and opened the door.

The smell of sautéing meat rolled out like a wave, all but dousing us with deliciousness. "Welcome to Taco Hole."

"Oh, mama," Lulu murmured. "I have come home."

We walked inside to squeaky floors covered in thin, grimy carpet. A long bar stretched across the wall opposite the door, every leather-and-brass bucket chair occupied. A couple dozen round tables filled the rest of the space, and restaurant staff were in matching yellow T-shirts and shorts.

It was . . . a supernatural dive bar.

Shifters in their NAC leathers at the counter, fairies at a high top, River nymphs in their tiny dresses toasting each other in a low banquette.

"How is this possible?" I asked, amazed and curious and still hungry.

"It's neutral territory," Connor said, using hand signals to order drinks from the man behind the bar after we'd taken seats at a small table.

"I can't believe I've never been here before," I said.

"Look around again, Elisa," Lulu said.

I lifted my brows at her, but did. And realized that, for all the magical diversity, I was the only vampire in the room.

"No vampires allowed?" I asked, glancing back at Connor. And wondering if I was going to have to fight someone for a damned burrito.

"Vampires allowed," he said and poured something red from a small carafe on the table into a little bowl. "But vampires not encouraged—most don't like the setting. Not quite fancy enough for the average vamp."

That was a damn shame, although I couldn't say I was surprised, having grown up in, let's be honest, a vampire mansion. It occurred to me that since we were surrounded by Sups, at least one of us might be uncomfortable with that. I glanced at Lulu.

"You okay being here?" I asked quietly.

"This is for food," she said, snagging a tortilla chip from a communal bowl. "Sanctuary means no Sup drama."

"Correct," Connor said and passed the little bowl to me, then did the same with the others.

"Salsa?" Lulu asked, eyeing it warily.

"Hot sauce," Alexei said. "Be careful with it."

"And it's *Alexei* saying that," Connor said. "So be careful." Then he pointed to an old-fashioned menu over the bar, with little plastic letters that clipped into slots. Options were limited. Burrito. Taco. Torta. Tamale. Menudo. I glanced around at the other tables, curious about the bestseller, and found a lot of people hunched over plates, and very devoted to their food.

A woman came over, her skin the palest shade of green, her hair and eyes dark. She put down four bottles. Dark liquid, no labels.

"House root beer," Connor said. "It's exceptional."

"Know whatcha want?" the waitress asked. Sup she may have been, but her accent was one hundred percent Wisconsin.

"Special," Alexei said. "Burn me up."

"Same," Connor said, then looked at me, brows lifted.

"Oh, do I get to order for myself?" I asked with a smile.

"Only if you hurry up," he said, smile teasing.

"Special," I said. "I don't want the full burn."

She snorted. "How much?"

"Light slap?" I asked, and she nodded, scribbled.

"Lightweight," Alexei muttered.

"No," I said, unashamed, "I just like to taste my food. It's not a competition."

"Burn me up," Lulu told the waitress, eschewing the bowl of hot sauce and pouring it from the bottle directly onto a chip. She crunched in, and her eyes watered immediately. And she smiled like a woman deeply satisfied.

"So you do have some good qualities," Alexei said. "Good to know."

She presented her middle finger, prepared another chip.

I munched one without sauce, looked around. The sheer diversity of bodies was amazing; I'd never seen so many different types of Sups gathered in one place.

"Thanks for bringing me here," I told Connor. "I'd have hated to miss out on this."

"You're very welcome."

The waitress brought a round tray of shot glasses filled to the brim with cloudy green liquid. She managed to slap them on the table single-handedly without spilling a drop. Alexei slid one across to each of us.

"Wolfsbane," he said, and lifted his glass, waited for each of us to do the same.

"Is this . . . poison?" Lulu asked, head tilted as she studied it.

"Only slightly," Connor said with a smile and drank.

"See you on the other side," I told Lulu and did the same.

It was like drinking a novel. A story with a beginning, middle, and end, with conflict along the way. And the faint aftertaste of wintergreen. There was no alcohol in it; the potency, I guessed, came from herbs and bitters. And it was very definitely potent.

I put the glass on the table. "Was that good or disgusting?"

"It was . . . yes," Lulu decided on, smacking her lips as if to study the taste. "One or both of those."

"Lightweight," Connor said this time, then drained his glass.

As if on cue, steaming platters of food were placed in front of us, the peppers so strong my eyes began to water. But god, the smell of it. Roasted meat and pale masa, flecked with salty white cheese and sharp cilantro.

"We'll see about that," I said and dug in.

I ate more than I needed, but less than I wanted, which I figured was about right. Alexei challenged Lulu to a round of pool at a table that looked like it had seen one too many fights. It was squeezed into a corner of the bar, so aiming took a lot of maneuvering around walls and literally bullish-looking patrons.

It was just . . . wonderful. "Can I swear fealty to this place?"

"No. But they do have a punch card." To demonstrate, Connor pulled one from his pocket. Eight of the ten little squares had been punched through with a hole the shape of—

"That's not a hot dog, is it?"

"No, brat, it is not." He smiled, put the card away. "I'm glad you like it. Not surprised, but glad."

"Are you talking about the punch card or the restaurant?"

"Both," he said and leaned forward, elbows on the table, and rubbed a thumb across my jaw. He liked doing that; seemed to find comfort in doing that. And his face had gone suddenly somber, suddenly grave. And a little bit sad. "I want you to know . . . I won't let anyone hurt you."

"I didn't ask you to protect me. We help protect each other." And saying the words aloud proved to me the truth, engraved that truth upon my heart.

"We protect each other," he agreed. "You know it's possible the killer will hurt someone else and say it's for you."

I searched his troubled eyes, trying to find the root of the sudden concern. "Maybe," I said, and that admission was a vise around my heart. "And I probably won't be able to stop it."

I'd been trying not to think about it, trying not to consider that every person behind me, in front of me, around me, might have been watching me. But it was undeniable: The stalker, the killer, was out there. Even if I'd never seen them, they were out there, relying on an emotional connection that wasn't real, but had been enough to drive them to violence.

This was vulnerability. Not physically; I had as good a chance at beating an attacker as anyone, especially if the monster played along. But there was an intimacy to being watched, to being seen in moments I'd thought I was alone, that made me feel exposed. And I didn't like that.

"I don't want you to think I'm like the killer," Connor said.

I blinked, stared at him, absolutely baffled. "What?"

"Whoever is doing this." He ran a hand through his hair.

"Why would I think that?" But understanding dawned when I asked the question. "Because you'd do what you needed to do to protect me."

He nodded.

"Connor, we've both killed, but not to prove a point. Not to prove love, or what someone believes to be love. That's not what love is. That's not who you are."

He looked at me for a long time, then squeezed my hand. Before he could speak, his screen buzzed. He pulled it out, glanced at it. His expression didn't change, but I saw the heat in his eyes.

"What's up?" Alexei asked, as he and Lulu returned to the table.

"The Compliance Bureau vamps are at the NAC building."

I hadn't even had time to ask a question—or be irritated that Theo hadn't warned us—when my own screen buzzed: CON-FIRMED BUREAU STAYING AT PORTMAN GRAND. TAIL BEING SET UP.

Better late than never, I thought. And gave them a head start. GO TO PACK HQ, I suggested. BUREAU ALREADY THERE.

His next message was mostly cursing, and a warning that the Ombuds couldn't touch the Bureau unless they did something. I had a feeling that wouldn't take long.

"They're staying at the Portman Grand Hotel," I said and put my screen away. "I asked the OMB to tail them. That's all they'll do for now. All they can do."

"Why does the AAM care about the Pack?" Lulu asked, taking her seat again. "Because of Elisa?"

"I assume they're trying to intimidate us into giving away her location," Connor said, sipping his drink.

Lulu snorted. "Have they never met shifters before?"

"Right?" Connor asked, his smile warm. "We're happy to give them a fight. It's kind of our thing."

"Are you going to headquarters?" I asked.

He brushed fingertips across the back of my hand, the sensation sending a shiver through me. "I'm going to continue enjoying my evening. The Pack will meet them if they choose, or they'll ignore them. Either way, the AAM will learn a valuable lesson."

TEN

When dinner was done, we drove to Humboldt Park in the SUV Alexei had picked up outside the loft, pulled to a stop on a snug residential street.

Both sides were lined with town houses, some old and distinguished pale stone, some sleek and modern glass and steel.

Connor walked to one situated firmly in the middle of those two styles. Three stories of red brick that sat stoically on the corner, each level with three narrow windows topped by rough-hewn stone. A line of dark green molding trimmed the roof, and there was a small plot of green in front, hemmed by a short black fence and accented by a low Japanese maple, its leaves already turning brilliantly red.

"Nice," Lulu said, as we ascended the stairs to the front door. Connor unlocked it, and we followed him in.

Old, honeyed wood gleamed nearly everywhere: the floor; the stairs that led immediately to the second floor; and in long, horizontal beams that crossed the foyer. I peeked into the room on the left, found built-in bookshelves and a fireplace surrounded by dark green tile with a hint of sheen. A low velvet couch looked perfect for reading. It led to a dining room with more warm wood, more bookshelves, and a long pendant lamp of glass and iron.

"It's like modern Frank Lloyd Wright," Lulu said, giving it what I'd come to think of as her narrowed artist's stare.

"It is," I agreed. It was old-fashioned—missing the round edges and gleaming white surfaces that were popular now—but it was beautiful.

We walked through to an open kitchen where more tile gleamed above copper countertops. Modernity took over again with sleek appliances. A few steps led down to a sitting area nestled in a bay window nook that was open to the floors above it. An enormous artscreen hung on the side wall, blues and greens shifting and melding until they became waves crashing rhythmically against a rocky shoreline.

I put down my bag, walked to the bay window, looked out on the back of a grassy walled garden that appeared to flow down the side of the house, bounded by an ivy-covered brick wall. A glass and steel conservatory, total Victorian luxe, bumped out from the building into the yard.

"Damn," Lulu said, standing beside me. "Seriously nice."

It was a gorgeous house, but having the luxury of a yard in a tight Chicago neighborhood? Much less the conservatory, the bay atrium, the wood . . . And all of it elegant, but not fussy. Antique, but also modern. Someone had taken great care to make every detail in this house matter; they'd wanted it to last, and last it had.

Lulu turned to Connor while I goggled at the yard. "So, does the Pack own this place or what?" she asked.

"No," Connor said. "It's mine."

I looked back at him. "Yours? Like, an investment property?"

"Mine, as in, I bought it. To live in."

"You're moving out of the Keene house?" I asked. The house was full of shifters—three generations of them.

"I moved out when we came back from Minnesota."

It took a full minute before I was able to speak again. "You bought a house, and moved out of your family home, weeks ago."

Lulu cleared her throat, reminding us we weren't alone, then picked up the bag I'd dropped. "Alexei, do you know where the guest room is?"

Alexei nodded, gave Connor a look, and they made their escape through the house. Through the house Connor owned, with the honeyed wood and the huge yard and the conservatory.

"Is there a problem?" Connor asked when we were alone.

I felt a thousand emotions at once. Surprise that he'd left the home shared by three generations of his family, shocked that he had the financial chops to up and buy a town house in Chicago, anger and hurt that he hadn't thought to share either of those things—huge, life-changing things—with me.

My parents hid the AAM's interest in me. Connor shut me out. Was there anyone left I could trust?

"Left home," I repeated. "Moved out. Bought a house. Those are huge decisions, Connor. And you didn't tell me about any of it."

"I'm telling you now," he said, pulling his screen from his pocket, putting it on the counter—and avoiding eye contact. "It's not a big deal."

"So completely rearranging your life is just an average Tuesday for you?"

He looked up at me. "Don't be ridiculous."

I glared at him. "Don't minimize my feelings."

"I'm not minimizing them. I'm trying to understand them." He swore, put a hand on his chest. "It was time for me to get some space from the Pack. I need a place that's mine. A place that's away from the Pack. It was time," he said again.

I could see in his face he didn't realize he held the knife, and had just twisted it a little more. "And that's it?" I asked.

"I don't know what you want me to say."

I had to make a decision between flight or fight, between letting this go or pushing back. And letting this go wasn't really my style.

"I want you to want to tell me when big things happen. Or when little things happen. I want you to *need* to tell me."

"It's not that simple."

"Isn't it?"

He must have seen the hurt in my eyes, because his softened. "Look, this is not how I wanted this to go. But the sun's about to rise, and I don't want us to say things we're going to regret. We can talk more at dusk."

If I'd been human, that would have been unlikely. I'd seen Lulu bleary-eyed after a night of lovelorn sleeplessness. But the sun would put me under. On nights like this, that was a relief.

"Fine," I said. "Where do I go?"

He looked at me for a long moment, jaw working while he considered the things he might say. "Second floor, second door on the right."

I nodded at him, walked back toward the hallway and the stairs. Then I stopped. "Thank you for giving us a place to sleep tonight," I said, without looking back.

And moved through silence up the stairs.

The second floor was more of the same. Gorgeous, warm, and an interesting mix of tech and antiques.

The door to the second bedroom was cracked, and I opened it, found Lulu sitting up in a large bed with an upholstered headboard in a tweedy gray fabric, gaze on her screen. I came in, closed the door behind me.

"You okay?" Lulu asked.

"Need a minute," I said. I walked toward the door I assumed led to a bathroom, found a large closet. I growled, tried the other door. This was the bathroom, with blue-gray tile and a slate vanity. The shower was an angular tower of glass with more dark tile. It was oceanic, I thought, not unlike the video on the artscreen downstairs.

I washed up and changed into pajamas, and by the time I emerged into the bedroom again—and confirmed the windows were covered by thick blackout-lined drapes—I was ready to form coherent words. "He moved out of the Keene home and *bought a damn town house.*"

"From your expression, I don't need to ask how you feel about it."

"Angry. Hurt. Shocked. Confused." I wished I could tell Lulu about my parents, about the things they'd hidden from me. But that would lead to uncomfortable questions about Testing and the reason for my fear.

"And what did Connor say?" she asked.

"That it was time, and he needed space from his family. Something that was his."

"Okay," she said, putting down her screen and crossing her legs. "That's reasonable. Would have been more reasonable for him to tell his damn girlfriend about it."

"Exactly," I said and sat down on the edge of the bed. "What the hell, Lulu? We have all this shared history, and I thought we were going somewhere." I turned to look at her. "Have I been reading this wrong?" The possibility reignited that ache beneath my ribs. And just pissed me off.

"If you read it wrong, then so did I." She frowned, shook her head. "We didn't read this wrong, Lis. He's crazy about you. And he trusted you enough to take you to Minnesota. He relied on you to help the Pack."

That was all true. But still . . . "He bought a house."

"Yeah," she said. She put her screen on the nightstand, lay back against the pillows. "It's weird. You can't fault the decor, though."

She looked up at the coffered (coffered!) ceiling. "He has surprisingly good taste for a man whose closet is mostly tight T-shirts and leather jackets."

I snorted.

"I mean, his tile choices alone?" Lulu kissed the tips of her fingertips. "Very squee."

I sat back, found the pillows almost irritatingly comfortable. "It's just not normal not to tell your girlfriend that you're literally *living somewhere else.*"

Lulu snorted. "When did that happen? Normality?"

I considered, came up with a possibility. "There was an entire week in Paris when it was too hot to move, even at night. People lay around, sat around, and couldn't be bothered with pretty much anything. So there wasn't any drama."

"That wasn't normal," Lulu said. "It was a meteorological aberration. That's what I'm saying—nothing is really 'normal.' It's just an average, a shortcut to explain common things." She paused. "Normal is a con created by people without imagination."

"You're a genius."

"I know," she said sleepily.

"Talk to him about it tomorrow," she said. "After your mean wears off. Dawn is nearly here."

I turned off the light, but stared at the ceiling, even as dawn threatened.

I could feel the tension in the house. Partly because of me and Connor. Partly because Lulu and I weren't here by choice but by necessity—because I had enemies outside. The AAM. The person who'd killed Blake. And the person who believed we were "friends."

It would make even the strongest vampire uneasy. But being here was most unfair to Lulu. This wasn't the life she'd signed up for, and I needed to get her home.

I needed to get the AAM off my back. I needed leverage, something that would force them to consider things differently and to withdraw their ultimatums.

But dawn stretched its grasping fingers above the horizon, and I had no better ideas.

ELEVEN

When the sun fell again, I wanted to get out of this house. The pain in my shoulder was gone, and I wanted action. And if I was being honest, wanted *control*. But I didn't actually have anywhere to go. I wasn't setting foot in a vampire House, my own house was off-limits, and I'd been fired from the OMB. What were my other options? Hanging out at a coffeehouse all day? Playing water girl while Lulu worked? Volunteering for the Pack?

Zero chance. If I wanted to be bossed around by animals, I'd go hang out with Eleanor of Aquitaine.

I found a message from Carlie checking in, and my heart melted a little more. VAMPIRE MOM, she said. EVERYTHING OK WITH THE AAM? WE AREN'T HEARING MUCH AND WE'RE WORRIED.

IT'S A MESS, I admitted. I wanted to shield her from pain, but shielding her from the truth wouldn't do that. At least the AAM wasn't pestering her, blaming her for what I'd done.

CONNOR AND LULU HAVE MY BACK, I assured her. Or she did, anyway. God knew where he and I stood.

SO DO WE, she said, and I could all but hear the earnestness.

I closed my eyes, grateful I'd had the opportunity to save her. And newly furious that the AAM—or at least Clive's part of it—didn't think that was worthwhile.

THAT MEANS A LOT TO ME. STAY CAREFUL, AND STAY SAFE.

My luck must have turned, because I got a message from Theo: IT WOULD BE REASONABLE FOR A CERTAIN CIVILIAN VAMP TO FIND HER WAY TO OMB TO REQUEST ASSISTANCE FROM SAID OMBUDS AND OBTAIN AN UPDATE. WE AIM TO SERVE.

"A certain civilian," I murmured with a grin, feeling hugely relieved by both the contact from Theo and by the invitation. They weren't shutting me out, at least not now. That mattered to me. Might not matter to Connor, but that was . . . Well. I'd deal with that later.

Maybe I'd pick up coffee and doughnuts en route to the office. Not as an apology—I had nothing to apologize for—but just to smooth the way.

Since the weather had cooled and today was for action, I pulled my hair into a knot and paired today's tank with leggings and knee-high boots. The house was silent, so I went downstairs, checked the kitchen for something to drink. Found a copper canister labeled COFFEE, but it was empty. I heard footsteps behind me and, given the lack of greeting, assumed it was Lulu or Alexei. "Do you know where he keeps the coffee?"

"He doesn't have any coffee."

I froze, every muscle tense, and then looked back.

Connor stood in the doorway in running shorts and nothing else, his body slicked with sweat. He'd probably gone for a run, and apparently without much clothing.

He walked to the fridge, took out a bottle of water, drank deeply, his eyes on me over the rim, and I couldn't look away. There was something nearly palpable in the power that radiated around him. His body exceptional, from strong arms, muscular back, flat abdomen, to his smooth and muscled flank inscribed with a tattoo in elegant black capitals: *Non ducor, duco.* I'm not led; I lead.

The idea of it—the arrogance in it—flipped desire into anger again.

When he'd taken his fill, he put the bottle down, lifted an eye-brow. Expecting—no, *demanding*—that I make the first move. Concede the first thin sliver of ground.

Instead, I ignored it. "I'm on my way out."

"You're sneaking out."

I lifted my brows at him. "I don't need to sneak, as I'm not a prisoner here."

He met my gaze with a stony stare of his own, but didn't re-spond.

Even the monster was irritated, my muscles quivering as if it was stomping around inside. "I'm going to the OMB. I want to find out what they've learned about the notes, and Theo invited me to come by."

"Do that," he said. "I'll be at the NAC building, because the AAM has taken up its position again to irritate my people." There was an edge in his voice. I wasn't the only one angry.

"They're still there?"

"They left before dawn, returned. There was a very good fight inside the bar last night, so the Pack felt no need to start one out-side with, and I'm quoting Eli here, 'chalky vampires.'"

"I'll deal with it," I said, heading toward the door. I wasn't sure what I'd do, but harassing the Pack was unacceptable.

Connor gripped my arm as I walked past. "I'll take care of it. They think they can intimidate me or the Pack, they need to be corrected. It's important that we, the Pack, send that particular signal. Maybe it's important that I do it."

I looked down at the fingers around my arm. "Are you looking for a fight here or there?"

"You tell me," he said, eyes glittering.

I wanted to push his fingers off my arm, to rail at him for push-ing me away. Even the monster was excited about the possibility. But I knew my anger—our anger—was just a symptom. So I took a breath, and opted for honesty.

"Did you not trust me enough to tell me you were moving?"

He stared at me with wide eyes, and I watched his anger drain into what looked like bafflement, then mortification. "Jesus, Lis. No. No." But he crossed to the sink, braced his hands against it. Then he ran a hand through his hair, and I worked not to be distracted by the clench and release of muscle.

"After Minnesota," he said, "and all the shit we went through, I considered taking a leave of absence. A sabbatical. I needed a break from the Pack."

My brows lifted. "You did?"

He looked back. "Yeah. I thought about going to the desert. Live in the heat. Spend time in silence on the bike under an empty sky."

"So, like most of your teenage years?" He'd frequently disappear for a few months at a time. Apparently most shifters did the same before taking on the obligations of adulthood.

He smiled a little. "Only two of them. I wanted all that because I was sick of the politics and the backstabbing. And you know what made me stay?"

I shook my head, even while my pulse quickened.

"You, Lis. You wouldn't be happy out there, and it would have felt empty—and not the good kind of empty—without you." He looked up. "So I decided to try a different way. A place where the Pack wouldn't always be . . . underfoot. A place of my own."

Having grown up in Cadogan House with nearly a hundred vampires, I understood that.

"There are two kinds of shifters," he said. "Those like my parents, who live and breathe the Pack. And those like the Breckenridges, who barely acknowledge its existence. They prefer to live like humans. Alexei and I—I think we're trying to find a different way. A different kind of balance. Because we want different lives. I have lived a very privileged life so far—privileged in that my parents let me be myself, let me get away with more than they should have, and helped clean up the mess. And the money."

"I guess so," I said, and felt my lips curve.

"So I didn't have to do much planning. Someday I'd fight for Apex, but that was far off, and I figured by then I'd know what to do. Most people think of the Apex as the ruler. The person in charge. While there's some truth to that, it's not the entire truth. The Apex is the voice. Strong, of course. Physically capable. But also able to speak for the collective based on what they want, and what they need."

"What if they don't know what they want or need?"

"Then it's the Apex's job to help figure that out, for the good of the people involved." He walked to me, put a finger beneath my chin, lifted it. "What do you want, Elisa Sullivan?"

"To learn who I am."

The words were out before I'd given conscious thought to the answer. So I knew they were the truth. My soul's truth.

"And the AAM would take that away, because they would tell you who you have to be."

"Yeah."

He cleared his throat. "I didn't tell you about this place because I thought you'd tell me to stay at home, with the Pack."

"I— What?"

He actually looked . . . bashful. Knitted brows, lopsided half smile. "It wasn't just important that I get some space from my family. I wanted to make some space for us. To give us a chance. And I figured if I told you what I was doing before I did it, you'd tell me not to uproot my life for you."

I just stared at him. "I . . . probably would have said that exactly."

His smile was brilliant. "I know you, Elisa Marie."

"My middle name isn't Marie."

"I know that, too." He grinned, lifted a shoulder. "But it sounds right." He moved toward me, took my hand, and squeezed. "It's early. For us, I mean. But I like the way this feels." He put my hand against his chest, above his heart. It pounded beneath my palm, strong and steady.

"I do, too," I said with a grin. And if the monster had had toes, they'd have curled at the invitation in his eyes. "I'm glad you finally came to your senses about me."

His laugh was full and hearty, and I loved the feel of it beneath my fingers. "The delay was all you, brat. You had to mellow the type A."

"Oh, it hasn't mellowed. You just matured."

"Maybe we both changed."

"Maybe we did."

He looked up, let his gaze pass around the room. "The house is pretty good, right?" That this man, strong and powerful, wanted me to approve of the den he'd made, nearly made up for the secrecy.

"It's gorgeous."

He looked inordinately relieved. "Good," he said with a nod. "Good."

My screen buzzed, and I pulled it out, anticipating a new horror. And found an alert I'd set the day before. "Damn it. I need to feed the starter."

He blinked. "Is that a sex thing?"

The laughter bubbled out of me, loosening the tension around my heart. And I caught the glint in his eyes. "You own a restaurant," I said. "Of course you know what a starter is."

"I do, because Georgia taught me." A shadow crossed his face, probably a memory of the very dysfunctional den of shifters in Minnesota, where she lived. "When did you bring it?"

"It was in my duffel bag when we left the loft. It's now in a jar in the refrigerator."

"Sneaky." He frowned. "I don't know if we have flour. I ordered a bachelor kit, but I'm not sure what's in it."

"You—" I shook my head to clear it. "You ordered a '*bachelor* kit'?" The images that moved through my head were decidedly not safe for work.

"Of food," he said. "Local mom-and-pop store sells themed grocery bundles."

"And bachelor includes . . . ?"

"A beginner's kit of cooking supplies," he said and flicked a finger down my chin at the relief on my face. "You have an admirably dirty mind."

"It's called a bachelor kit. If I'd ordered a bachelorette kit, what would you have imagined?"

His grin was wide and smug. "Many things, Lis. Many things."

I skimmed my fingertips across his bare abdomen, watched the muscles flex in response.

"Be careful," he said, lips near my ear. "If you start something, I will see it finished."

I cast a glance to the stairs; I assumed his bedroom was up there somewhere.

And then Lulu walked in and made directly for the refrigerator.

Connor's sigh was haggard. "Bell."

She grunted.

Alexei followed, took an apple from a basket on the counter. He tossed it in the air, caught it with his teeth, crunched.

"Nice trick, tabby," Lulu said, having plucked a bottle of juice from the fridge.

"Panther," Alexei said. "You wanna see?"

"No," she said, but her cheeks were pink when she looked at me and Connor. "Everybody good in here?"

"Fine," I said. "You?"

"Heading to work."

"Alexei," Connor said, without taking his eyes from Lulu. "Go with her."

"With me?" Lulu said, moving toward them. "Oh, no. Absolutely not."

"You need protecting."

Lulu spun, turned to Alexei. "I don't need anything from you. I need to work, and having someone hanging over me isn't exactly helpful. Plus, the clients aren't going to want some random guy hanging around."

"Someone is stalking Elisa," Connor said. "And the AAM thinks she killed Blake. They'd probably be happy to take you instead, and use you for leverage. Let's not take the chance. He won't get in your way."

Lulu snorted. "He is in my way by his very existence."

"That hurts me right here," Alexei said dryly, mimicking pulling a knife from his chest. "Magic would be handy. And without it, weapons."

Lulu's eyes flashed with temper. "I'm not using magic. You're insufferable."

"You're stubborn."

"I have work. And I'm not going back on a contract because goddamned vampires are fighting again." Her hands were clenched into fists, her teeth bared.

"Take him or stay here," I said. "Your life is worth more to me than your anger."

She grumbled, exhaled loudly. And for a brief moment, I knew how my mother felt when I was a teenager.

"And you're going to be late if you don't get moving," Connor said.

She made a little scream. Then pulled the cap from the juice bottle and drank, throat bobbing, until she'd finished nearly half of it.

Alexei watched her with avaricious eyes.

When she stopped, she ran the back of her hand across her mouth, recapped the bottle. "Hangry," she said, when she'd returned it to the fridge. "Still pissed at all three of you, but at least I won't be hangry anymore."

Connor smiled thinly. "We'll take whatever miracle we can get."

Connor had arranged a driver for me—*We protect each other*, I thought again—just as he'd arranged protection for Lulu. That might have felt stifling, but he hadn't demanded I stay in the town house. Probably knew that would have resulted in more angry words, as it wasn't the right thing for me.

I climbed into the front seat of the SUV, found Daniel at the wheel. He wore a dark V-neck sweater and slacks today, his dark hair pushed behind his ears. "Good evening."

I felt a pulse of guilt that I'd inconvenienced yet another person. "I guess you lost another bet?"

"You need security," he said. "And I need to learn the city."

"And do a favor for an Apex candidate."

"Vampires are strategic. But also, yes. Where shall I take you?"

"To the Ombuds' office, please. You know the address?"

"I do." He pulled into the street and turned on the radio. The song that emerged was slow and seductive.

Connor trusted me a lot, I thought with a smile, and relaxed into the seat for the ride.

We stopped for pastries at a diner not far from the brick factory, a place where Theo and I had grabbed truly atrocious coffee a dozen times while investigating. The memory clutched at my heart—and strengthened my resolve. I had to finish this. Deal with the AAM and get back to work.

There were no vampires lurking over the doughnuts, and no sign of the AAM in the small parking lot outside the guarded gate at the brick factory; and in the unlikely event they'd been invited inside, someone would have told me.

"Thank you for the ride," I said, as I slid from the car.

"Would you like me to stay?" he asked.

"No, thank you. I'll get a ride back. And if he asks, yes, I'll be careful."

His smile was wide now. "I'll tell him you said so. Good luck," he said, and he waited until I'd made it through the gate. I waved back, watched as he drove off toward one of his rendezvous.

The parking lot was empty but for a white sedan. No sign of the AAM or its member vampires. Stupid enough to loiter outside the Pack's enclave, but not the OMB? It was a very strange line to draw.

I walked toward the building, decided it was a good night for beautiful men as another came toward me. This one was tall and on the lean side, with suntanned skin, golden hair, whiskey eyes, and a faint sense of magic. Probably related to the sharp cheekbones and slightly pointed ears. I'd have said they were elvish, but that came from fairy tales and preconceptions. I'd heard there were elves in Chicago, a small and tightly knit group that generally avoided contact with other Sups—primarily because they believed themselves superior to others—but I'd never met one before.

The man wore perfectly tailored trousers, paired with a white button-down shirt that skimmed his trim torso, along with the strap of a gray messenger bag. He made eye contact, his smile vague and distracted. Then something flickered in his face, and he offered a tentative smile. "Elisa Sullivan?"

"Yes?" I asked cautiously, my guard already up.

His smile was brilliant, and undeniably beautiful. "I've been hoping to meet you."

The smile, the words, sent a shudder through me. Was it a coincidence the note I'd received had said something similar? Or was I now being paranoid?

"Oh?" I asked, as blandly as I could manage.

"Jonathan Black," he said and offered a hand. I shook it and felt nothing unusual in the warmth of his hand beyond the faint tingle of his magic.

"In addition to being half elf," he said, "I'm an attorney. I represent various interests in Chicago, most of them supernatural. Your work stopping the fairies was greatly appreciated."

"Interests?" I asked.

"Sorry," he said with an apologetic smile. "Their identities are confidential. But you saved them a lot of trouble and expense— not to mention loss of life—by sparing Chicago returning to a more rural existence. You're owed a boon."

"I didn't help with the fairies in order to collect a debt."

His smile was broad and generous. "I know. That's why they'll give it to you."

I cocked my head at him. "That was weeks ago. Why are you telling me this now?"

That smile erupted into laughter, full-bodied and contagious. I couldn't help but smile, too. "In addition to being naturally suspicious, Sups are very stubborn folk, especially the older ones. They're more accustomed to getting their way. It took some . . . convincing . . . for them to appreciate my argument. I was actually planning to send you a letter—to formally acknowledge the debt."

"I appreciate the offer, but that's unnecessary."

He winced. "But it took me so long to convince them," he said with a slightly pouty smile that I bet worked wonders on the dating scene.

Then his eyes widened, and his gaze went a little vague.

"Are you okay?" I asked him.

"What?" He blinked. "Yes, sorry. I had meetings just after dusk and haven't eaten yet, and my mind tends to wander when I'm hungry." He pointed at the box. "And those smell delicious. Doughnuts?"

I nodded. "There's a diner down the street. The coffee is atrocious, but the glazed are phenomenal."

"Then that will be my next stop." He glanced at his watch, an old-fashioned anachronistic accessory when screens offered a world of information in seconds. "I'd love to chat more, but I've got an appointment." He pulled a thin card from his pocket, offered it. A business card, another old-fashioned relic. "Until I manage to get that letter written, you can use this. Like a 'get out of jail free' card. But much less effective."

I nearly told him that I could have used it yesterday. But I didn't know this man, or who he represented, and some needs didn't need sharing.

"Thanks," I said noncommittally and took it, feeling the raised text with a fingertip.

"No," he said, adjusting the strap of his messenger bag as he walked toward a white vehicle. "Thank you."

TWELVE

I was cleared into the offices by the human guard, who managed a sympathetic look but still required me to sign in and show identification. I refused to write "civilian" on an OMB form, and opted for "vampire" instead.

He let me walk down the hallway unattended, so I offered him a doughnut, then carried the box through the window-lined hall and into the office shared by the Assistant Ombuds.

We worked—I *had* worked—in a long room with four screen stations on two long tables, and additional work spaces. There weren't any assigned desks; screens were communal, and mostly used for research and paperwork. Most of our time was spent in the field, and none of us had been the type to install pencil cups or motivational pics. Or hadn't, in the little time I'd been working there.

Sadness threatened to rise again, and I pushed it unmercifully down. I didn't have time for that. Not with the AAM on my trail.

Theo and Petra sat at two of the comp stations. Roger, lean and compact, stood in front of the wall screen, sliding his fingers over the small handheld device that controlled it, and reviewed photographs of what looked like the interior of a bank vault. Evidence from the robbery, I assumed. He had medium brown skin and short dark hair and, like his Assistant Ombuds, had opted for business casual.

"Doughnuts and rolls," I said lightly, holding the bag. "An offer of appreciation from a tax-paying vampire to the Ombuds who represent her."

Roger glanced back and I met his gaze, saw the apology there. But he slid the device into his pocket and walked over. "It's good to see you, Elisa."

"You, too," I said and nodded toward the wall screen. "Fairies?"

He glanced back. "Yes."

"I thought they confessed."

"They did," he said. "But there were some inconsistencies I didn't like." He looked back at me, expression pained. "And I'm sorry, but that's all I can tell you."

I nodded, and it was at least comforting to know the shut-out was as difficult for them as it was for me.

Petra came toward us, her dark hair in a bouncy tail, and took the bag, peeked inside. "Oh, you get extra-good representation now," she said and pulled out a cream-filled log nearly as long as her forearm.

"Dibs on sprinkles," Theo said, rising from his own chair. He squeezed my arm, made his own dive, came up with a cake doughnut covered in them.

"You want?" Petra asked Roger.

"No, thanks," he said, patting his flat belly. "I'm not much for sweets."

"Perish the thought," Petra said, moving back to her desk.

I plucked an old-fashioned from the box, took a seat at one of the empty chairs, spun to face them.

"Let's start with Jonathan Black," I said, pulling off a chunk of doughnut. "I met him on the way in. Who is he, and what does he want?"

"He's delicious," Petra supplied. "All blond and dreamy. Like a caramel sundae. Part elf, but I don't know the details."

"Is he trustworthy?"

Theo came around the desk. "You have reason to believe he isn't?"

"I don't have reason either way. I just got a vibe. And he said he'd hoped to meet me."

"Is that a bad thing?"

"The first note sent to me said almost the same thing."

Theo frowned. "It's a pretty general thing to say. But . . ."

"But," I agreed. "He said he represented some interests who owed me a favor," I told them, and offered the details. "Do you know who he represents?"

"Not specifically," Roger said, frowning. "We've worked with him in a few minor matters. He's been vague to maintain his clients' confidentiality, which isn't surprising. I presume they're well funded since they have the money to act through an intermediary."

"Or they want to hide their identities."

"It's not impossible," Roger said. "But why would they? There are Sups with arrest warrants, sure, but no one who'd have power like that."

"Maybe it's nothing," I said and paused. "He said he wanted to meet me, but he didn't mention anything about the AAM or the fight at the Grove."

"He didn't want to bring up sour grapes?" Theo asked. "Something that might hurt you?"

"Maybe." I was suspicious, and I didn't like situations without clear boundaries, clear rules, when motivations were cloudy. But it seemed there was nothing more to learn at the moment. "Never mind," I said. "What about the stalker?"

If I called him "the" stalker, instead of "my" stalker, it was less personal. Less disconcerting.

"Very little," Theo said. "No fingerprints, no DNA on the paper." He tapped his screen, and an image appeared on the glass panel. Pale shadows on white I could hardly make out.

"What is that?" I asked. "A building?"

"The Water Tower," Theo said. "It's the watermark from the

notepaper, scanned and enhanced. We were able to trace it, but it's common. Available online and at dozens of shops in Chicago alone. The ink was just as common. Basic office supply pens."

"Who writes a creepy love note with a basic office-supply pen?" Petra asked. "You need a fountain pen and wax seal *at a minimum*."

"So," I said, "he's not into high-end writing implements, or he was smart enough to pick something difficult to trace."

"One of those," Theo agreed with a smile. "And the postage mark from the first note doesn't do us any good. The postage was purchased from a kiosk, paid with cash. No other way to track it."

"What about the loft security camera?"

"Proves you didn't leave the apartment when Blake was killed. Doesn't show anyone unusual who might have delivered a letter."

"Maybe he's a ghost," I said with a sigh.

"Ghosts rarely obsess over humans," Petra said. "That's actually a myth."

I had been joking, but decided I'd take her word for it. "What about Blake?"

"There's no surveillance video of his death; he was left in a security camera blind spot," Theo said. "So either the killer got lucky or knew where the cameras were located."

"Maybe he works in the building?" I wondered.

"We're going through the list," Theo said with a nod.

"I still think it's weird he was in the Brass & Copper building ten minutes before dawn to get coffee. Why did a member of the AAM walk into that building for coffee when there are a dozen coffee shops on the street within a few blocks?"

"Maybe because it's across the street from the Portman Grand," Petra said.

I stared at her. I'd known they were both on Michigan, but hadn't realized their proximity. "It's across the street?"

"Give me a sec," she said, frowning as she began typing, pulling data onto the wall screen. A search, a map, an image of that block of Michigan. And the Portman Grand sitting right across the street from the gleaming Brass & Copper building.

"Awfully convenient," I murmured, thinking about the rising sun and the very short time the victim—and killer, if a vampire—would have had to make their escape.

"Still—why would you risk it?" I asked again, the same question that had been gnawing at me. And then I realized—he didn't have to risk it.

"The Pedway," I said. "Does it connect the buildings?"

The Pedway was a system of under- and aboveground walkways through downtown Chicago that allowed Chicagoans to get around even in the depths of winter. What would a vampire like better than a safe underground passageway between your hotel and a little caffeine?

"Well, holy shit," Petra said, looking at the map of crossing red and blue lines she'd pulled up. "It totally does. It's not part of the marked Pedway," she said, gesturing to the screen. "That's why the section is yellow. But if you could find the access points, I bet you could get in."

"I bet you don't even need to look for them," I said and glanced back at them. "They aren't the first vampires to stay at the Portman. I bet Pedway access is something they use to sell vampires on staying there. Move around the city without fear of sunlight or something."

There was a gleam in Roger's eyes now, and he nodded at me. "Good, Lis. That's good." He looked at Petra. "You make that call. Theo, see if we can get security feed in the hotel or tower near the access point. Maybe that will give us an ID."

Maybe it would give us something.

I sent Connor a message, assuring him I was on my way and that Roger was giving me a ride. He was out on Pack business, he responded, and said he'd meet me at the NAC building. Traffic was light, and we made good time across the city.

I recognized the roar as we neared the building; sure enough, Thelma came toward us from the opposite direction. Low and dark, its rider equally so.

Yuen had nearly reached the curb when I heard it. The sudden acceleration, the screeching of tires. And saw in the side mirror the white sedan that turned onto the street somewhere behind us and was now barreling toward us.

No, I realized with horror. Barreling toward Connor.

My heart simply . . . stopped. In that second, the world slowed, Connor nearly to the curb, the sedan racing, the driver's hair color—blond—the only thing I could see.

And when time snapped back again, I had the door open and was out of the car before Yuen had even come to a stop. I heard his shout behind me, his confusion, but screamed toward Thelma. Screamed toward *him*. "Connor! Move!"

Still wearing his helmet, his head popped up to find me, then behind to find the threat, and I saw the brace of his shoulders.

I'd never known fear before. Never known real and icy terror until I'd seen him realize a vehicle was bearing down and there was nowhere to go.

He leaned to his right, bringing Thelma into a slow skid that put bike between shifter and sedan. Undeterred, the car struck. Metal met metal, met concrete, met man as the vehicle spun Thelma around, taking Connor along for the ride. They hit the sidewalk, then the building wall, and the car accelerated, took off.

Tires squealed as Yuen slammed his door closed, sped after it.

It was the monster that gave me the push to move, that sent me running across the street, just as shifters—drawn by the noise— emerged from the building to investigate. Curses, then they were lifting Thelma, the back of its frame half-crushed, the back wheel nearly folded in half.

I hit my knees, ignored the sting of concrete against tender skin, and unbuckled his helmet. "Connor."

"Hold his head," someone said, and I nodded, kept his head and torso steady while they pulled away his helmet.

His eyes were closed, his body still.

"Connor."

Nothing. Seconds passed, but it felt like hours.

Then brilliant blue eyes blinked at me. "What . . . the fuck . . . was that?"

"A sedan," I told him, when he'd refused an ambulance and was sitting up against the building. He'd let me check him for injuries, and I felt nothing broken. He had plenty of scrapes, and probably some broken ribs I couldn't feel.

"Whose fucking sedan?"

We looked back, found Gabriel in the doorway, rage in his expression. "Whose fucking sedan?" he asked again, moving closer, gaze on his son, his child.

"Don't know," Connor said, pushing a hand through his hair. "Maybe an AAM asshole. Maybe some other asshole."

"Yuen was dropping me off," I said. "He followed the car."

Gabriel crouched in front of Connor, looked him over. He touched a hand to his son's face, his brow, looked relieved that his only son was still alive. And furious that someone had tried to take him away.

"You'll shift," Gabriel said, a prediction and an order. "And you'll heal."

"I will," Connor said and offered his father a hand. Father pulled son to his feet, gave him a moment to steady himself.

"Inside," Gabriel said. He looked back at Thelma. "And get that into the garage."

The Pack wasn't shy, but nor did it want to spill Pack business out on a public street. Gabe sent most everyone back to work, and those who remained, mostly family, to the lounge.

"Shift," he told Connor. "And let's discuss."

Connor nodded. "We'll be in."

When we were alone, I looked back at him, afraid to touch him for fear of causing pain. "You're all right?"

He looked around to ensure we were alone. To ensure, I thought, that whatever weakness he was about to admit was for my ears only.

"I took a hit," he admitted, "but I'll be fine. Shifting is going to hurt like a son of a bitch." And he winced at the thought. "But once that's done, it'll only be bruises and aches. Thelma's going to need more work than me."

"I'm sorry for that, too."

He nodded. "Did you see who was driving?"

I shook my head. "I got a glimpse of blond hair. I think it was a guy, but it was too dark to see anything else."

Jonathan Black had blond hair, and he'd gotten into a white sedan at the OMB. But why would he have tried to hurt Connor right after trying to convince me to accept a favor from his clients?

"I haven't heard from Yuen," I said. "Did you see anything? Or anyone?"

"Just the damned car," he said, wincing as he rolled his shoulder.

Raised voices—some concerned, some angry—echoed down the hallway.

"The Pack's going to have a lot to say about vampires. But you have nothing to fear," he murmured and kissed my temple. "Don't let them push you. Show the monster if you have to, but no fear."

That he was trying to help me face down the Pack after what had just happened . . . I didn't have words for my gratitude. So I nodded, sucked it up, and promised myself I could let it out later.

They were gathered in the lounge. "What happened?"

Connor told them about the AAM, the attack on my apartment. And Miranda spun toward me like a hurricane, with fury in her eyes.

"You did this," she said, stalking toward me. "This happened because of you."

"She didn't drive the car," Connor said. "Or order anyone to do so."

"Maybe not," Miranda said. "But without her, it wouldn't have happened."

My screen buzzed, and I checked it, found a message from Yuen. He'd lost the vehicle in a jam in Wicker Park, but put out an all-points bulletin. He'd search the plates, and the CPD would also pull traffic camera feeds from the route they'd followed and try to nail down a shot of the driver.

The CPD had already been watching the AAM, and the Ombuds hadn't gotten an alert that the group had left the hotel. That suggested the driver wasn't part of the AAM.

Yuen offered to come back, to take an official statement, but I told him to wait. If Connor wanted that, if the Pack wanted that, they could ask for it specifically.

"Miranda," Connor was saying, "we don't even know if a vampire was driving the car."

"Who else would do it? Who else would dare try to take you out?"

I wanted to point out the members of her own Pack in Minnesota who'd done just that, but knew I needed to stay quiet. This conversation wasn't for me.

"Quit making excuses, Connor! For all we know, this is a vampire plot to take down the Pack." She gave me a suspicious stare. "This is probably because the Pack denied her sanctuary for her little vampire troubles."

That had the shifters who watched us whispering to each other.

"She didn't request sanctuary," Connor said. "So there was no denying to be done."

"Whatever. The point is, every time new vampires come into this city, bad shit goes down. Shit that hurts us."

There were a few rolled eyes, but also a few nods of agreement. They didn't trust me. And if they didn't trust me, they wouldn't trust Connor. I couldn't let that happen.

"We don't know who did this," I said, and every eye in the room turned to me. "But if it was a vampire, or if it was because of the AAM, I will handle it. That makes it my problem, and my responsibility, and I will handle it. And if any of you have issues with that, you can talk to me."

Silence for a moment. Then, "Agreed."

I looked back, found Gabriel at the back of the room, arms crossed. "If it's your problem, you fix it. If it's our problem, we fix it."

"Agreed," I said with a nod, sealing the deal.

He shifted alone. Not because he was too shy to do it around me—I'd seen him shift before, and the nakedness that preceded and followed it—but because he was afraid the pain would scare me.

I didn't hear him scream. But I felt its vibration, the earthquake of magic and rage and agony across the building. And was immensely relieved when he walked toward me again. He'd changed clothes, given the beating taken by the other ones, and his hair was damp.

He reached me, kissed me, pulled me against him. Tears welled, but I held them back. We were still in Pack territory, and the Pack was still angry. Still hurting. It permeated the air.

"I'm good," he said and ran a hand down my hair. "A little food, a beer, wouldn't hurt. But I'm fine. Let's get out of here, and we can talk." I had the feeling he wanted away from the scene, and away from the magic.

We walked outside to the SUV, and my screen buzzed. I pulled it out again, expecting another message from Roger, an update on what he'd found.

And because I'd been expecting that, I wasn't prepared for what I found there.

Elisa:

How could you pick shifters over vampires? I've admired you and wanted so much to be your friend, but you're being disloyal! I'm beginning to wonder if you appreciate what I've done for you. I'm protecting you, Elisa. Ensuring your future.

I remain, with hope that you'll understand,

—A friend?

What he'd done for me, the note said. But he'd done nothing on my behalf, only his delusion of it. And that delusion had nearly gotten Connor killed.

My heart roared, a timpani drum of anger. "It was him."

"What?" Connor asked, and I showed him the message.

"I'm— Connor, I'm sorry." Horror and fury and fear battled in my chest, squeezing hard against my heart. "It was the stalker. He hit you. He tried to kill you. This is all my—"

"No," he interrupted, sliding a hand behind my neck and lowering his head to look directly into my eyes. "No. You are responsible for your actions, not his. You gave me the warning, and you were there to pick me up. Not that I needed picking up."

"Because you're a big, strong shifter."

"Damn right. He wasn't the first one to take a shot at me, and probably won't be the last. And how many of my Pack members tried to take you out in Minnesota?"

I paused. "That is a point."

He nodded. "So if you so much as suggest this was your fault, you'll just piss me off."

I sucked in a hard and shuddering breath, nodded.

"I'm okay," he said. "It's gonna take more than a shitty sedan to break me."

I put my screen in my pocket, scrubbed my hands over my face until I'd regained some composure.

I understood logically that I hadn't caused this; I hadn't driven the car, or asked anyone to hurt Connor. But that didn't mitigate the fear, the fury, that someone had tried to hurt him—or that they believed hurting him was something I wanted. It couldn't have been further from the truth.

Connor had become part of my life. An essential part. Despite our beginnings, despite at least fifteen years of mutual irritation, and paths that diverged almost completely. I'd come home to Chicago unwillingly. But I'd found a kind of home here, and he was a major part of it. And in seconds, someone had nearly ripped him away.

Tears breached my lashes. "Damn it," I said, swiping at them. "I hate crying. And I've done entirely too much of it this week."

"You are having a bit of a week," he said and wrapped an arm around me. "Sometimes tears are inevitable. But I'm okay."

I nodded. "It's just..." I swallowed hard, opened my eyes, and looked up at him. And it took all the bravery and composure I had left to let myself be vulnerable, and tell him how I felt. "I've never had this much to lose."

The look in his eyes was . . . majestic. Pride and triumph and joy combined, and I felt myself sink a little deeper in his thrall.

He smiled slowly, with more of that Connor-trademarked satisfaction. "How much did that little admission cost you?"

I curled my lip at him. "Watch it, wolf."

Still grinning, he brought our joined hands to his mouth, pressed his lips, soft and promising, to my fingers. "I don't want to lose you, either, especially to a coward like the one who sent you that note. But life isn't fair. So we enjoy what we can, and we fight when we must."

"I'll pay for the damage to Thelma."

"Offer accepted." The corners of his mouth lifted. "She deserves a little pampering. And possibly a few upgrades."

The fear had passed; the traces were still there like salt on tear-stained cheeks, but I could think again. And those thoughts were . . . disturbing.

"The stalker is not sane," I said quietly. "Someone else has to have noticed they're pretty seriously disturbed. So how are they out and driving and able to send notes via mail and electronically?"

"Maybe the stalker's a loner," Connor said. "That wouldn't be hard to believe."

"No, it wouldn't." I pulled out my screen again, forced myself to read the note again and think about the message. I saw what I'd missed the first time. "The stalker is a vampire."

"Yeah," Connor said. "I agree. You should send that to the Ombuds."

I did. There was only a moment's delay then Theo responded: PETRA SAYS MESSAGE WAS ANONYMIZED, SO WE CAN'T TRACK DIRECTLY. WE'RE GOING TO LOOK FOR SERVER DINGS AND WE'LL APPRISE ROBINSON.

"What's next?" Connor asked.

"The Ombuds and CPD are on the stalker," I said. "And I'm not going to sit around and cry in the meantime."

"That's my girl," he murmured.

"I'm glad you think so, and I'm going to apologize in advance for this," I said, and I put a message on my online public profile, as big and bold as I could manage:

Hurting people in my name doesn't help me. It hurts me.
If you're a true friend, talk to me directly. You know how
to get in touch.

I let him read it; he went still, every muscle tense, a predator considering his strike. Slowly, he lifted his gaze to me. "I'm not sure if that was stupidly reckless or brilliantly strategic."

A corner of my mouth lifted. "I'm not sure, either. But I'd rather have him—assuming it's a man—aimed at me instead of hurting others. Including you."

"I'm not leaving your side until he's caught."

"Deal," I said. "But first I need to talk to my parents."

"They're back?"

"Messaged me at dusk. I told them not to travel, but . . ."

"They're your parents."

I nodded. "Yeah. I need to tackle this one myself—by myself. And you need a beer and some brisket and to put your feet up."

"I like all of those things," he said and pressed a kiss to my forehead. Gentle and sweet this time. One in the spectrum of ways he showed that he cared. "I'll stay. But you have to do me a favor, lover."

"Yes to the favor. No to the nickname."

But I knew I was doomed.

THIRTEEN

The favor was in the front seat of an SUV, looking handsome in a white button-down and black suit.

"Mr. Liu," I said, belting myself in.

"Ms. Sullivan."

He was quiet beyond that greeting, and didn't speak another word until we pulled up in front of Cadogan House and he stretched to peer out the windshield. "No sign of the AAM, or anyone else."

"No," I agreed, opening the door. "And no unfamiliar magic."

Though there was plenty of the familiar version. The latent power of a century and a half's worth of vampires in residence seemed to have seeped into grass and iron and stone, a marker of the power of this very tight family. A family that had welcomed me warmly, but I'd never really felt part of, through no fault of theirs.

"What was it like?" he asked. "Growing up in there."

"Probably not a lot different from growing up somewhere else," I said. "Good times, bad times, blood orgies, the whole thing."

Now his grin was wide, a spark in those dark brown eyes. "You paint an interesting picture, Elisa."

"Lulu's the painter," I said and climbed out, katana in hand. "I call it like I see it."

*　*　*

Cadogan House. Several graceful stories of white stone in the middle of grounds large enough to be a park, albeit one surrounded by a tall iron fence.

The House was accessible only through the narrow gate where guards stood duty twenty-four hours a day. Humans when the sun was high, vampires when the world was dark. Two guards, katanas belted at their sides, watched warily as I approached. And relaxed a little when they realized who I was.

"Elisa Sullivan," I said, when I reached them. "I'm here to see my parents."

"Of course," the guard said, and the gates whirred open.

I walked down the familiar sidewalk, where I'd once attempted to draw princesses fighting dragons with chalk. Inside, I found a second guard beaming at the small reception desk tucked into the grand foyer.

"Ms. Sullivan," said the vampire, a female I didn't recognize. "Welcome back to Cadogan House. Your parents arrived a short time ago, and they're in your father's office. You're welcome to join them."

"Thanks," I said, with a smile I tried to make pleasant.

Below me, down several feet and through layers of wood and concrete and tile, my mother's sword—steel and leather and gleaming scabbard—beckoned to the monster. And it seemed louder than the last time I'd been here.

It was the sword used to bring down the Egregore. The sword that now held some portion of its essence, and called to my monster with a power that scared me, that tugged at some thread deep inside my body. And threatened my control.

No, I told the monster. *Don't even think about it.* And sent a clear image of what would happen if it tried to take control while we were in Cadogan House. It would be identified and rooted out, and we'd see which of us survived.

That must have done the trick, because it settled down.

I walked down the hallway, thickly carpeted and painted in pretty pale colors, to my father's office. He sat at his desk in his usual business attire while my mother, her long dark hair flowing down her back, stared through the windows that took up the opposite side of the room.

At the sound of my footsteps, or their sensing me, they both lifted their heads, met my gaze.

"Parental units," I said with a smile, and was surrounded by embracing arms when I'd barely crossed the threshold.

"Okay," I said after I'd judged they'd gotten their fill of reassurance, "now you're being suffocating."

I pulled back, and still my mother touched my hair, my father squeezed my hand, ensuring themselves that I was safe and whole.

"It's good to see you," my father said. "We've been worried."

"You didn't have to worry," I said.

His stare was bland. "Let's go sit," he said and gestured toward the seating area across from his desk. Leather couches and chairs that surrounded a glass coffee table and had been the site of innumerable meetings with Sups and mildly rebellious daughters—me and Lulu both.

We took seats, and I jumped into business.

"Have you talked to Nicole again?"

"Unfortunately," Dad said, "we haven't been able to reach her."

That set off alarm bells. "Why not? Where is she?"

"According to her admin, she's in New York, meeting with the Masters in that city."

"That seems convenient," I said. Was she trying to avoid us, or had the Compliance Bureau been trying to avoid her?

"The visit has been planned for months," my father said dryly. "The admin assures us our messages have been forwarded, and Nicole will be in touch regarding our 'concerns' as soon as her schedule allows."

Nicole and my parents had been opponents when the AAM was founded, but they'd only had positive things to say about her leadership since then. I hadn't met her, but that she was steady and reasonable was the sense I'd gotten from them. I didn't think she'd have ignored the murder of an AAM vampire to focus on administrative issues.

"You didn't tell the admin everything," I surmised.

"No," he said. "The admin either has no idea what's going on here or is doing a very good job of hiding it."

"Is Nicole being played by her staff?" I wondered.

"Even good leaders can have bad employees," he said grimly. "We've sent Luc to New York to talk to her and speed a resolution." Luc was the House's former guard captain. He became House Second when Uncle Malik became a Master.

"What about more generally? Is there anything I can use? Some rule of the AAM I can twist around?"

"We've learned the Compliance Bureau was created for a one-year trial period," my father said. "Unfortunately, that means there's no *Canon* law that applies to it."

"So no regulations I could say they're breaking?"

"Not that we're aware of yet."

Frustration had me rising, stalking to the end of the room and looking through those dark windows to the grounds beyond, to the stands of trees and late-season flowers, the lights that dappled the grass. It comforted me, to see the space, to know it was bound by the rules of nature, not of vampires.

I exhaled, turned back. "Saving a human life is more important than a rule. And locking up vampires who don't agree with them is just wrong."

"We don't disagree," my father said. "But changing the rules is going to take time. It's *supposed* to take time," he added at my impatient look, "to ensure that rules are thoroughly considered, that the process isn't manipulated to serve someone's whim. Until we hear from Luc, it would be best to avoid the Bureau and let the OMB investigate." He paused. "Would you consider joining a House as a temporary measure? Just until we can gather the necessary support?"

I just looked at him. "Dad."

"What about staying here temporarily?" my mother asked.

"*No,*" I said, more forcefully now. "I'm not going to put you at risk like that. It's not fair to you or anyone else in the House. And giving in to the Bureau's demands is an admission I did something wrong. I won't apologize to them for making Carlie. And I shouldn't be punished for doing the right thing."

Dad's expression was pained, but he nodded. "We had to try," he said with a lopsided smile. "It's the best way to protect you."

No, I thought, it wasn't. Because whether Nicole Heart knew it or not, Clive had other ideas. Other plans. Other missions.

"What about seclusion?" I asked, already seeing the strain around their eyes.

"I would presume they mean incarceration," Dad said. "But the AAM doesn't have a facility for that, or not that they've told the Masters."

"They might have contracted with a facility in Atlanta," my mother said.

"So they'd just incarcerate me until I cave. Until I swear allegiance."

"That's the threat," my mother said. "And you would be the first they'd handled that way. Or maybe they're just bluffing because they think you'll be frightened enough to join a House."

I could see in her eyes that she wanted me to take that step because, she thought, it would ensure my safety. But I wasn't so sure.

"There's still Testing," I said. "If I fail, they'll say something's wrong with me. That I was born broken. If I pass, they'll say I'm too strong for my own good. And if there's anything unusual, seclusion will be the least of my worries."

Because they'd see who I was.

I glanced up and saw my mother watching me, gaze narrowed. And I knew she'd seen something. I didn't know what—not the monster, which was bored by more talk—but something of my concern, of my fear.

Maintain, I ordered myself, and gave her the only smile I could manage. Small, and probably not convincing.

"Clive won't stop," I said.

"What do you mean?" she asked.

I thought of what I'd told Gwen. "He believes in what he's doing. Not just that rules are important, but that rules are the only thing that is important. It goes beyond me. If Nicole Heart broke a rule, no matter how innocuous, I think he'd do the same to her. Not because it would mean no favoritism, but because he has no real loyalty to her. If she broke a rule, he'd punish her, too. Maybe it's a kind of obsession," I suggested. "Maybe it's about control. There was nothing unusual in his background that you found? The Ombuds didn't, but . . ."

"We found nothing on Clive," my mother said. "We did the full run. And speaking of the Ombuds," my mother said, "we know about the stalker. You should have told us."

"I didn't know until after we'd talked." And damn whoever had told them first. "I haven't seen him—only the notes—until tonight."

"Connor's okay?" my mother asked.

"He says he is. He wanted to come with me, but I told him to rest. Lulu and I are staying . . . at a second location," I decided on. "It was offered by the Pack." I didn't want to get into the details of Connor's purchase, or the reasons for it, when I was still dealing with those myself. And the less they knew, the less could be used against them.

"Good," my father said. "It's secure?"

"It is." I was basically living with two strong and capable shifters, but it didn't seem appropriate to mention that, either.

My father rose suddenly, moved to the door. My mother did the same, as if positioning themselves between me and some danger. Given the silence, I presumed they'd gotten telepathic messages.

"They're here," I guessed. "The Bureau." So much for not bringing the trouble to their door, I thought with disgust, anger rising like a moon-pulled tide.

"They're outside the gate," my mother said, no doubt informed by my father through their silent telepathic connection. She strode to my father's desk, plucked his mounted katana from the wall.

"Sentinel," my father said, the blade singing as she unsheathed it. "Let's not provoke war."

She glanced back at him, eyes silvered, fingers clenched around the sword's handle. "They threaten my child, they provoke me."

I cleared my throat, feeling both too young and too old for this conversation, standing in my father's office, in this House. Here, I was an overgrown child, still not quite adult enough. And it made me itchy.

"Any chance you'll let me handle this on my own?" I asked.

My dad gave me a look I'd seen at least a hundred times. Eyebrow arched, imperious stare. Every bit the Master in control.

"No." There was no meanness in his voice, but there was plenty of determination. "You are our child. Perhaps," he said, "we're learning to let you fly when you're away from here. But *here*, in our home, we will protect you."

There was a knock on the doorjamb. The vampire who stood

there was blond and pale and pretty, her jaunty ponytail a strange foil against the black fatigues. Lindsey was my mother's closest vampire friend and one of the House's guards. She and Luc were married.

"Report," my father said.

"Liege," Lindsey said. "The guard towers are staffed. Dozen outside the perimeter. None have breached."

"Cowards," my mother muttered, then looked sheepish when we all glanced her way. "Sorry—I don't mean they should attack. I meant they'll strike at Lis, the others, when they're alone, but not at the House."

"Perhaps they're wise enough to understand there are lines even they shouldn't cross."

"I wouldn't bet on it," I murmured.

Lindsey gave me a sad smile. "It's good to see you, Lis. Sorry about the circumstances."

"Good to see you, too. And same."

"Thank you, Lindsey," Dad said and looked back at me, offered a supportive smile. "We'll see what they have to say."

I nodded, and he looked at my mother. "Ready, Sentinel?"

Her smile was wide. "Yes, please. I never get to do the fun stuff anymore."

I loved my parents. But sometimes, they were a lot.

We made our way through the House, which was quiet now. That was the case, I discovered, because virtually every vampire was on the lawn, swords belted, waiting for orders.

The Bureau vampires were, as promised, on the other side of the fence. Clive stood in front, as was his way, and didn't seem to appreciate the katana blades currently aimed at his neck by the duty guards. But there was a bright cut on one guard's face, and Clive's knuckles were white around the handle of his katana.

We strode down the sidewalk, my father in the lead, flanked by Lindsey and my mother. I was behind them, and it didn't take a vampiric load of strategy to realize they'd formed a wall to protect me. Some of that was bravado; my parents didn't want war against the AAM. But some of it, I knew, was parental ferocity. And I hoped it wouldn't get them hurt.

At the sight of me, the vampires behind Clive moved forward. Two of the three who'd come to my doorway that first night were with him—Levi and Sloan. Their third, Blake, was gone. And each of them gazed at me with hatred born of their belief that I'd killed him.

"Johnson," Lindsey called out to the guard with the injury. "You good?"

"Fine," Johnson said, with a curl to his lip. "This excuse for a vampire believed he could trespass on Cadogan property. I corrected him."

"Well done," she said, then nodded at my father.

"I am Ethan Sullivan," he said, stepping forward. "Master of Cadogan House and member of the Assembly of American . . . *Masters*," he stressed after a dramatic pause, emphasizing the fact that he outranked Clive.

If Clive was shamed, he didn't show it. "Clive. Compliance Bureau, AAM. We are here on the authority of Nicole Heart."

I couldn't see my father's face, but guessed it held great displeasure. "You have surrounded a registered House with soldiers and weaponry without invitation. I very seriously doubt Nicole Heart authorized that."

"We have business with Elisa Sullivan."

"Who is on private property," my father pointed out. "And who, as she's told you before, is not a Novitiate of Cadogan House. You have no business here."

"We have business with Elisa Sullivan," Clive repeated, either too arrogant or too stupid to hear the threat in my father's words. "The longer it takes to resolve this issue, the more people will be injured."

My father's head tilted. "Is that a threat?"

"It's a statement of fact."

"Please trespass," my mother called out. "Please give me an opportunity." My mother loved a good fight.

"Sentinel," my dad said, a gentle rebuke that carried no heat.

But the Bureau vamps exchanged glances, looked not entirely sure it was a good idea to take on Cadogan's famous Sentinel. Levi stepped forward, whispered something to his brother that had Clive's expression tightening.

My father allowed silence to fall again, watching the vampires with the mildest expression. Clive swallowed hard; the tips of the katanas were millimeters from his skin.

A minute passed, then two, while they watched each other. Twelve Bureau vampires against the several dozen currently on the House's lawn, all of them silent and still and ready to fight for their Master, their House. And for me, I thought guiltily. Even though I wouldn't join them.

Clive blinked first. His jaw worked as he swallowed down harsh words, but he released the katana. It fell to the ground, the steel like a bell against concrete.

"He should be punished for that alone," Lindsey murmured. "Dropping a katana on the ground. Disrespectful."

I bit back a grin. I had missed the trademark Cadogan House humor.

"Because I believe in the rule of law," my father said, "but I do not engage with those who threaten our House or our people, I will allow you, and you alone, through the gate. You will leave that sword on the ground."

Clive and the others discussed; after a long pause, he stepped forward. The gate was opened to allow him to slip through, then closed and locked again.

He strode toward us with hatred in his eyes, all of it centered on me. "We are here to take Elisa Sullivan into custody."

But my father, much like the Pack, was no pushover. He slid his hands into his pockets, and his stare was blank and mild. "No. You are not."

"She is a murderer."

"Wrong again," my father said. "As I'm sure you're well aware, she was nowhere near the scene of your colleague's unfortunate demise, nor did she have any motive to wish him dead."

But Clive read the truth as a lie. "Cover-up. The Ombudsman's office is tied closely to the Chicago Houses and can't be trusted."

"Yet you'd allow Elisa join our House to satisfy your conditions?"

"There are rules," Clive said, like it was a mission statement.

"So there are," my father said. "And I'm aware of no rule that authorizes you to require a vampire join a House or to demand they be tested."

For the first time, something like uncertainty showed on Clive's face. "A lie. Nicole has afforded us authority to act for the AAM."

"While I have questions about the scope of that authority, and I'll communicate those to Nicole, it certainly does not extend to brandishing weapons at my people."

"Masters are obliged to submit to the authority of the Compliance Bureau."

"No," my father said, as magic and anger began to rise, mix, in the air around us. "We *are* the AAM, and you are no Nicole Heart."

Clive's eyes flashed silver, his hands squeezed into fists. "Your daughter will submit, or she will be arrested and confined. If you afford her protections, you will be punished accordingly."

That was when realization struck, hard and bright as one of Petra's shocks. Clive had already decided the "facts," and nothing we said was going to change his mind. Actual reason and logic were lost on him, ignored due to his unwavering conviction that he was right, and I was evil. I admired conviction, but not obsession. Not willful ignorance.

Victory and defeat were the only things he understood. So defeat it would have to be. But I'd be damned sure he made the first move this time.

My parents stepped forward together, but I reached out, grabbed their arms. "Enough," I called out. "Enough of this."

They both looked back at me. "You will not—" my father began, but I cut him off with a shake of my head.

"We can't ignore this any longer," I called out, but squeezed his hand, willed him to understand.

I released him, stepped in front of my parents. And felt my mother's anger at the movement. She'd been trained as a soldier, and didn't like anyone, much less her child, shielding her from harm.

I put on my most frazzled and defeated look. "I'll fix this," I said to Clive. "But I need time to get some things in order." My father began to speak, but I held up a hand. "Give me"—how much time would it take to find a way out of this?—"three days."

Silence followed.

"One," Clive said, finally.

"Two," I said. "And no magical summons."

Clive's brows lifted. "So you can use your family's considerable resources to run away and avoid punishment? No."

An insult not just to me, but to my family. "Sullivans don't run."

"She will not leave Chicago for the next forty-eight hours," my father said, probably working hard to guess my game. Then looked at me with trust enough that my throat tightened with love. "You can bond the House if you wish."

Clive liked that possibility, it seemed, from the glint in his eyes. "Forty-eight hours," he said, looking at me. "At which time, you will swear allegiance to a House other than Cadogan—assuming any will still have you. You will be Commended, after which you will immediately be taken to Atlanta for Testing. Should you fail to do so, you will be taken to Atlanta and placed into seclusion until such time as you have atoned for your crime." Then he looked at my father again. "Cadogan House as bond."

"She will meet you in forty-eight hours," my father agreed.

Unless I came up with a better plan, I silently amended. Unless I figured some way to wiggle out of this in the meantime. Which I damn well would.

"I will meet you in forty-eight hours," I said, and the deal was made.

FOURTEEN

Well, daughter mine," my dad said when were back inside his office. "I hope you have a plan?"

I winced. "Not yet. But I will within the next forty-eight hours."

"I'll talk to Luc," my father said. "Nicole will need to know about this, too."

"While he's doing that," my mother said, "let's take a walk."

We both looked at her.

"A walk?" my dad asked.

"A walk." My mother came to me. I searched her eyes, wondering what she might tell me, or what she might ask. What she might have seen. But she was my mother, so I nodded, took the hand she offered.

"We'll be back," she said, giving my father a look, and led me out of the office.

We walked through the kitchen, out into the yard, where path lights glowed and trees swayed in the breeze, not yet ready to give up their leaves for winter.

She stopped when she reached a small fountain, gurgling water illuminated by small in-ground lights, with benches placed around it.

"Sit," she said. An order. Polite, but an order.

I lifted my brows, but did as she requested.

"What's wrong?" she asked.

I stared at her, felt my heart begin to race. "I think Clive laid it out pretty well?"

She sat down beside me, looked at me with pale blue eyes. "I'm your mother, and I know when something's bothering you. And it's not just the AAM."

"Being pressured to join a House isn't helping."

"We aren't trying to pressure you," she said after a moment. "It's just . . . hard for both of us not to take personally that you don't want Cadogan."

"It's not an issue of want."

"I know," she said and put a hand over mine. "I know. I said that wrong, and I'm sorry." Frowning, she rose, walked to the fountain, looked down at it. Then she looked back at me—and I knew she knew.

Not exactly—not that the monster existed—but that I was hiding something. She knew I hadn't told her, or either of them, the absolute truth.

"You know you can tell us if something is hurting you. We won't judge. And we'll hold your secrets if need be."

"I'm just . . . figuring some things out." It wasn't the entire truth, and probably a lie by omission. But it was all I was willing to say.

Her shoulders seemed to relax, as if my admission was enough to soothe some of the worry. I'd validated her concerns, even if I hadn't shed much light on them. "Nothing you can talk to me about?"

"Not really," I said, and watched light dance across water.

"Connor?"

"He's good. He's great. And the Pack has been supportive."

"Good. In the olden days," she said dryly, joining me on the bench again, "before I joined the House, the Pack was standoffish. Trust had been lost between the Pack and other Sups, and they didn't involve themselves with others unless they had to—unless there was some very specific reason for it. But then I joined, and Gabe and I became friends of a type. Not hanging-out friends, but we had a camaraderie." She smiled, gaze vacant, as if revisiting old and comforting memories. "Probably in part because it irritated your father. Which made it that much more fun. It changed more after the House and Pack became allies. And after Connor hit puberty," she added.

I snorted, thinking of the number of times I'd heard about teenage Connor "borrowing" another shifter's bike without their knowledge, or keeping someone's daughter out a little too late. He hated bullies, and loved picking fights with them. He'd tested every boundary he could find—and was on a first-name basis with the local CPD officers who walked the beat near the Keene house. He'd washed a lot of dishes during the summer to pay the fines he'd accumulated over the year.

"Because they had to apologize to so many people for his behavior," I said.

"It's one way to socialize," Mom said. "And then we had you, and you and Connor were close in age, and you spent time together, or with Lulu. Even if you hated each other. Strong emotions," she said, "even then."

She'd been smiling, but her smile fell away. And when she looked at me, there was fear in her eyes.

"What's wrong?"

It took a moment for her to speak. "I don't know if I should tell you this. I don't know if it will help or hurt, or if it's something you should know or shouldn't."

"Tell me," I said without hesitation. I'd always rather have the truth, and quickly. And yeah, I realized the hypocrisy. But that I was willing to listen to hard facts didn't mean I wanted to deal them out.

"Gabe came to Cadogan House one night when Connor was

little. And he said something then . . ." She trailed off, as if gathering courage.

I leaned forward. "What did he say?" My voice was quiet, as if words spoken too loudly would break through the mist of the moment.

"He showed me my future—or a part of it. A child with green eyes."

Those green eyes—my green eyes—widened. "How did he know?"

"Some shifters can prophesize. He's one of them. And he said we—me and Gabe—were like family." She swallowed. "And then he said, 'But we lose them always, don't we'?"

I stared at her, trying to make sense of the words, of the questions. "He meant me and Connor?"

"We didn't know either of you, yet," she said and squeezed my hand. "But yes, I do think that's what he meant. And I don't think it's some harbinger of problems for you or Connor. I think he knew, even then, that I was going to be pregnant, and that you and Connor would play a role in each other's lives. I didn't really believe him then—how could I? No one else had done what he thought would happen. And then it did. You were born, by whatever miracle of magic and biology.

"After you were born, I didn't sleep much. I had this fear someone or something would take you away. You were so rare, and so loved." She touched my cheek. "I was worried, at least in part, that the magic that helped make you would sweep you back up, that Sorcha would return and steal you like a fairy in the night. But then I started sleeping again, and logic returned. And when that happened, I decided by 'losing' he meant your growing up."

She shook her head clear, looked at me. "I think he knew you were going to be part of their family—that you and Connor would bring us all together, even as you and Connor formed your own unit." She sighed. "And that's a very long way of saying, if you can't hold to Cadogan, hold to the Pack. Let them be your allies, even when we can't. And whatever it is, know that we love you."

I nodded and smiled, but knew the truth: My monster—the magic that remained inside me—was her nightmare.

I walked back through the House, paused at the stairs to the basement, and almost considered going down.

The armory was down there, the room where the House's collection of weapons was saved. Including my mother's former sword.

Maybe, if I had the sword, if I wielded it, I could serve both ends. Give comfort to the monster. Take comfort from the AAM.

please

The word, or the idea of it, echoed in my head. I could feel the bare need, the desire, and I wasn't sure which of them I was feeling. Probably both.

I closed my eyes for a moment, listened to the sound, felt them both reach out for connection. For . . . completion? And the monster, by now, knew me. Knew what I valued. I saw myself walking through the House, down the stairs, through the basement hallway.

And when I opened my eyes, I stood outside the closed armory door, hands raised as if to push it open.

I took a stumbling step backward, heart racing as I realized where I was, and what I'd almost done. I'd walked downstairs with my eyes closed, down the hallway with my eyes closed. Had let the monster and its kin—or whatever they were to each other—lead the way through my childhood home.

"Lis?"

I glanced back, found Lindsey looking out through the guard room door, which was just down the hall. She came toward me, lips curved into a smile, but eyes narrowed.

"Are you okay?" Lindsey was empathic, could feel others' emotions.

She didn't, as far as I was aware, know about the monster. I hadn't even known it existed until I was nearly a teenager, and my awareness of it had been sporadic for a few years after that. Now that the monster and I were in closer contact, the risk was higher she'd sense it and tell someone.

Cover, I ordered myself, and pushed the monster down, smiled. "I'm fine. I visited my parents and was just kind of . . . wandering around."

She looked at me, then the door, then back again. "Thinking about weapons, were you? Not surprising, given what assholes the AAM are being right now."

Thinking about weapons was one way to put it, I thought, but realized with some comfort the AAM gave me pretty good cover. It was entirely normal to be flustered and worried about that. "Yeah. I thought about going in." Entirely true.

"You want me to unlock the door? Couple of good blades might set you right up."

"No, thank you." I took another step backward. "I need to figure out a way to deal with this without weapons. Without war."

"Okay," she said and gestured back toward the guard room. "I need to get back on a call, but if you change your mind, just let me know. I'll send down a guard."

"Thanks. I appreciate it, but I'm going to head out now."

I felt her gaze on me as I walked back to the stairs, began the climb up. But I didn't feel better until I was out of the House again.

And then I saw the SUV waiting at the curb, and the man standing beside it, and I felt almost ridiculously relieved.

The gate opened slowly, and I slipped through the gap sideways, too impatient to wait. Connor pushed off the car, frowned at my expression.

"What?" he asked.

"First, are you okay?"

"I'm fine," he said and brushed a thumb across my cheek. "Even the aches are mostly gone. What happened?"

"The AAM showed up."

His eyes fired, and he cast a hard look toward the grounds, the street. "They didn't stay long."

"Didn't make it past the gate. Either because Clive was afraid of my parents, which wasn't unwise, or he knew he didn't have the authority to actually fight Cadogan House." I paused. "So, to put an end to it, I agreed to meet the AAM in forty-eight hours."

Connor went very quiet, and very still. But the magic around him, around both of us, roiled like a storm-tossed sea. I could hear the guards come to attention behind us, wary of the power that now permeated the air.

"Am I losing my mind," he asked, voice dangerously low, "because I think you just told me you agreed to meet the AAM?"

"I did agree," I said, standing a little straighter. "And it was the right thing to do."

"It gives them an excuse—"

But I held up a hand, cut him off. "It doesn't. It gives me two days without running—at least from them—to find a way out. I'm not actually going to give myself up." And I hoped my father and I had worded our acceptance carefully enough for that. "But they were threatening the gates, and my parents were threatening them. It was . . ."

"A de-escalation?"

I nodded, watched him.

"You should have talked to me," he said, and looked amused to be parroting back my words. And I got to use the same tactic.

"I knew you'd tell me not to do it," I said. "And I'm not used to getting permission just to do the right thing."

Connor snorted. "Lis, even the AAM is aware of that. And I'm not in a position to offer you permission to do anything. You're your own person, and I'm not your keeper. But." He stepped closer, tugged a long lock of my hair. "I worry about you. Keeping me in the loop makes me worry a little less."

"I'd have called you if I had time," I said. "And I'll . . . try to do that in the future."

His smile warmed. "Maybe we could both do better on that end."

"Apology accepted."

Connor rolled his eyes.

"Speaking of checking in, I am in need of some ideas to avoid having to surrender to the AAM, so I think we need to have a team meeting."

"Do we have a team?" he asked, opening the passenger door for me.

"Right now, we have a Lulu and an Alexei. So we'll make do."

We went back to the town house and found Lulu at the round table in the dining nook in the bay window, picking vegetables from a take-out box with a pair of tear-apart chopsticks. The house smelled like pork and pepper, and my stomach rumbled.

"Team meeting," I called out. "I don't suppose you ordered extra?"

She just grunted, dug in the box for more. And I saw the mountain of take-out boxes and bags on the kitchen island.

"Uh-oh," I said.

"Jackpot," Connor said, then looked at me. "What? Why?"

"I'm pretty sure this is a breakup binge." I unfolded the box tops, found half a dozen different dishes that ran the gamut from fried pork to wobbling tofu in spicy sauce. "Damn."

"What should we do?" Connor's words were garbled, and I looked back to find him chewing pork. "What? I was hungry and it's here. And it's my house." He swallowed. "I can't help having a shifter appetite."

I rolled my eyes, walked to the dining area, sat down at the table beside her. "What happened?"

"I was at Mateo's." She speared what looked like peppered beef with a chopstick. Aggressively. "He said I had too much drama. It was messing up his artistic juju. He decided Nadya would be a better match."

"Prick," I said, but felt a wave of guilt. I was certainly the reason for some of that drama. "How can I help?"

She slumped a little as she looked back at the take-out containers. "I might have ordered too much food."

"Fortunately," Connor said, joining us with a container and fork, "you've brought it to the right house."

"Thank you," Lulu said, tears brimming.

"You're welcome. Want to throw darts at a picture of his head later?"

She gave me a watery nod.

"Then that's what we'll do."

We moved the take-out boxes to the dining room table and ate directly from them, sliding them around to get the combinations we wanted. Connor turned on music, and we ate through Nina Simone and Otis Redding, the heartfelt crooning he preferred to the jarring guitar usually played at the Pack's bar.

I turned at the sound of footsteps, found Alexei padding through the kitchen, naked but for a pair of very snug boxer briefs.

His body was remarkable, every inch toned and taut, from strong shoulders to flat abdomen to the hard lines of muscle that ran past his hips toward his . . . other apparent assets.

I glanced at Lulu, found pink on her cheeks and her gaze very focused on her food.

"As his grandfather liked to say," Connor mused, "Alexei is . . . unburdened by humility."

"I mean, if you look like that," I murmured, "why would you be? You might be the third-prettiest boy in the Pack," I whispered to Connor. I'd teased him before that one of Lulu's exes, Riley Sixkiller, was in second place.

Connor flicked my arm. Which I probably deserved.

Lulu worked very hard not to notice, but her gaze followed as Alexei moved across the kitchen.

"Chinese take-out leftovers," I said. "Help yourself."

He looked across the spread, then back at us, gaze settling on Lulu. "What happened?" he asked, and there was no irritation in his voice now, and no teasing sarcasm. Just concern.

"I was dumped," Lulu said, and she broke open a fortune cookie, spread the tiny paper between her fingers, read it. Then scoffed and tossed it into the pile with the others she'd pillaged. "But it's fine. I'll stuff myself with broccoli beef now, and we're going to throw darts at his picture later."

"No," Alexei said and, without another word, walked out of the kitchen.

"Hmm," was all Connor said. We waited in silence for the two minutes it took him to come down again.

He'd added jeans to his ensemble, carried a small black case. He walked to Lulu and, while she stared, set it on the table in front of her. Tapped it once.

Blinking, she opened it. The case spread into three sections, each holding a throwing knife of gleaming silver.

"I don't have his picture," Alexei said. "But these are more satisfying than darts. I'll show you how to use them."

Silence, then Lulu swallowed hard, nodded once.

When he turned to walk back to the kitchen, I took his hand as he passed. His eyes widened in surprise, darting down to the contact.

I almost pulled my hand away, afraid I'd insulted him or that physical contact just wasn't his thing. But he squeezed my fingers, nodded, and headed for food.

Shifters and vampire made a decent dent, but Lulu and I would be eating leftovers for many nights to come. Or would, once we were able to go home again. And because there was no chance of that without dealing with the AAM, I called the meeting to order.

"Why did we need a meeting?" Lulu asked, rubbing her belly.

"Because your BFF," Connor said, "offered to meet the AAM in forty-eight hours."

Lulu stared at him for a minute, then turned her icy gaze to me. "She did what?"

I told her about the AAM showing up at Cadogan House, the threats Clive had made, and what I'd agreed to. She slugged me in the arm.

"What the hell," I said, rubbing it and looking between them. "I'm pretty sure I don't deserve that for being incredibly noble."

"You should have told me," Lulu said.

"*Supernatural shenanigans*," I said with emphasis. "I was trying to protect you."

Lulu rolled her eyes. "There are obvious exceptions to the no-shenanigans rule when my now rent-paying roommate is in danger."

"So your interest is financial," I muttered. "Maybe you shouldn't have spent the difference on Chinese food." I held up a hand to stop more argument. "We are under a literal deadline, so let's skip the blame and get to the solution. Given the running from attacks and stalkers, I haven't had a lot of time to brainstorm."

And forty-eight hours would slip by quickly. Especially since I'd be unconscious for a good chunk of it.

"Do we get T-shirts like the OMB has?"

We all looked at Alexei.

"What?" I asked.

"Our team. We can call ourselves 'Lace.' L, A, C, E," he said, pointing to Lulu, himself, Connor, and me in turn.

"Can we put 'Sups against Fangs' on the back?" Lulu asked.

Alexei grinned, but I shook my head. "Obviously not," I said, "since one of us—in literal point of fact—has fangs. And I'm calling this meeting to order. The floor is open for suggestions."

Connor's grin went wicked, his blue eyes drowsy.

"Strategic suggestions," I clarified.

"What about a duel?"

We all looked at Alexei.

"If they're good enough for secretaries of the treasury, they're good enough for vampires. I'm just saying, if you and Clive had it out in some kind of winner-take-all scenario, would he pack up and go home?"

That was along the lines of Uncle Malik's thoughts. "I don't know," I said honestly. "I could probably take him one-on-one. His katana skills weren't that impressive."

"Not slick enough," Alexei said.

"Not nearly," I agreed. "And I'm sure I could provoke him into a fight. But I don't think that would resolve the other issues."

"Blackmail?" Connor asked.

"I'm also not above blackmailing a bully," I said, "if we had any information to use against him. Which we don't."

Connor and Alexei looked at each other. "Maybe we could obtain something from the Consolidated Atlantic Pack."

The shifters of the eastern seaboard. Their territory abutted the NAC's. "You think they'd be able to dig something up on an Atlanta vampire?" I asked.

"Maybe. Relations between shifters and vamps out east are a little . . . testier . . . than those here," Connor said. "If there's information to be found, the Atlantic may be able to find it."

"I don't want to damage the AAM," I said. "Just put a little pressure on Clive."

"Understood," he said, and nodded at Alexei, who took out his screen, slipped out of the room.

"If that doesn't pan out," Lulu said, "you could go the bargaining chip route. The stalker killed Blake, right?"

"Right," I said.

"So you find the stalker—and Blake's killer—first, and we offer him up to the Compliance Bureau. A trade."

"That's not bad," I said, sitting up. "Except that we aren't any further in figuring out who that is. And we don't have any leads independent of the OMB."

"So make him come to you. Lure him out. And when he shows up, kick his ass and deliver him to the AAM for a price—your freedom. And Bob's your uncle," Lulu said and mimicked wiping dirt from her hands. "All is well in the kingdom again."

"My uncles are Ben and Christopher and Derek and Eli," Connor said with an admirably straight face.

She just rolled her eyes. "Don't you have a squeak toy to gnaw on somewhere?"

"Ah," Connor said, stretching out his legs. "Just like being fifteen again." He slid his glance to me. "Except you aren't tattling nearly so much this time."

"I have no idea what you mean," I said primly, since he was well aware I'd gotten him in trouble often enough as a teenager. "And because this meeting has degraded into childishness or the reminiscence thereof, let's wrap it up. Alexei is going to check with the Consolidated Atlantic for information we can use on Clive. My parents are trying to reach Nicole. Connor and I are working on the stalker." I glanced at the wall clock. Two hours until dawn. When I woke up again, we'd be down to thirty-six. "Let's find something."

Connor rose, stretched, glanced at me. "Let's go sit on the patio."

I looked at him. "What?"

"The patio outside." He cleared his throat. "Past the conservatory."

"With the pipe, Ms. Scarlett?" Lulu asked.

Connor's brows lifted. "You like *Clue*?"

"The movie? Of course. It's genius, and I'm a woman of obvious taste and discernment. I'd say I'm surprised you do, but then, you also like comic books."

"We all have our pop culture weaknesses," Connor said and held out a hand to me, as if the warmth in his eyes wasn't enough of an invitation.

I glanced back at Lulu, who stared out the windows, the sadness in her eyes obvious, and worried that Mateo had compounded her sadness.

"Give me a minute, will you?" I asked quietly and looked back at Connor.

"Of course," he said, and he pressed a kiss to my forehead. "I'll be outside."

FIFTEEN

I waited until he was gone, looked over at her. "You want to go past the conservatory, too?"

"I want to not regret having eaten my way through half of China Palace's menu."

"Same." I waited a moment, trying to figure out my strategy, decided to stick with the truth. "Out with it."

She looked back at me, brows lifted. "What?"

"Out with it. Tell me what's bothering you—has been bothering you, since Minnesota."

"Nothing is bothering me." But she rose, gathered up containers and carried them into the kitchen, began to consolidate rice boxes and toss the empties.

"Yes, I can tell by your relaxed tone and chill manner."

She looked up, misery in her eyes, and it broke my heart a little. I went to her—taking boxes on the way—and put them on the counter.

"Lulu. Talk to me."

She looked at me for a minute, then took my hand. "Come with me," she said and pulled me through the kitchen, the dining room, into the small front parlor with its fireplace and bookshelves. "Look."

She hadn't given me the chance to object, but I had no idea what

I was looking for, or ought to have seen. "The couch is nice?" It was low and boxy, covered in emerald-green velvet.

Lulu muttered, stalked to the bookshelves, pointed. "Look," she said again.

Confused, but trusting, I walked closer, looked at the books, the titles. They included *The Care and Feeding of Vampires* and *The Official Guide to Vampire Etiquette.*

Connor *had* been reading about the care and feeding of vampires. And since that had been on his screen, he must have had both electronic and paper copies of the book. While I knew there was no chance in hell he'd willingly follow formal vampire etiquette, that he cared enough to look into it made my heart flutter a little.

But I didn't think that was the point, so I looked back at her, watched as she settled onto velvet cushions.

"I think Connor might be loaded," I said quietly, sitting cross-legged on the floor in front of her.

"Shifter money," Lulu said. "They're quiet about it, but they've got plenty. They rarely buy anything but beer, bikes, and leather."

Saving plenty for lush town houses, I thought, but didn't say it aloud. "So what's wrong?"

It took a moment of silence, another wiping of tears I knew she didn't like to shed around people. "I feel like life is just . . . moving around me. I'm scraping by to make a living as an artist, and you've got this legitimate OMB job—or did before they put you on leave. Connor, the prince of werewolves, is mad about you, and I just got dumped."

She crossed her arms. Not petulance, but protection. A shield. Lulu had always been more private than me. More gregarious, but still holding something back. That was, I thought, the reason she cut her hair the way she did. The shoulder-length bob, one side always falling across her face. It was another shield.

"You guys have your own vibe, and I feel very much apart from it." She held up a hand. "That's not a complaint about you. It's fine that you have people, and I know you'd include me more if I wanted to be part of the shenanigans."

"I would."

"But I don't have that kind of group. Growing up, I was too Sup for the humans, not Sup enough for the sorcerers. And Mateo . . . That was new and exciting and I really like him. And he's part of this cool art collective, and I'm thinking, 'These are my people!' And then he dumps me, and there goes my plan for community building and gallery openings."

I sat with that for a minute. "Is that why you wanted to have the potluck? For community building?"

"Yeah," she said with a sigh. "It was."

"It was a good potluck. A good party. I'm glad your artsy friends were gone before the vampires showed up."

"No shit."

"As to the rest of it, do you want comfort, commiseration, or contradiction?"

She half laughed, which I thought was better than nothing. "Right now, commiseration."

"So, when I came back from Paris, I was lost. Everything I was going to be, everything I was supposed to be, was back there. I had to find myself all over again—and still am. You gave me a place to stay—a home," I amended. "The OMB gave me a job. Connor gave me . . . understanding."

"And Hot Boy Summer."

I snorted. "And Hot Boy Summer. And then I got fired and someone tried to kill Connor today. Someone who thinks we're friends, that I've maybe never met, tried to take Connor's life to win some kind of favor with me."

"This commiseration is becoming depressing."

"Yeah, this week has been a lot." I looked over at her, found her looking back, and offered my hand. "Circumstances are going to be shitty as long as people exist on this planet. But you've got family to help you through. You've got me."

She took my hand. Squeezed. "Okay," she said. "You can move to comfort."

I smiled. "You've given me a home and a devil cat. What do you need to make your dreams come true? How can I help?"

She cleared her throat. "Maybe we could start doing more stuff in the art community? Like, I don't know, gallery openings or something?"

"Done."

Lulu looked at me, brows lifted. "Seriously?"

I shrugged. "It's snacks and champagne on someone else's dime. If the art's good, you can enjoy it. If it's not, you can mock it."

"A cruelly practical approach."

"That's me," I said. I sat up again, looked at her. "I'm sorry if we don't spend enough time doing Lulu stuff. There has been a lot of my nonsense since I came back. Not caused by me, but I end up in the middle of it."

"You put yourself in the middle of it."

My first instinct was to respond with a sharp, defensive denial. But she was right. "I do. I have to," I admitted. "I can't just stand around and let other people do the dirty work."

"I know. You're good people, Lis." She sat up, scrubbed hands over her face, looked at me. "It's just damned inconvenient some-times."

I smiled. "I can't argue with that. We good?"

She nodded. "We're good. You think Benji would let us have a party here?"

"No, not if you call him Benji."

"Lassie?"

"Quit while you're ahead, Lulu." I gave her a hug. "Does going to those paint-your-own-pottery places count as artistic? I've always wanted to do that."

"Sure. If your pottery turns out good enough."

I was getting judged on *everything* this week.

I walked through the conservatory, a narrow room of framed glass with pretty rattan seating, to the stone patio outside, where several chairs fanned around a stone firepit. Connor wasn't at either, so I took the path along the ivied wall that bounded the yard and found him on a blanket in the middle of the long rectangle of grass.

I'd already pulled off my boots, and the grass was deliciously chill beneath my feet.

Connor lay on his back, hand beneath his head, gaze on the sky—and the few stars he'd be able to see through the haze of Chicago's lights.

He turned his head to look at me. "She's okay?"

I nodded. "She will be. She's getting used to my working for the OMB and dating and then there's this house. I think she's feeling . . . left out. She needs to find her people, and thought she had with Mateo."

"Alexei would be happy to entertain her."

"I know. And she does, too, believe me. I think she needs more time with me right now. More time on Lulu activities."

"Which would be?"

"I think I'll be painting mugs."

He blinked. "If that's a euphemism, I don't know what for."

I sat cross-legged on the blanket beside him. "Not a euphemism. Artsy stuff."

"Ah."

"I saw the books," I said, when we were nearly eye to eye again.

His brows lifted. "Books?"

I poked him in the shoulder. "The ones in the front room. About vampires."

"Ah."

I brushed a lock of dark hair from his temple. "I think it was very thoughtful. And I look forward to lengthy discussions about the order in which ranked vampires can enter a room."

"Not in a million years."

"Speaking of millions," I said, grateful for the segue, "can I ask you a personal question?"

His grin was wicked. "Of course."

"Not that kind of personal question." But still, very personal. And awkward. I gestured around us. "How did you pay for all this?"

His brows lifted in surprise; whatever he'd expected me to ask, it hadn't been that. "With money?"

"I mean—I can't believe I haven't asked this—I assume you get paid by the Pack for working at NAC or . . . ?"

"Pack members get a portion of the profits from NAC Industries and the businesses that make it up. They've been mostly very successful. Our family's share is larger because we put up the initial investment money."

I could buy that, and knew they operated several businesses, but his individual sliver of Keene family profits still didn't seem to be enough for all this. "And?"

"And," he said flatly. "Other means."

I thought of the leather, the bikes, and what little I knew of old-school motorcycle clubs said they ran heavy in drug and protection rackets.

"That's an ignorant stereotype," he said, apparently having read the look on my face. "And no, I didn't use those other means to buy the house. The funds were entirely legitimate."

"From the profits of NAC Industries?"

To my absolute surprise, faint pink rose across his cheekbones. "And other sources in my account."

"Do you . . . have a trust fund?"

More pink, which made my grin widen.

"Are you . . . rich?"

"You don't have to say it like that."

I grinned at him. "I kind of think I do."

"I'm comfortable," he said, squirming a little. "My parents knew how to invest their funds." He tapped my chin. "So if we can't meet the deadline, and I need to whisk you out of Chicago, we can make other plans."

His turn for a decent segue. "And where would we go?"

"Wherever you'll go with me," he said and pressed a kiss to my lips. "Come here." He patted the blanket. "Let's enjoy the night and the air and the breeze. And the peace and damned quiet."

I adjusted to lie beside him, fitting perfectly into his arms. And he was right. It was peaceful and quiet. The brick wall or house or greenery, or all three, seemed to soften the sounds of the city, so it hummed softly around us. The air was cool, the breeze delicious, and a few stars had been strong enough to pierce the haze and shine above us.

"I can't believe this is inside the city," I said. "It's really remarkable."

"I thought so. It felt like . . . an oasis. But we won't get many more nights like this. Not when the cold sets in."

"You have fur."

"So I do. And rolling in the snow is a lot of fun. But traversing hard-packed and filthy snow on a Chicago sidewalk in February is not."

"Picnic dinners and moonlit chats," I said. "You're a lot more romantic on dates than I'd imagined."

He turned to look at me, grin full of masculine satisfaction. "You imagined?"

"Let's just say, the girls you used to date didn't seem very interested in romance, and you didn't seem very interested in supplying it."

"What did I want to supply?"

I snorted. "You don't need me to tell you that. You were a player, and the girls lined up for a chance with the prince."

"I can't help my natural appeal."

"Again with the modesty," I said, but I felt some of the tension leaving my shoulders. "I talked with my mom about you."

"You did?"

"We were discussing the AAM, the Pack, vampires. About trouble for all three, and the trouble you'd gotten in as a teenager."

"Growing pains," he said, and there was no regret in his smile.

"That's one way to look at it. You got in trouble so often I kept a list."

Connor looked down at me, brows raised. "Excuse me?"

My smile was wide. "In my journal. Only the times I knew about, of course. So if you told me or Lulu or my parents." I slid him a glance. "Or if I actually watched you get hauled off by the CPD."

"That only happened a couple of times."

"Four that I'm aware of," I said, correcting the record. "And it was a good thing your father was friends with the Ombudsman. I also kept a top ten list."

"Worst crimes, or most impressive?"

"Both."

"Why were you so obsessed with me, brat?"

I was torn between humor and insult. "I was not, and have never been, obsessed with you."

"You had a list."

"Because you kept getting in trouble. And those were only the times you got caught."

His grin was wide again. "Those were halcyon days. Before screens and responsibility."

"Before actual consequences, you mean?"

"Yes."

"My favorite was probably when you replaced the bottled blood in the Cadogan cafeteria fridge with ketchup and hot sauce. Or when you marked all the cards in the Pack bar, then spent the evening emptying your uncles' pockets."

"Those were good nights," he said with a very pleased smile. "My uncles were pissed. Or all except Christopher, who said they should have known better and checked the deck first. Said it was a good lesson for them. I was grounded for a week after the blood because someone snitched."

"I do not admit to snitching"—I totally had snitched—"and even if I had, there was plenty of evidence. You'd been in Cadogan House that night asking about how blood tasted."

"You snitched," he said. "And I got in trouble. Thing was, it wasn't me."

"Right," I said dryly. "Who else would it be?"

He looked down at me, and there was honesty in his eyes. "You tell me."

Puzzled, I thought back. I remembered that night, because Lulu had stayed over, and we'd spent a good chunk of the time complaining about Connor and eating ice cream. Until we'd snuck him inside, and let him join us. So Connor and I weren't the only ones there . . .

"Lulu," I guessed. "She did it—and you took the blame."

He shrugged, as if he might have shrugged off the gallantry. "Her parents were stricter than mine."

"Everyone's parents are stricter than yours," I muttered.

"Shifters," he said, unrepentant. "She usually played by the rules, and didn't like getting in trouble. She's"—he frowned as he searched for a word—"softer than us that way."

"I didn't like disappointing my parents."

"No one does. But I mostly ignored punishments, and you usually tried to negotiate your way around them by citing House rules or whatever."

"Now who's got the list?" I asked.

Connor snorted. "The point is, it was no skin off my hide to take responsibility. Lulu was relieved she didn't get in trouble, and very irritated that she owed me. It was a total win-win." He frowned. "I think that's when she was spending time with the necromancer kid."

"That was—" I had to work to remember the girl's name. "Ariel, I think. Her mother, Annabelle, was a friend of my parents. She helped them, and the Ombuds, before she retired."

Her daughter, I recalled, had been a hellion, and not an especially good influence on Lulu. Necromancers didn't come into their magic until they hit seventeen or eighteen, and it could be a rough road before and after.

"Maybe the entire thing had been her idea," I mused.

"I take it you aren't in touch."

"No, and I don't think Lulu is, either."

"I think I kissed Ariel during her wild-child phase."

"You're still in your wild-child phase and just as incorrigible."

He turned to me, gaze narrowed, but eyes gleaming like blue fire. He touched my face with a gentle fingertip, tracing the line of my jaw, lips hovering near my ear. "Shall I prove just how incorrigible I can be?"

"Yes," I said and grabbed a handful of his T-shirt.

Next thing I knew, I was on my back, a prince above me, his eyes outrageously blue. He nipped at my bottom lip.

"We are outside," I reminded him. "People can see us."

"No, they can't," he said. "Check the windows."

Instinctively, I glanced up, realized the only windows that

faced the courtyard were from his town house, and they were all closed, the curtains drawn. No one could see.

"Clever," I said, as anticipation rose on my skin.

"Shifter," he said. "We enjoy all manner of naked outdoor romps."

And in case I didn't believe him, he proceeded to prove it. He pulled his shirt over his head, then rose. His feet were bare, and he unbuttoned his jeans, more slowly than I thought fair or necessary, and then there were boxer briefs, and then there was nothing but smooth, tan skin.

He was glorious.

I'd seen him naked before, but that had only been brief flashes before or after he'd shifted. Having him stand there, the prince of wolves, staring down at me with that fallen-angel face, was something altogether different. Altogether more powerful.

Broad shoulders, strong arms. His chest, each muscle defined as his lean torso narrowed to his abdomen. Strength rippled there, dark ink calling out his challenge to the world. *I'm not led; I lead.* The sentiment matched the daring in his eyes, the strong brace of his legs, and the hand that dipped from abdomen to arousal, the fingers that gripped.

"No modesty," I said, barely able to form words.

"None needed," he said, brow arched in authority, and dropped to his knees. He looked at me for a moment. Gaze raking over clothing like he might see through it.

But he still bore the bruises of the attack on him, and I traced fingers lightly over the mottled skin on his torso, near his shoulder. "Are you sure you're okay for this?"

"More than fine," he said and lifted his gaze back to me. "Are you?"

"Oh, definitely," I said with a grin.

"Good. I want to see you."

I matched my expression to his, proud and sure, and pulled the sleeveless top over my head, then removed my leggings. His gaze followed the line of my neck and down to the bits of dark satin and lace that remained.

"Beautiful," he said. "And mine." He beckoned me forward with a finger, and I joined him on my knees.

I put a hand against his chest, felt his heart race, blood and magic and desire rushing beneath taut skin. I closed my eyes, reveled in the sensation of it. And when I opened them again, I knew they were silver, my fangs descended.

His lips parted, his eyes brilliantly blue as desire and shock flared.

I knew what I read there. "You've never been with a vampire."

Connor shook his head. "No," he said, the words a ragged exhalation.

I leaned forward, pressed a kiss to his neck, above the artery that pounded there just beneath the skin. Could feel the power beneath it, roaring like an engine. He would be Apex, king of the Pack. Not just because he would demand it, because he would accept nothing less, but because his power was too potent to allow for any other possibility.

So much power, I thought drowsily, and scraped my fangs against his neck.

Connor went absolutely still, and I mentally cursed, afraid I'd gone too far in the thrall of his own magic, and nearly pulled back to look at him. But he held me tight against his body.

"Again," he demanded. His voice was ragged, as if I'd scraped at it, too, and that nearly broke my own control.

I had to force myself to focus on giving pleasure, not taking what he hadn't offered—what I'd never take unless he offered. I curled my fingers into his hair, flicked my tongue over his ear, felt his rumbling approval. Then used my fangs to ignite, to entice. To remind him who and what I was. And who and what he'd taken on.

And then I was on my back, the stars wheeling overhead, and Connor above me, body braced on strong arms that framed my head.

I smiled at him, and his answering grin was stunningly beautiful. "Of all the places I ever thought I'd be," I said, "this wasn't one of them."

"Then we'd better make it worthwhile." His mouth found mine, body sinking, lowering, until we were aligned. I gripped his back, felt the muscles contract as he deepened the kiss, mouth plundering, tongue dipping with mine, every inch of him trying, I guessed, not to snap.

"I want you," he said, and his hand found my breast, and I arched beneath him. I felt electricity, potent as any spark that magic could fathom, as he teased me. I opened my eyes, found his gaze on me, watching, intense.

"Say it," he said and lowered his mouth, suckled. The stars seemed to spin faster.

"I want you," I said, and his growl was a triumph.

He moved his way down my body, slipping away any remaining satin, fingers, hands, mouth giving pleasure with slow and deliberate movements. And when he reached my core, I burst, nearly joined those wheeling stars. Another grumble of satisfaction, of victory. Of pride.

He climbed above me again, kissed me with a gentleness that was just as shocking. "I've dreamed of this," he said, "for a very long time."

It was my turn to go still, to be shocked. I put my hands on his face, searched his eyes. "What? What do you mean, for a very long time?"

His smile was slow and wide. "Even when you were a brat, Lis, you were desirable. I seriously considered trying to seduce you before you got on the plane to Paris."

"You did not," I said and brushed a dark curl from his forehead. "You were at the going-away party for, like, twenty minutes."

He just looked at me expectantly.

"You left," I said again. "I didn't even get to say goodbye."

"Because you were leaving. And it seemed wrong to, I don't know, interfere. That's why I've never touched another vampire. I've never known one who could compare to the possibility of you."

The words staggered me, left me as breathless as the kiss. "I'd have said yes."

He stared at me, his eyes darkening. "Yeah?"

"You were hot," was all I managed.

His grin was exceptionally wicked. "Then we both have time to make up," he said, and found my mouth again. Whatever tether he'd used to hold himself back was broken now. There was only desire, only love, as he aligned himself. And then we were connected, and he fought for control again, forehead against mine.

"Connor," I said, a plea, and he began to move, and we began to move together, as the moon tracked across the sky and the stars turned and we soared through the universe toward our fates, whatever they might be.

I gripped his back like I could capture him, us, this moment in time. One of his hands was braced near my head, the other on my jaw as he kissed me, seduced me, destroyed me.

Stars burst again, and he cried out his triumph, with the darkness above us.

I didn't consider myself prudish, but I also wouldn't have predicted I'd be lying naked on a bed of grass in the middle of Chicago, feeling very smug, and with an equally naked and smug prince beside me.

"Well," I said. "I guess I can check 'outdoor sex' off the list."

He turned his gaze to me, surprise in his eyes, chased by what looked like sympathy. Made sense, coming from a shifter. "Seriously? You never—"

"I never," I finished, and narrowed my eyes. "And you never had sex outdoors that was as meaningful as this, right?"

Connor rolled on top of me, a lock of dark hair falling rakishly across his forehead, his eyes brilliantly blue. "It is the most. The only."

And proceeded to prove it again.

SIXTEEN

We slept together in his third-floor bedroom, which was as luxe as the rest of the house. A bed big enough for a Pack of wolves, covered in sumptuous fabrics, a sitting area near a silver-tiled fireplace of large pillows and faux-fur blankets, a glass artscreen across one large wall of a deep and foggy forest.

He was gone when I woke, and the hallway was dark and silent. When I made my way downstairs, it took my brain a moment to understand the scene in the living room: Lulu and Alexei twined together on the couch, both still in yesterday's clothes, both still asleep.

They weren't embracing. His head was at one end, hers at the other, their legs tangled in a position that looked remarkably uncomfortable. But Alexei held one of her legs, his cheek snuggled against one of her socked feet like it was the softest pillow a shifter could ask for.

I stared for a full five minutes, confident Lulu would raise her head and explain she'd lost a round of truth or dare. But still they slept.

I was going to need coffee to emotionally process this. And since Connor hadn't stocked any, I grabbed a jacket, pulled it on over jeans and a fitted V-neck T-shirt. Then I used my screen to search for the nearest Leo's, confirmed the location, and headed for the door. Thinking it would be better if I didn't disappear without a word, I left a note on the counter: WHY IS THERE STILL NO COFFEE?

I didn't bother to sign it. They'd know it was me.

I checked the street through the window before stepping outside, and closed my eyes to focus on the presence of magic. The only power I sensed was behind me among the still sleeping. I opened the door as quietly as I could, closed it the same way, and walked into the darkness.

The weather had changed; there was a new chill in the air. Winter would be here soon, bringing its tough wind and layers of ice and snow. Not that a few months cuddled up with Connor would be a hardship.

Lights were on in the town houses I passed as I walked, families visible in some as they worked through their evening routines. Dinner. Homework. Toys. Catching up.

Normalcy. And it was wonderful to see—to remember. This had been a good idea, I thought, and walked into the coffee shop, which smelled of smoky beans and vanilla. It was tiny, a narrow slice between larger restaurants, and just big enough to host a few small tables and a glass-fronted counter of pastries.

I bought coffee for the group because I was a thoughtful soul, and moved aside to wait while paper cups were filled. And felt my screen buzz.

Given the kind of messages I'd been getting lately, I considered chucking it into the recycling bin and being done with it. But I didn't have the privilege of ignoring it, so I glanced at the screen.

THIRTY-SIX HOURS REMAINING, it read. WE LOOK FORWARD TO YOUR COMMENDATION OR SURRENDER.

My hand shaking with sudden anger, I stuffed the screen back in my pocket. God forbid I should forget our bargain, or the amount of my remaining freedom.

"Troublemaker," a woman nearby muttered. "Typical vampires."

Startled, I looked up, thinking she'd seen the message. Then I followed her gaze to a large screen mounted near the counter, with the sound off, but the closed captions on.

"*Elisa Sullivan*," the screen read, as video of me stepping off the plane from Paris played, "*daughter of Ethan Sullivan, the head of Chicago's Cadogan House, has agreed to surrender herself after a tense standoff at Cadogan House last night. Sullivan is accused of breaking vampiric protocols and assaulting those sent to capture her. More on this story as developments occur.*"

It was lies. All lies, if effectively spun by Clive or his colleagues to whichever reporter decided to listen. Vampires causing trouble was a much sexier story than vampires paying their bills on time.

"Troublemaker," the woman murmured again. "I'm sure she did whatever they're accusing her of. She looks the type. Spoiled."

"She's not so bad," said a man at a nearby table. "Didn't she help with the fairies?"

"She probably started the fight with the fairies in the first place."

My drink tray was placed on the counter. I snatched it up and fought back the urge to slink through the coffeehouse so the woman wouldn't recognize me. And realized that would let her— and her ignorance—win.

So I walked toward her, waited until she lifted her gaze to me, and watched the fear widen them.

"I'm Elisa Sullivan," I said. "They want me because I saved a human life. If they punish me for that, you'd better hope the next life that needs saving isn't yours."

I turned on my heel and walked out, and left her sputtering behind me.

Connor was sitting at the kitchen island, gaze on his screen, when I walked inside again. He looked up at my foot-stomping stride.

"What happened?"

"Vampires," I muttered and put the tray on the counter.

He stood up, leaving his screen behind. "They found you?"

"No. They fired back," I said. "Sent me a message about my deadline and planted a story about how my 'surrender' is imminent." I handed him my screen. "You read. I need to freebase this caffeine."

While his gaze tracked across the screen, and angry magic began to pepper the air, I took a cup from the holder, drank deeply, and closed my eyes. "There we go," I murmured, as warmth and the bite of coffee and caffeine settled in.

"They're going to be sorely disappointed when you don't surrender."

"Oh, they absolutely are. And then they can fuck off right into daylight."

Connor's mouth quirked. "That's a good one."

"Thought of it while I was muttering on the walk back." He handed my screen back, and I saw the two new messages from *Tribune* and *Sun-Times* reporters wanting a statement.

"You going to respond to those?" Connor asked behind me.

"I'm going to do one better," I decided.

In response, I told them to direct any inquiries to Roger Yuen and Theo Martin. That would keep the media off my back. If the OMB wanted to keep the investigation in-house, and to keep me out of it, it was only fair that I send reporters their way.

I put my screen away, promised myself not to look at it again for a good hour, and looked at him. "Did you pick this place because it's a three-block walk from Leo's?"

He gave me a very satisfied smile. "It didn't hurt."

"Clever boy."

"I try," he said, sipping his own coffee. "What else?"

"Nothing," I said, an automatic response.

But he put his cup down, looked at me with the imperious glare I had no doubt he'd be using as Apex in the future.

"That look doesn't work on me, due to Ethan Sullivan being my father."

"Okay," he said. And to my surprise, he pulled up his shirt, revealing his flat abdomen. He ran a hand across it, winged up his eyebrows in obvious invitation, magic rising in the air like heady perfume.

I swallowed down a wave of lust. "That, however, is incredibly effective."

"Everyone has a weakness."

I looked up at him, batted my eyelashes. "And what's yours?"

He snorted. "As if I'd reveal that to a vampire."

I took a step closer and, before he could put his shirt down, trailed my hands along his abdomen, felt muscles tense beneath, the magic grow more potent.

He tugged me forward, but I evaded, put another foot of space between us.

"Everyone has a weakness," I said with a polite smile.

Connor blew out a breath, looked at me beneath dark lashes. "We'll call that a draw. So what else is bothering you, vampire?"

My smile slipped away. But because I knew he was in earnest, I tried to put my feelings into words. "I'm worried about you, about Lulu. I'm angry at vampires. I'm sick of wondering who might be skulking around in the dark." I looked at him. "Darkness is supposed to be mine. Ours."

"We enjoyed the dark pretty effectively last night."

"You know what I mean. The AAM is stalking me. The stalker is hunting me. I'd take a straight battle over this shadow nonsense any day." I tried to roll the tension from my shoulders. "Maybe Alexei will find something."

"Or maybe your parents will, in the *Canon*. Or maybe we'll have this out in a big, bloody battle and the AAM will finally come to its senses." He sat again, put his arms around me, drew me between his thighs. "We'll figure out a way through it."

I rested my head atop his, breathed in his cologne. Then glanced toward the sitting area, found it empty of shifter and sorceress. "Did you see?"

"Trouble on the horizon?" he asked. "Yes. Yes, I did."

"I mean, they're both free agents, right?"

Lulu padded in. Her bob of dark hair gleaming, her clothes paint-splattered but tidy. She held up a hand as she aimed for the coffee. "I don't even want to discuss it."

Connor snorted. "Who said we do?"

She just grunted, pulled off a lid, and drank, throat working. When she'd properly self-medicated, she put the cup down, looked up again. "We just fell asleep. It wasn't a big deal."

"Okay," I said, as casually as I could manage.

"We were watching this show about guys finding junk on old farms. And we fell asleep. That's it."

"Okay," I said again. "You're talking about this much more than we are."

She narrowed her gaze at us. "Oh. You'd love that, wouldn't you?"

"No," Connor said. "We definitely wouldn't. Is he upstairs?"

"How would I know?" she asked, a little too loud.

"Because you just came from upstairs," I offered, feeling the need to defend him, "and it's a finite space." I drew a box with my index fingers. "So it's not unreasonable that you'd be aware of another person in said space."

She just growled at me. Maybe she was missing the cat.

"He goes with you to work," Connor told her, sipping again.

"Oh, great. Another night with baggage."

The baggage walked in. He'd paired jeans with a tight-fitting T-shirt that showed off his leanly muscled body.

Connor flicked my ear.

"Stop doing that," I said, sticking a pointed finger in his face and trying hard not to laugh.

"Stop staring at my Packmate," he said.

Alexei took the other coffee, looked at us, looked at Lulu, and rolled his eyes. "Ready?" he asked her. Lulu grunted and followed him out.

"Have a good night at work," I called out, and they both ignored me. Which was probably for the best. I looked at Connor. "What's on the prince's agenda for the evening?"

"Helping my girlfriend escape the wrath of the AAM, probably."

"Good call."

A buzzer sounded. Doorbell, I assumed, and cast a wary glance back toward the stairs, hand on my dagger. "Expecting someone?"

"As a matter of fact," Connor said, and I followed him to the front door. And found Petra and Theo smiling through the glass.

"Damn nice digs," Theo said, glancing around as Connor gave them a quick tour. "You have good taste."

"Thanks," Connor said. "There's no coffee left, but—"

"We're fine," Theo said, shifting his gaze to me, still full of apology, as we followed Connor into the dining room.

Not the sitting area or the kitchen island, where we'd talked with Alexei and Lulu. Because those were for family. And Petra and Theo weren't. At least not right now. Not yet.

Petra and Theo exchanged a heavy glance, but pulled out the upholstered chairs around the burled oak table, took seats. They'd understood, too.

I wanted to comfort everyone, but there wasn't time for it. Not now.

Connor and I sat on the other side of the table, hands linked. And I wondered how many nights we'd sit together and face worries and tragedies. Hopefully always on the same side.

"We found the vehicle used to hit Connor," Theo said. "It was dumped in the North Branch of the Chicago River. Divers found it during the day."

"That doesn't sound like an accident," I said and squeezed Connor's hand. "In case we needed any proof this was intentional, we have it."

Theo nodded. "They're searching for evidence, fingerprints that weren't ruined by the swim. The make and model are common, but it happens a vehicle matching the description was stolen from the Brass & Copper building. It belonged to a human found inside a janitorial closet off the building's lobby. Car key taken, along with a pint of his blood. But he's alive."

"A little snack," I said, fury now hot. "Confirming the person who stole the car—and made an attempt on Connor—was a vampire." My anger rose again. I'd have preferred the stalker come after me, put me in his sights, instead of taking aim at innocents.

"And because the stalker already took credit for Blake's death, confirming he was also killed by a vampire," Theo said.

"Why kill a vampire, try to kill a shifter, and avoid killing a human?" Petra asked. "The human would be the easiest to kill."

"Because the human didn't try to hurt me," I said. "And the stalker's goal is punishing those who hurt me, or so the notes say. Did the guy see anyone? Or is there video of the attack?"

"No video," Theo said. "The closet isn't far from the spot where Blake was killed, and there's no video in that portion of the building. He remembers seeing a man coming toward him, but that's it."

"So male vampire," I concluded. "Anything new about the origin of the text message?"

"Not yet," Theo said. "It was routed through an overseas server, and we're not having much luck getting cooperation on that end."

"What about the Pedway?" Connor asked.

"Elisa nailed it," Petra said. "There's an underground walkway between the Portman Grand and the Brass & Copper. It's sixty years old and needs repairs, so it's not accessible to the general public. Used only for employees, maintenance crews, road crews, that kind of thing. At least officially."

"Officially?" I asked.

"They don't get supernatural guests very often, but they do tend to mention the Pedway to vampires because the coffee shop in the Portman opens earlier than the one in the hotel."

"Allowing vamps to get coffee before dawn in safety," Theo said.

"But wait," Petra said, holding up a finger. "There's more. A concierge named Burt, which is such an old-school, conciergey name, recognized Blake from a picture. Says he mentioned the Pedway when the vampires checked in."

"Mentioned to one of them specifically?" I asked, and she shook her head.

"The group, generally."

"So coffee kills vampires," Connor said.

I knew he was trying for humor, but I wasn't in the place for it. I was glad to be right about the rest—glad to be one step closer to finding the killer—but that didn't lessen my frustration, or my anger.

"I have a feeling I know what you're going to say, but was there video of the tunnel perchance?"

"Neither of the access points nor the corridor itself has a camera, probably since they're supposed to be closed to the general public. But there are sensors on the door that register when it's used." Theo consulted something on his screen. "It was opened ten minutes before and four minutes after Blake's time of death; it hadn't been opened for hours before that. It was opened ten minutes before the human's attack, and not again until the next day."

I sat back, closed my eyes, let what they'd told me percolate a bit. I thought of the stalker, the building, the steps he might have taken to kill his quarry.

"So Blake leaves the Portman Grand sometime before dawn, walks through the Pedway to the Brass & Copper building. He gets coffee. An unknown vampire kills him, and walks back through the Pedway to the Portman. The next night, the killer opens the door, goes through the Pedway into the Brass & Copper building again, drinks from a human, and steals his car. And doesn't go back through the Pedway."

"Because he has a vehicle now," Theo finished. "Good. That's *very* good, Lis."

"And I don't think the killer is local," I said. "Otherwise, if his feelings are so strong, why not try to contact me before now?"

"So a vampire temporarily in Chicago needs a place to stay?" Connor asked.

I nodded.

"Put all that together, and the killer was staying at the Portman Grand," Theo concluded. "Learned about the Pedway, used it to get to and from the Brass & Copper building. Snuck up on Blake?"

"We all saw him fight," I said, thinking of the battle. "He was quick, made smart moves. The killer had to get close to decapitate him. I don't think anyone could have snuck up on him, especially not ten minutes before dawn."

"So he let someone get close," Connor said. "Let his guard down."

"And maybe walks with the killer from the Portman Grand to the Brass & Copper building," I said, and let the implication hang.

"A vampire visiting Chicago and staying at the Portman Grand," Theo said. "A vampire Blake knew and trusted."

"Someone from the AAM killed Blake," Petra said quietly, and silence fell heavy over the room.

"But why?" Theo asked.

Connor looked at me. "You could be reason enough. The imagined slight by Blake showing up at your door, fighting with you at the Grove. We know the killer is disturbed. Maybe those were enough to push him over the edge."

It wouldn't have been to any rational person or vampire, but there was nothing rational about this.

"Then why not also take out Clive, or the rest of the AAM?" I asked. "They all want me in chains or, if not that, dead. Clive is plenty bloodthirsty."

"Aren't all vampires?"

We all looked at Petra, who shrugged. "I don't mean that as an insult; it's literally true. Literally and figuratively in this case."

"You're not wrong." I looked at Theo. "You need to talk to the AAM. Tell them about Blake, about the attempt on Connor. That you think Blake was killed by a vampire he trusted."

"We can talk to them," Theo said, "and will. But while we've made some logical leaps, they're still leaps. There's no physical evidence the killer was an AAM member."

I knew he was right, but that only increased my frustration.

Connor's screen buzzed, and he pulled it out, cursing as he looked at the message.

"What now?" I asked and emotionally braced myself.

"Miranda was attacked by a vampire at NAC headquarters."

I just blinked, trying to make sense of what he'd said. "What? Is she all right?"

"Lacerations, or so the message says. Vampire had a blade."

"If it's Elisa's stalker, he's attacked someone less than a day after his unsuccessful attempt on Connor," Theo said. "He's escalating."

"Maybe the stalker was frustrated he couldn't get to Connor," Petra said. "Tried again."

"Has the AAM left the Portman?" I asked.

"I haven't gotten an alert," Theo said. "It's not impossible the stalker, assuming he's there with them, snuck out again and we missed it. Did you get a message taking responsibility?"

I pulled out my screen, found nothing. "Not yet, but it wasn't immediate last time."

Connor rose. "I have to check it out."

Theo did the same. "I'll go with you, if you're amenable. She's a shifter, and she's accused a vampire of attacking her. That puts her in our jurisdiction."

Connor watched him for a long moment.

"We're on your side," Theo said. "And hers."

"All right," Connor said, resigned to his bureaucratic fate. "Let's move."

Petra took Theo's car back to the OMB office to continue working the case. We drove to NAC headquarters in the SUV Connor had used the night before, Theo in the backseat. There were no shifters outside, no commotion, and no sign of a scuffle. But the magic that bloomed in the air was powerful . . . and angry.

We reached the building at the same time a squad car pulled to the curb. Gwen Robinson climbed out, her uniform nearly the same as last time I'd seen her: Hair pulled back, trim suit, her badge clipped to her waist. And that unmistakable air of competence and authority. Which might come in handy.

"You called the cops," Connor accused when we emerged from the vehicle, that unresolved anger flaring again.

"I asked the CPD to join the investigation," Theo said, "because one of your people was assaulted. If she's telling the truth, it's more ammunition against the stalker or the AAM, or both. But we need it clean and on the record."

Connor just watched him in fulminating silence. But Theo was unbowed.

"I know you care about Elisa," he said. "But I'm not the asshole here. Roger and Gwen aren't the assholes, either. The asshole is the killer who's doing this, who's putting her in the spotlight. The tighter we draw this net, the easier it will be for her."

"And you."

"Side benefit," Theo agreed with a nod. "So check the ego, and let us do our jobs."

"You interrogated her," Connor said, eyes flashing, hot and predatory. "Like a criminal."

"Like a party we needed to clear," Theo said. "You know exactly why we did it, so cut the possessive bullshit. It's insulting to both of you, and it helps the enemy. Whether the stalker is part of the AAM or not, they both win if you're off balance. They want you off your game, because if there's trouble between you, all the easier it is to convince Elisa to fall into line. Or so they think." He gave me a speculative glance. "They obviously have no idea how stubborn either one of you can be."

I just grunted. "Should I go inside to investigate this assault, or do you two want to continue arguing about me in my presence?"

For a hot, piercing minute, Connor just stared at Theo, his eyes brilliantly blue and dark with anger. And then he took a step backward, the wave of magic receding once more.

"Fine," Connor said. "You're right."

Theo's shoulders dropped. "Then I'll say I'm sorry. Not for questioning Elisa, but that it came to this. That you're both in this situation."

They exchanged nods. Not as positive a development as tough handshakes, but I'd take it for now.

"Theo's right." Detective Robinson stepped onto the curb, having waited for the duo to work out their issues. "Dissention helps them—the AAM and stalker. You need to be a team right now. A unified front."

Theo lifted his brows. "And you're, what, the neutral arbiter?"

Her smile was thin. "Always. And whatever this was"—she said, circling a finger between Theo and Connor—"gives me an idea. I understand interviewing the victim may be a challenge, and that she has some animosity toward Elisa. If that's correct, showing a little tension between Elisa and Connor—vampires versus shifters—might encourage her to be more forthright."

Theo nodded at the idea. "Miranda will probably be more comfortable if she thinks the Pack has her back—and that Connor is picking the Pack over vampires."

"Make Miranda the heroine," Gwen said with a nod.

I glanced at Connor, who was already watching me, brow furrowed. It was easy to see he didn't like the idea, but Theo and Gwen were right.

"I don't like it," I said. "But they're right. You'll get more out of her—more information, maybe more details—if she thinks it might hurt me. And it's entirely understandable you'd be frustrated at vampires right now."

"I'll send a message to Dad," Connor said and pulled out his screen. "It will be more convincing if he plays along."

"Agreed," I said. "But if you overplay your hand, you'll pay for it later. And either way, your town house gets a coffeemaker the second we're done here."

He grinned at me, leaned in, kissed me hard. "You're a cheap date, Elisa Sullivan."

Poor boy, I thought. He'd obviously never priced Italian espresso machines.

SEVENTEEN

Connor led us inside, through the NAC building to the lounge where we'd talked to Gabriel. Miranda sat in a recliner in a tank top and fitted jeans, dark boots. A shifter I didn't recognize applied cream to a nasty slice on her arm. She'd definitely been injured. Add to that the half a dozen more shifters in the room, including Gabriel, who watched suspiciously as I moved in behind Connor, and I was beginning to feel uncomfortable.

"Keep that bitch away from me," Miranda said, teeth gritted against the pain of her treatment.

"She'll keep her distance," Connor threw out, sending me a glare. "We don't need any more vampire theatrics today."

Theo moved a little closer, as if protecting me from Connor and the rest of them.

I made a show of looking embarrassed, but couldn't quite manage a flush.

Miranda smiled, but it dropped away when she realized Gwen had followed them inside. "What the fuck?"

"Miranda, this is Detective Gwen Robinson," Connor said. "None of us want the CPD in here, but we do want your story, your injuries, documented. And I want it official, so we can bury them with it."

Miranda looked warily between him, me, Gwen, then managed a nodding scowl. "Fine."

"Ms. Mitchell," Gwen said, sitting down on the coffee table across from Miranda, gaze slipping to her laceration. Just the right amount of sympathy clouded her eyes. "I'm sorry you were attacked." She pulled a small silver disc from her pocket, showed it. "I'm going to record this conversation, okay? That way I don't have to take notes or ask you to repeat things I'm too slow to write down."

"Okay," Miranda said warily.

Gwen nodded, pressed the disc until it glowed green, placed it on the coffee table beside her. "Tell me what happened tonight."

"Asshole vamp with a silver blade," Miranda said, teeth gritted as more cream was applied to her arm. "I'd just come back from a delivery. Got off the bike, and he just came at me. Had a blade. I blocked, but he got through my jacket, got my arm. Nearly put me on the ground. I got in a shot, and when I pulled my own blade, he took off." She looked past the other shifters, aimed her eyes at me. "He was a coward."

"And where did this happen?" Gwen asked.

"Why? You don't believe me?"

Gwen looked taken aback. "Of course I believe you. You said you got off a shot—perhaps the attacker left blood, DNA, that we can trace."

"Outside the bar. Near the corner."

"Great," Gwen said, nodding. "That's helpful."

"What did he look like?" Connor asked.

"Mr. Keene," Gwen said sharply. "I'll handle the questions."

He nodded stiffly.

"He was pale as a ghost," Miranda said. "But I didn't see his face. He was wearing black. They always do," she said, gesturing in my direction.

Gwen cocked her head. "How did you know he was pale if you didn't see his face?"

"He didn't wear gloves. Had on a jacket with a hood, long sleeves. But no gloves," she said again.

So it was light enough that she could tell the color of his hands, but not catch a glimpse of any part of his face?

"Got it," Gwen said. If she found anything weird about Miranda's answer, she didn't dwell on it. "What happened after he hurt you?"

"Like I said, he ran off."

"Which direction?"

She lifted a careless shoulder. "Away from the bar. South, I think. I was bleeding, and wasn't really paying attention."

"You haven't shifted yet," Gwen said. "I understand that would resolve the injury."

"It will. I wanted to, you know, preserve the evidence."

Gwen nodded with approval, crossed one leg over the other. Just two women having a chat. "That was smart. Very smart. Now, did you recognize anything about the attacker?"

"Other than the fact that he was a vampire?" Her tone was dry, and had several of her allies chortling.

"How do you know that?" I asked, and all eyes in the room turned to me.

"Remember where you are," Gabriel said, voice low and threatening. If I didn't know Connor had clued him in, I'd have slunk right out of the room.

"Hey, watch the tone," Theo said, moving a little closer to me. "It's a reasonable question."

"Can we please focus on Ms. Mitchell?" Gwen asked. "This isn't helpful."

Miranda's eyes gleamed with satisfaction. "I can tell when some asshole's a vampire. I can feel the magic."

"Did you see his fangs?" I asked.

"I said he had his hood up. Did you not hear me?"

"Elisa," Connor said, sharply, and I closed my mouth, made a point of glaring at his back.

"Did the vampire look familiar to you?" Gwen asked, drawing Miranda's attention back to her.

"I don't know. Maybe?" She looked at me speculatively. "Maybe there was something familiar about him."

"What something?" Gwen asked.

"I don't know. I said 'maybe.'" The words were quick, impatient. And didn't sound very convincing. What would have been familiar about a vampire whose face she couldn't see?

Gwen sat up straight, brows lifted. "So, do you think he was a local vampire? Not one of the vamps from the AAM?"

"I don't know. Could have been either." A shoulder rose, fell. "I don't pay attention to that political shit."

Another lie, and I could see it in the shift of her eyes.

"Believe me, I get it. It's always something with them." Gwen's eyes narrowed, then she slid her gaze to Connor. "Weren't you attacked by a vampire yesterday right outside the building?"

"We don't know it was a vampire," Connor gritted out. "Not for sure."

"He was nearly run over," Miranda couldn't wait to say. "They damaged his bike, too."

Gwen turned off the recorder, slipped it into her pocket. Then rose, straightened her jacket. "Thank you, Ms. Mitchell, for your time. Rest assured, we take these allegations very seriously."

"Will you tell me when you catch him?"

"We'll absolutely advise you of the results of our investigation. I know you'll feel better when it's complete." She turned, looked at me, gaze narrowed. "Ms. Sullivan, let's step outside."

Her tone was harsh, the words an obvious order—and a threat. Behind her, Miranda's smile was deep, victory in her eyes.

"Why?" I asked, feigning suspicion.

"Because your . . . colleagues . . . have been implicated in the attack on Ms. Mitchell. We'll need to discuss that." She stared at me until I relented, cast Connor a look of betrayal, and stalked to the door, magic in my wake.

I took a moment to shake off the heavy shifter magic, and when I emerged into fresh air, found Gwen standing beside her vehicle. She gave instructions to uniformed officers and a crime scene technician, who began the process of inspecting the crime scene.

Then she turned to me.

"I'm going to do a lot of pointing and accusing," she said mildly. "And you're going to look sheepish."

I looked at the ground, as if chagrined. "Why am I doing this?"

"We're keeping up appearances while we're still in their view, because she definitely doesn't like you." Gwen pointed at the car, as if demanding I get in it.

I shook my head, glared at her. "You're pretty smart for a cop."

"I guess you owed me that."

"I guess I did. Why does how she feels about me matter to you?"

"Because it provides her a motive to lie."

I *knew* it. "You didn't buy it?"

"Not even with a coupon. Now I'm going to chastise you. Do that sheepish thing again."

"You're enjoying this, aren't you?"

"It's made those two years of community theater worthwhile," she said, and pinned me with a glance.

I waited for a moment, then took a step back, lifted my hands as if in peace. My face was a model of contrition.

"You aren't bad yourself," she said. "Vampire thing?"

"Constantly playing a role," I agreed. "Why don't you buy it?"

Gwen looked back at the door. "Because I'm a skilled and experienced investigator. She shows none of the typical characteristics of a person who's been assaulted—no fear, no concern. She seemed very eager to put the blame on vampires without any hard evidence a vampire was involved. The attacker might have been familiar, except she couldn't actually see his face. And there's nothing near the corner of the bar that indicates a fight took place. None of her blood, none of his. Given the size of her cut, she should have left something behind."

"So what will you do now?"

"I took her statement, and I'll file a report, and I'll continue to investigate. Because my suspicions are just suspicions until I have more evidence."

I nodded. "Thanks for handling this carefully."

She moved to the door of her vehicle, opened it. "You don't know me, so I'll excuse that. But I handle everything carefully. It's kind of my thing."

Gwen left, and I waited outside for Connor and Theo to emerge, but ten minutes passed in relative silence, but for the thump of raucous music from the bar.

It took long enough that I was a little afraid Miranda had started some new nonsense that had embroiled my friends, so I walked inside again, found Connor and Theo with Gabriel in the lobby. His expression was fierce. And when I walked in, he aimed it at me.

"I'm not sure I should let you in here."

But when I reached Connor, I felt his fingertips brush against mine. Confirmation we were still playing the game, and it was the Pack's turn to take a little of theirs. At least, I presumed that was why the air roiled with magic.

Since I was potentially the root cause, I couldn't really blame them—and had my own part to play. I wouldn't take calling out without a fight, even from Connor's dad. So I tipped up my chin. "Since I'm not the one who hurt Miranda, there's no reason not to let me in here. You've got no evidence a vampire did this to her. And even if you did, I'm not that vampire."

Gabriel's lip curled. "They're in Chicago because of you."

"Wrong. If it's the AAM, they're in Chicago because of your Pack," I countered. "But for their bad acts in Minnesota, I wouldn't have needed to save Carlie's life."

I saw the truth in his eyes and almost regretted my words. But their truth insulated me from that guilt.

Something crashed nearby, and all eyes turned to the bar, where the sounds of a scuffle erupted. Then crashing, and the quick pop of magic. Fights were pretty run of the mill, but this must have been different, as Gabriel's eyes narrowed, and then he turned to me.

"You want to help?" Gabe asked, throwing back the promise I'd made after Connor had been hurt. "Go deal with that."

He stalked away; after a last look, Connor followed him.

There was another crash from the bar, a cloud of acrid magic.

"This is punishment, right?" Theo asked.

"Yes," I said and headed for the door. "Yes, it is." I glanced back at him. "You ever been in a shifter bar before?"

"No." He lifted his brows. "Should I be concerned?"

"Yes. And avoid the claws."

The bar lined the far wall, a stage at one end. Tables and chairs usually filled the space in the middle, squeezed together over hard concrete floors. It smelled like alcohol, cigars, and shifter. And right now, blood and magic.

Two of the tables had been upended, and Daniel Liu stood in the clearing with a shifter I didn't recognize. About the same age, with ruddy skin, shorn auburn hair, and blue eyes that gleamed at Dan with considerable hatred. A bruise was already blooming across his jaw, and blood from a cut above Dan's eye had streamed a line of crimson down his face.

Shifter blood, potent with magic and power, was more than a little tempting. But I pushed the desire back, lifted my chin, and surveyed the two men—and the twenty who'd gathered around them.

"Problem, gentlemen?"

Dan shifted his gaze to look at me, eyes widening. The stranger didn't bother. Just sniffed the air.

"No one asked a vampire to come in here," he said.

"Your Apex did," I said, and all eyes turned to me. "He heard the scuffle, felt the magic, and wondered why two grown-ass adults were fighting in his place."

Daniel looked thoughtful at the announcement. The stranger looked defiant.

"This asshole touched my girlfriend."

"Your name?"

"Castle. John Castle."

I looked at Dan, felt the shifters at my back move closer. Some because they were curious. Others because they still weren't sure if I was a threat.

"Mr. Liu?"

"She's his ex-girlfriend. And we spent a very pleasant evening together."

"You son of a—" was all John managed before he lunged forward.

He was bigger than Dan, broader in the shoulders, but Dan was faster. John tried to grab his waist, send him to the floor, but Dan sidestepped, stuck out a foot. John tripped over it, hit the concrete hard on his hands, but came up swinging.

There was fury in his eyes. But something else. Grief, it looked like.

"Enough," I said and whipped my sword out between them before they could go in for another round. And heard clicks around the room from blades being drawn, weapons being unholstered. Probably wasn't often that a vampire pulled a katana in this room.

John looked back at me, teeth bared. "Did you just draw a blade on me?"

"I did," I said pleasantly. "And I'll use it if you two don't stop being morons. How long ago did you break up?"

His jaw worked, hand reaching toward the holster at his waist, but I shook my head.

"Don't make me call the Apex. That would just embarrass both of us. How long?"

"A month." But from the sadness in his eyes, only just masked, I bet it felt much shorter.

"And what would be appropriate compensation?" I asked John.

They all looked at me.

"What?"

"Compensation," I said again. "For your . . . injuries."

The man's eyes narrowed. "His head on a pike."

"A very poor starting bid," I said. "Try again. You want booze? Usually helps to nurse a breakup."

"No, I don't want fucking booze. I can buy booze for myself." He ran a hand over his short hair, looked away. And I watched the fight die in his eyes.

The light in the bar wasn't great, but when he moved his hand, I could see his nails, while neatly clipped and trimmed, were dark around the edges, bore scrapes along the knuckles. That might have been from fighting, but it also had another possible source.

"You a bike mechanic?"

His gaze snapped back, narrowed suspiciously. "I know my way around. Do mostly bodywork. Why?"

"Because Connor's bike took a hit yesterday. It's going to need repair. You up for helping the prince with that?"

It was a gamble. I had no idea if Connor would want someone else touching his bike, much less if John would be interested in working on it. Maybe he'd see that as an insult, not an offer. But the Keenes were royalty, and I bet the opportunity for one-on-one interaction with the prince didn't come often. And work—especially hard, knuckle-scraping physical work—helped keep painful emotions at bay.

The bar had gone quiet now, probably with shifters wondering if I had the authority to make something like that happen, and whether John would accept, or if they'd get to enjoy a little more combat with their beers.

"I guess I wouldn't turn down a chance to work on Thelma," John said.

Disappointment spread behind me, but I had no doubt the Pack would get its chance again.

"Done," I said. "I'll make it happen." I looked at Dan, whose smile was considering, then the rest of the bar.

"I'm sure one of you is going to piss off someone else soon enough, and you can get back to beating the shit out of each other." I figured the company necessitated a little more salt in the language.

That got a few chuckles. "In the meantime, maybe don't screw around with each other's exes."

Connor was waiting in the foyer when Dan and I came out of the bar. Connor took in Dan's eye, and if he was surprised by the injury, didn't show it.

"Jealous ex-boyfriend," I said, glancing at Dan. "Dan is going to stay away from ex-girlfriends for a while, and John Castle, a mechanic, is going to be helping you repair Thelma."

Connor's brows lifted. "Is he?"

"It was the only reparation I could think to offer."

"There's an entire bar of booze."

"Offered, declined."

"Well, damn," Connor said. "That usually works in a bar fight." He considered, nodded. "All right. I'll talk to him. And nicely done."

"Thanks," I said and meant it. It had been fun to play the bad-ass Pack problem solver.

Connor looked at Dan. "You okay?"

"He dumped her," Dan said. "Said he was moving on. She was devastated, and I gave her what comfort I could."

There was sadness in his voice, and a kind of resignation that said this wasn't the first time Dan had played this particular role. And interesting that he hadn't mentioned that in the bar. Maybe it wasn't the kind of vulnerability that crowd would appreciate.

"Take it from one who knows," Theo said. "It's her responsibility to move on."

Dan nodded. "I know. But I enjoy myself, and so do they. And for a little while, we're both at peace."

Theo called an Auto, headed back to the OMB office.

"I get the sense you weren't the only reason Dan left Memphis," I said, when Connor and I were alone again.

"He's . . . working through some things," Connor agreed. He put an arm around my waist, pulled me toward him. "It's been a night."

"It has," I said. And as if to prove the point, my screen buzzed. I pulled it out, found a message from Petra.

TAKE A LOOK AT THIS, the message read. NO BUILDING-OWNED SURVEILLANCE, BUT POSTAGE STORE ACROSS THE HALL HAD A CAMERA. ONLY TAKES A PIC EVERY TEN MINUTES, BUT GOT THIS ONE.

I opened the image she'd sent, found a grainy color shot. Two men, both with lightish skin, talking near what I presumed was the coffee shop. I couldn't identify either from the wide shot, so I enlarged, focused on the man on the right.

It was Blake, coffee cup in hand, and still wearing the pendant. Based on the time stamp, this was minutes before he was killed.

So who was he talking to? Had he talked to the killer in those last moments?

I scrolled over, focused on the other man. And stared. There, talking with Blake in front of the coffee shop where he'd been killed, stood Jonathan Black.

"Holy shit," I murmured, and zoomed in on the time stamp again, the faces again, to confirm I hadn't misunderstood, hadn't imagined a coincidence. But I'd seen the truth. And the other pieces fell into alignment.

He'd said he wanted to meet me.

He had blond hair and a white sedan, just like the man who'd struck Connor.

And now, proof he'd been with Blake a few minutes before Blake's death.

Jonathan Black wasn't a vampire, but he was connected to this somehow. It was time to have a discussion.

"Elisa."

I blinked, looked up at Connor, whose head was tilted as he stared at me. "What did she send you?"

I showed him, but his expression was blank. "Who's the man talking to Blake?"

"Jonathan Black."

No sign of recognition, and I realized I hadn't told him about my meeting. I gave him the update, and he nodded.

"He's not a vampire, and the OMB trusts him. But he was the only person we know of who was with Blake before he was killed. Someone needs to talk to him."

"It doesn't have to be you," he said, "especially if he's the one who's stalking you, or he's involved in it." His voice was testier now. "Surely they can handle one interview with an elf."

"Black said his people owe me a favor," I reminded him. "He may be more likely to talk to me."

Connor stepped forward. "And if he's involved, more likely to hurt you."

"Then it's even more imperative that I find him and correct his misperception."

"What misperception is that?"

"That anyone gets to lay hands on you other than me."

Connor stared at me, nostrils flaring as he exhaled his frustration. "I'm going with you."

"No," I said, put a hand on his chest. "I don't think he'll be frank with you there. Or if you're flurrying magic into the air."

"Because he knows I could tear him apart with my own hands."

"That does tend to discourage conversation. I need to talk to him alone. But I'll be armed." I thought through my options, had a twinge of anger that I'd been dumped by the OMB. Theo would have been the natural choice to accompany me. But that wasn't one of my choices at present.

"What if Dan drove me? He's security, right? But he won't be as magically hyper. That way you can stay here and deal with"—I waved a hand at the building—"all of this."

He stared at me for a moment, hands on his hips and every muscle tense. "It would make me feel better if you were locked in the town house for the duration of the epoch."

We both knew that wasn't going to happen.

"I'm telling you about this ahead of time," I reminded him. "Involving you in the decision-making. We're running out of time; we're going to have to do some uncomfortable things."

"Such as it is," he said, but sighed. "Fine. Dan, if he's free and emotionally recuperated, will be armed. He's a very good shot. He'll keep me on the line, and you'll contact me when you arrive, and when you're back in the vehicle."

He tipped up my chin, looked into my eyes. "But if Jonathan Black lays a finger on you, he answers to me."

EIGHTEEN

Petra was able to give me Jonathan's address—he worked out of his home—and Dan drove me to his house on Prairie Avenue, one in a line of historic mansions built by Chicago's richest denizens during the Gilded Age. The house was pale stone with a green mansard roof, the lines ornate, and stood at the edge of a large lot big enough to be a park of its own.

I climbed out, belted on my sword. No point in being unprepared, especially if Black had powerful and magical friends.

"Any trouble," Dan said, "and send me a message. Via screen, rapid flip of the lights, his bloody corpse thrown through the front door."

"That would definitely send a message," I agreed. "But I'll probably go for something a little more subtle."

"Must be that Midwestern nice I hear so much about."

I snorted, closed the door.

The house was dark when I climbed the front steps, although thick curtains made it difficult to tell if the lights were on or off. I didn't know if he worked for humans and Sups, or if he kept human or Sup hours.

I knocked. Waited and listened. And knocked again.

Five more minutes, and the door opened. Jonathan Black stood in the doorway, naked but for the towel slung around his hips, blond hair damp, and a very sultry smile on his face.

"Elisa Sullivan. What are you doing here?"

"I had a question," I said, and I forced up a little blush.

"I was in the shower," he said and opened the door. "Come in and make yourself at home. I'll just go . . ." He looked down at himself. "Grab a robe, would be a good start. Five minutes," he said and trotted to the stairs.

It was possible he was going to try to sneak out the back, but he didn't seem concerned I was there. Or he was a very good actor. Vampires weren't the only ones who could use glamour.

I glanced around the house, found the front room mostly empty. Large and beautifully maintained for a house as old as this one, but empty. The space was at least thirty feet long. There was a sofa beside a gleaming malachite fireplace. An old-fashioned secretary, the top closed and locked. Boxes marked with room names, still taped. A lamp, its cord wrapped around the base. The few items were dwarfed by the remaining emptiness.

Two minutes later, there were footsteps on the stairs, the house creaking as if each step was a note, and then behind me.

I glanced back. Jonathan wore trousers and a V-neck sweater in a thin, dark fabric that looked very expensive. His feet were bare. A vulnerability. One he offered on purpose to show me he was relaxed?

"You just moved in?" I asked casually.

"Three weeks ago, actually." He walked in, ran a hand down the fluted molding that framed the door. "This house had been on the market for an hour when I learned it was available. I'd planned to rent until I was settled, but couldn't pass it up."

"It's not hard to see why. It's a beautiful space."

"It is. Extravagant for one person, but beautiful all the same." He walked toward me, and I made a show of finishing my circle of the room, gaze on the ceiling. I didn't trust him, and certainly not enough to put myself in a corner without an exit.

In fairness, the ceiling was gorgeous—large tiles of pressed silver metal that reflected the light of a delicate raindrop chandelier.

I made it to the room's threshold, leaned against it, and looked back at him. He stood in front of the fireplace, hands in his pockets, his expression a mask of cool reserve.

Time to make a play. "Can we skip the chitchat and posturing and get to the point? I'm sure you know why I'm here."

For an instant, his eyes widened in surprise, before settling back into reserved lines, but his smile was wide, sly. He tilted his head and let the veil of magic slip away.

The man who stood before me now looked the same, but the power he'd hidden had become very clear. It roared around him like an angry sea, waves crashing against hard and ancient stone.

I swallowed back a bolt of lust. Not for the man, but for a drink. I knew in that moment, certain as I was of my own heart, that his blood would be . . . intoxicating. Potent, imbued with power. The monster agreed, and shifted inside in a way that made me not entirely comfortable.

None of it was comfortable. And watching him, seeing that minute shift as the wave settled, I realized the bloodlust had been a trick of magic, too.

"A neat little trick," I said, when I was certain my voice wouldn't shake.

He gestured toward his ear. "It's the elvish."

"The hiding, or the unveiling?"

He smiled. "Both. Many find the magic distracting or the power . . . discomforting."

"Because it's greater than theirs?"

He nodded. "And revealing it can be a powerful tool. A seductive one."

Maybe there was a little incubus along with the elvish, I thought, but wasn't going to flatter him by asking.

"Now that we've skipped the posturing," Jonathan said, stepping forward. "What can I do for you?"

"Blake."

His expression didn't change, but for the slight flattening of his mouth. "The vampire who was killed?"

"We've skipped the posturing," I reminded him.

Silence. "What do you want to know?"

"You met with him in the Brass & Copper building shortly before his death."

Much to my surprise, he smiled. "Very astute. Security cameras, I presume?"

"There's an image," was all I'd agree to.

He walked to the couch, sitting fluidly with his legs crossed and his arms stretched across the back.

"What are you thinking right now?" he asked, gaze narrowed with interest. "And no posturing."

"That you move like a vampire."

His grin was wide, disarming. "I'm not entirely sure, Elisa, but I don't think you consider that a compliment."

"It wasn't intended to be one. What did you talk to him about?"

He frowned, smoothed a minute wrinkle in the knee of his dark trousers. "Business," he said, without looking up. "And before you ask, no. It had nothing to do with the AAM or their shortsighted persecution of you."

"Shortsighted?"

Jonathan raised his gaze, looked me over. Not in the way one lover gazed at another, but as a general might gaze upon a weapon. "You are unique among vampires. If they were smart, they'd make you an ally—bring you into the fold. They haven't, so they aren't." He cocked his head. "What's your interest in Blake's death? You're no longer working for the Ombuds' office, yes?"

I ignored the last bit. "The vampire who killed him says he did it for me, because Blake insulted me. He also tried to kill Connor."

He was up in an instant, the motion fluid again. "For you?"

"He believes we have a relationship, or should. Did you arrange to meet Blake at the coffee shop?"

"No. That was a coincidence. Or so I thought. Now I'm beginning to wonder." He shook his head, slipped the frown away. "I had business in the building with a client. I'd finished that, was leaving, found Blake in the lobby."

"You knew him already."

"Actually, I didn't." He cleared his throat, as if nervous, which I seriously doubted. Probably another tic to help him assimilate, hide whatever it was that roamed beneath his skin.

I understood the feeling.

"I became curious about the AAM's grievance. I did a bit of research regarding the Compliance Bureau, its members. It was a coincidence that I met him there—if a big one—so I asked him about the charges against you."

"And what did he say?"

"He said they were justified, regardless of what Chicago's vampires or the media said about it. He didn't seem interested in having a good-faith discussion, so I left him."

I wasn't sure how much of what he'd told me was true, but this, I believed. If he'd had more information, he'd have dangled it in front of me, a mouse to his cat. But I much preferred the company of wolves.

"How did you leave the building?"

He blinked. "How did I leave? I called an Auto, which brought me back here. Why?"

"Just curious," I said and pushed off the doorjamb. "Thanks for the information. I'll leave you to your"—I shifted my gaze to the boxes—"unpacking."

"You haven't asked me the most important question."

I went still in the doorway, glanced back at him. "Which is?"

"Who was with Blake when he was buying coffee."

I stared at him. "He wasn't alone?" The surveillance shot showed Blake by himself.

His smile was sly. "He was with a vampire."

"Who?" I asked, my voice low and heavy. My blood was running now, wanting the name. Wanting the chase. Wanting to throw this man bodily to Clive and let them destroy their own.

But Jonathan Black knew when he held the power. He lifted a shoulder, a movement that was both elegant and careless.

I turned around. "This isn't the time to play games. Lives are at stake."

"Life is a game."

"You said your clients owe me a debt."

"Ah, but this information didn't come from a client. It comes from me." He was smiling now, joy dancing in his eyes. I'd heard elves, not unlike their fairy cousins, were tricksy. Where fairies were the royalty, the soldiers, the purveyors of thick and green magic, elves were the jesters, the tricksters.

But I didn't have time for games, I thought, frustration growing. "What do you want?"

"Friendship."

Never take a supernatural deal at face value. "Meaning what?"

"Like I said, I haven't been in Chicago long. It's interesting to watch you fight back against entrenched power. If I provide information that helps you, perhaps that makes us allies."

I stared at him, trying to see through the words to the emotion beneath. To the intentions beneath. But he might as well have been a vampire, they were hidden so well.

"Is it so unusual, Elisa, that someone offers you a little help in exchange for so little?"

"It's unusual for strangers, yes."

He watched me for a minute, then turned away, walked back to the fireplace, propped an arm on the mantel. "An unfortunate outlook."

"A realistic outlook," I said. "We are not friends. We are not allied. But we are not enemies. That's the best I'll do."

Whatever he saw in my eyes seemed to satisfy him. "Your terms are accepted. He was with Greg Voss."

I stared at him. "Who the hell is Greg Voss?"

"Ah," he said with a smile. "That's for you to figure out."

I cursed under my breath. Nothing was easy with old magic. "Thank you again," I said through gritted teeth.

"Even if my motivations are suspect?"

"All Sup motivations are suspect. Magic is the best disguise."

I left him alone with those words, a mourning dove calling in the darkness as I walked back to the SUV. Dan stood outside, arms crossed and watching.

"There was a lot of power in there."

"Yeah, there was." I smiled at him. "Were you going to come to my rescue?"

"If necessary." But when he stood again, there was nothing pleasant in the dark gaze he aimed at the house. "Is he an enemy or ally?"

"Don't ask," I said. "Let's get out of here."

He glanced back at me, expression pained. "You smell of his magic."

I sighed. Of course I did. A parting gift from a new friend.

I texted Theo and Petra the second the vehicle was moving again, the inquiry simple: J. BLACK SAYS BLAKE WAS WITH 'GREG VOSS' AT B&C COFFEE SHOP. WHO IS HE?

They hadn't responded by the time we made it back to the NAC building, thankfully without incident. I thanked Dan and found Connor in the otherwise empty lobby reviewing his screen.

"No bar?" I asked, striding toward him. "No beer and lounge?"

"Too much noise, too much magic." He rose and put the screen away, crossed to me, and then sniffed. "There's magic all over you." And he looked, as predicted, displeased.

"Can you throw a supernatural breeze in my direction? Make it go away?"

He just blinked.

"That's what I thought. So if you're going to say something like, 'no foreign magic in my territory,' let's just skip it." I patted him on the chest. "I'll take a shower as soon as I can. Who is Greg Voss?"

His brows lifted. "Who?"

I cursed. "I had a feeling you'd say that," I told him, and relayed my byplay with Jonathan Black.

"Old magic," he cursed.

"That's exactly what I said." My screen buzzed, and I pulled it out, found an incoming call from Theo and Petra.

"We okay to talk here?" I asked Connor.

"Sure. But give them a heads-up."

"We're in the NAC building," I said, answering the call. "So guide yourselves accordingly." I narrowed my gaze at Petra. "Why do you have glitter stars around your eyes?"

"I had a date," she said with a smile. "And I'm pulling them off."

"You totally are. Good date?"

That smile went wide. "Her name is Jules and she is *exceedingly* into me. I'm bi," she added. "In case you didn't know."

"I didn't," I said, wishing I could give her a hug. "Thanks for telling me. And I'm going to need all the date details later. But for now, back to killer vampires." I looked at Theo. "And you?"

"No glitter stars. No date. But Greg Voss was a human who was turned fifty years ago. It doesn't appear he goes by that name any longer. But I think you'll recognize his face."

He and Glitter Stars disappeared, their images replaced by a white guy with blond hair. Average features, good smile, square jaw.

And I'd seen all those features before.

"Son of a bitch," I muttered, staring down at the man who—

according to Jonathan Black—had stalked me, killed Blake, and tried to kill Connor.

Greg Voss was Clive's goddamned brother—Levi, one of the vampires who'd come to my door that first night.

It took me a full beat to understand that, to grapple with it. I'd spoken to him for, what, seconds in the doorway? That I knew so little about him, had seen so little of him, and yet had become an object of his obsession, seemed . . . worse . . . somehow.

What scenes had played out between us in this man's mind? Didn't matter, I told myself. I had to deal with my immediate circumstances.

"Levi," I said finally.

"Yep."

"Pick him up," Connor demanded. "Now."

"We told Gwen before we called you, and she's on it. Cops stationed at the Portman Grand say he's not at the hotel."

"Is he at the NAC building?" I asked.

"I'll handle that," Connor said and pulled out his screen.

"Clive will know where he is," I told Theo. "Sequester the vamps at the Portman Grand and find out."

"Did Jonathan Black say Levi killed Blake?"

"No," I said, irritation rising, because I knew what was coming.

"So you've got a person who saw Blake with another vampire. Possibly the killer, but that's supposition. We have no hard physical evidence Levi was with Blake, or that Levi killed Blake. We don't have a basis to hold Levi, much less anyone else. But we're looking for him," Theo said again, "and we'll find him. In the meantime, don't do anything rash."

I ended the call before I started screaming, then stuffed my screen into my pocket and paced down the hall, considered seriously punching a fist into drywall.

Seriously considered but didn't actually. I was sick to death of vampires. But I'd made enough problems for Connor with the Pack, and exacerbating it wasn't going to do anything.

Connor moved in front of me when I paced his way again, put his hands on my shoulders. "Let's go back to my place," he said, voice soothing. "We'll take a break and process this, decide what we want to do next."

"I don't want to process. I want to end this. I want justice for Blake, for you."

"In that order?" he asked, lips curving.

"Most justice for you, slight justice for him. And I want Clive to piss off." I leaned my forehead against his chest. "Fucking vampires."

"Fucking vampires," Connor said and drew me into his arms. "Thank god you aren't dating one."

"Can you imagine?" But the sentiment made me smile. "You're right. We should let the CPD do this part of the job. Clive knows about Levi now, and that might be enough to send him running." I shook my head. "He won't leave. Not until this is done. So we have to figure out a way to end it. To wrap this up, close this circle, et cetera." I sighed haggardly. "But first, we have to feed the cat."

Lulu and I had agreed to take turns checking on Eleanor of Aquitaine, and my turn had come, so we drove back to the loft.

We circled the block once, then twice, looking for prying eyes, waiting vehicles, found none. We climbed out of the SUV, looked around.

The loft was dark, as it should have been. The street was quiet of magic; only humans stirred here, some preparing for work at this dark hour, some returning home from work or entertainment. But most lights were off, the steady drum of traffic from the streets on the edge of the neighborhood the only real noise.

"Anything?" Connor asked, voice a whisper in the night.

"No. You?"

He shook his head.

We went inside, glancing right and left, then cautiously took the stairs to the loft. The building was quiet, probably much to the delight of Mrs. Prohaska. And since it smelled like cabbage again, I could guess how she was spending her time.

We reached the door, and I put a hand on it, felt for any magic inside. Found nothing but the belligerent whine of a cat who was angry either that we'd left her behind or that we were trespassing in her fortress of feline solitude.

I unlocked the door, let it swing open. The loft was dark and the hallway was empty but for the pile of mail on the floor and the angry goblin-cat. Eleanor sat in front of the threshold as she so often did, tail swishing furiously.

"I'm here to feed you," I said. "Do you prefer we leave again?"

She flicked that tail in the air and disappeared into shadows.

"She's probably a fairly good guard," Connor whispered. "But let's go check."

I nodded and we slipped inside, closed the door as quietly as possible. I picked up the mail, and we crept through the hallway, looked right and left. He motioned me toward the bedrooms, gestured toward the kitchen area.

We split, searched our areas, found nothing and no one out of place. And she hadn't peed in my shoes, which was its own miracle.

Mood lifted, I made my way back to the kitchen. "Clear," I said aloud, when I found him standing in the loft, hands on his hips, looking around.

"Same."

Still. There was something mildly creepy about being in here; like the loft had been abandoned and left for dead. Something dystopian. "Let me feed her and check her water, and we can leave."

"No argument," Connor said and rubbed his belly. "I could eat."

"Pizza and coffee."

"No. And you have a problem." He nodded toward the pile in my hand. "Any more notes?"

I flipped through it, found the usual advertisements and garbage. "Nothing," I said, but that didn't make me feel better. The stalker might not have found Connor's town house, but he knew we weren't staying here. He'd been watching.

Goose bumps lifted on my arms, and I shook the fear away, put down the mail. Fear was what he wanted, and I wasn't going to give him that victory.

"Good girl," Connor said, trailing his fingers over my hair, as if he'd understood my silent battle and the result of it.

His screen buzzed, and he pulled it out. "Damn it. Fight broke out in the bar."

"As they do," I said.

"Yeah, but this time two humans were hurt, and they're threatening to sue the shifters they fought with. I need to make a call, and it's likely to get loud and magicky. I better step outside." He glanced at me, frowning. "Will you be okay in here by yourself?"

I dumped old water in the sink, turned on the tap. "Alone in my empty apartment? Yes. I'm pretty sure I can handle that difficult assignment."

"I'll just be outside." He came toward me, covered my mouth with his, left me little doubt of the extent of his affection, his concern. "Be careful. Or I'll mete out the punishment."

I heard the door close, replaced the water dish, filled the cat food.

And wondered that Eleanor of Aquitaine didn't come running. Fresh food, even if not the delicately sautéed line-caught Atlantic salmon she preferred, was a beckoning she rarely ignored. Probably still pissed.

Still. It was weird. I walked back into the loft, looked around. The cat had disappeared. "Eleanor of Aquitaine?"

I didn't know there'd been magic until it was gone; I didn't know I hadn't been alone until I heard the voice at my ear.

"I'm very disappointed in you, Elisa."

And then the world went dark.

NINETEEN

I felt pain before I could hear, before I could see. Then tried to move, to shift against new pains, and realized I couldn't.

I blinked my eyes open, vision blurry from the strike, and knew from the ringing pain that radiated down my back, my arm, that he'd struck my neck. Hit the vagus nerve, probably, and I'd gone down. I was still in the loft, sitting in a chair, shoulders pulled back, hands bound behind me with what felt like fabric. The room spun, and I shook my head to clear it, used the fingers of one hand to pinch the other. The bright pain helped clear the fuzziness away.

"You're awake."

I looked up at the man who stood in front of me, stared at his face until it resolved from blurs to features. Pale skin, blond hair, black fatigues, and a hunting knife gleaming in the glow of street-lights through the windows.

Levi.

I was tied to a chair in the loft with my stalker.

My shoulder ached anew from being dragged behind me, and I clung to it, used it as fuel. I had to focus, because I had only a moment to decide what to do, how to play this. I opted for sympathy, hoping he was just crazed enough to buy it.

"Levi?" I asked and blinked my eyes a few times. "I'm sorry, I'm dizzy. I didn't know you were here."

Brown eyes smiled beneath blond hair that was shaggier than he'd worn it before. "It's my particular version of glamour. I'm rather good at it."

So he'd been hiding in plain sight. Connor and I had expected the loft to be empty, so a little glamour just made us think we were right. Pushed us just enough. He'd watched me talk to Connor, watched me feed the cat, until it was time to reveal himself.

"Connor will be back . . . in a minute," I said slowly, as if still unable to focus.

"The dog will have his own problems," Levi said. And the fear that slid through me was a cold and silver thread. "And you really, really need to stop thinking about him, Elisa." The words were tight, pinched off, angry.

He started pacing, and I glanced down, around, looking for something to use. The weapon I needed—that gleaming knife—was in his hand. But that wasn't going to happen, so I rubbed my wrists together, trying to scrunch up the fabric enough to get a hand free. Keep him talking, I thought, and figure out a way to get free.

"I'm sorry," I said. "I didn't mean I wanted him here. I just wanted you to know that he'd be back. He'll come looking. So you have to be careful."

I kept my lids lowered, playacting drowsiness, and tried to listen to the world outside, to any scuffle below. But there was only silence, at least for now. Behind my eyes, the monster watched, waited. It wasn't foggy. And it was *pissed*.

Soon, I told it. A promise.

Levi moved across the loft, hunting knife in hand. "I'm supposed to be your partner. Your friend." He stopped, looked back at me. "You're friendly with shifters—with dogs. I'm disappointed in you. So angry that I gave you my trust."

I stared at him, trying to pick my way through his rambling

words, the sentiment behind them. He was past logic and rationality.

"I'm sorry," I said. "I'm very sorry that I hurt you." I softened the words with glamour, just enough to make him believe. "It's just, I only got your note a few days ago. So this is a bit of a surprise."

"I suppose I did take my time. But I had to wait until everything was in place." He stopped, looked back at me. "Why didn't you do what Clive asked? You just had to pick a House, and then I could join you. We'd be married and Masters one day, together."

"Levi, Clive didn't give me any time to think. He just showed up and made demands."

"He is impulsive," Levi agreed. "Not nearly as strategic, as intentional, as me. He doesn't think things through," he said, tapping a finger to his head. "Nicole wanted the Compliance Bureau, but he wanted it more. He doesn't like cheaters. Rule breakers."

And I didn't like the gleam in his eyes when he said that.

"You're an experiment," he said, and my blood went cold.

"What do you mean?" I asked, struggling to keep my voice steady. Was this about Testing? Had they wanted to conduct scientific experiments on me?

"For the Bureau," Levi said. "To see how far its authority extends, how much Nicole will let them do."

That . . . had nothing to do with my making, or my monster. "You're sure?"

"Of course. He tells me everything."

I doubted that was true. But there was no point in asking Levi more questions about it. He'd just get suspicious.

He walked to the kitchen island. Sat down on a stool. "And Clive just hates you." There was a hint of dark joy in his eyes when he said that. Was he happy to pit us against each other, with him in the middle?

"He hates me?"

"Of course. You're from Cadogan House. Spoiled." He leaned forward conspiratorially. "He doesn't know you like I know you."

You don't know me at all, I thought. Didn't know me or the monster, and was more than willing to offer up his brother as a foil for his devotion.

"Maybe we were too late," he muttered to himself. "You saved him—Connor Keene—yesterday."

While fury burned, I kept it off my face, leaned in conspiratorially. "You tried to hit Connor?"

"Maybe," he said, pleasure on his cheeks.

"To protect me," I said, and he nodded, looked relieved.

"Just like I'm protecting you right now," he said, "from that roughneck you've been spending time with. I don't get why you're dating a dog. You could have any *vampire* you wanted. After all I tried to do for you—getting you on the right path, saving you from the den of iniquity you grew up in."

I blinked in feigned confusion. "The den of iniquity? You don't like Cadogan House?"

"They wouldn't let me in," he said, his laugh a bubble of madness.

I stared at him. "What?"

"They wouldn't let me in. I applied. I wanted to be in Chicago; it was close to home. They let you run wild, but they wouldn't let me in."

My parents hadn't said a thing. Had they known, but not told me? No. They absolutely would have. So, assuming he was telling the truth, they hadn't made the connection.

"Clive said the House was never good enough for me," Levi continued, "that it was full of lawlessness and disrespect. But look at me now. Now I'm here, in your place, with you. I've come full circle."

How much, I wondered, had Clive fed his brother's madness?

His obsessions? Clive had to have known. A man this troubled didn't go through life without family noticing. Without having hurt someone before. Was that why Clive was so focused on rules? On control? Because that's how he kept Levi in line?

"So you know I'd decided to stay in Chicago," I prompted, trying to keep him talking.

"Of course. I'm older than you, had to wait for you to grow up. But then you were in Paris, and I had to wait for you to come back here. And now we're here together."

And now I was creeped out in a completely new way. I had to get out.

"We could make it work," I said, softening my voice. "I didn't know you were . . . ready for that kind of relationship. We could leave here right now, and be together. Just me and you."

I could see that he wanted to believe it, the struggle on his face as truth and falsity warred in his troubled mind. But he shook his head. "You chose them over me. You're a traitor, just like Clive said."

"He called me a traitor?" I actually made my lip quiver.

"*You picked the shifters,*" Levi said again, emphasizing each word with a shake of the knife.

"But I didn't," I said and nodded to the room. "It's just me and you in here right now. I didn't know you'd be here, that you would be waiting for me. But that was a nice surprise."

He watched me for a moment, hope blooming. "Really?"

"Of course. Shifters are really rough. They don't have nearly as much class as vampires."

The scrape of metal on metal rose up from the street, and my blood went cold. *Connor.* But even as my heart pounded, I had to fight not to struggle. If I broke character, I knew I'd lose Levi, and have no chance to get out of here—or to get to Connor.

He can take care of himself, I repeated silently, a mantra, and nodded, all the while working to loosen my bonds, even as fabric scraped raw skin. I frowned, feigned confusion. "But what about Blake? Why did I need protecting from him?"

In a flash, the pleasure was replaced by anger again. "He hated you even more than Clive. Wanted to tear you apart. He played nice, sure, but that was just his play. His face. Sometimes we wear faces that aren't who we really are."

Like the innocuous vampire who showed up outside my door the night of the party, I thought. Like you.

"What about Miranda?"

"The girl who turned you in?"

"The girl . . ." was as far as I made it before my own fury exploded, and brought the monster with it.

It hadn't been a shifter from Minnesota who'd called the AAM. It had been Miranda. She'd set all of this—the AAM, the stalker, Connor's injuries, Blake's death—in motion. Oh, we were going to have some fucking words, Miranda and me.

"Did you attack her? That girl?" My voice was shaking now as anger burned. I pushed one wrist against the other, trying to force one hand through the fabric, and wanted to scream with frustration.

"No," Levi said, oblivious to my struggle. "She brought me here to you. Why would I?"

Because she was all of it, I thought. *She* was cause and effect and all the rest.

"I'm sorry. I'm just so confused. She was hurt, and blamed it on vampires. So typical."

"So typical," he agreed.

"I don't know how I should thank you," I said and looked coyly away. "Especially with the AAM hunting me."

"You just have to join a House. That's not hard. Pick one, and I'll stay here, and we can live in Chicago and be happy. You have to join a House," he said again, eyes reeling. "You have to. You have to. We need to be part of a House. It's crucial." He stopped in front of me. "It's everything."

There was something pitiable about him, about the world he'd created in his mind, that made it hard to loathe him. But I persisted.

"You don't think we'd be okay without joining a House?"

He backhanded me.

Knuckle hit bone, and flesh struck flesh, and the insult of pain was nearly blinding. "I just said you have to join a House. You have to. Don't you understand?"

I understood plenty, I thought, as my face throbbed, the skin tingling. I understood I'd run out of patience. I'd run out of time to play nice, to wait. To hope we could get out of this without death.

Go, I told the monster. And it wasted no time, pushing forward through me with a speed that had me jerking in the chair.

I lifted my head, let Levi see what I was. That would be his punishment, or part of it. To watch his dream dissolve in fear, in the haze of my red eyes.

Horror smeared across his face like a stain, contorting his brow. "What are you?"

"Not like you," I said, and the monster had us rocking forward in the chair, slamming my forehead into his.

Levi stumbled back to the kitchen island, swore. He braced his hand against it, then used the other to wipe the blood now pouring from his nose.

"You bitch!" he screamed, spittle flying with rage. The words were loud enough that I hoped someone would think to call the CPD, but I'd have to protect myself before he did.

Still tied to the chair, the fabric around my hands looser from working but not yet undone, I swung to the side, trying to strike him with the tall ladder back.

It grazed him, but he just reversed the momentum, throwing me to the ground. I hit the floor on the shoulder I'd injured at the Grove, pain ripping through it again. Nausea rose, but I refused to acknowledge it.

The fall had buckled the chair. Levi came closer, lifted his leg to kick, and I gathered up all the power I could and slammed it into the floor. The chair's back shattered. The monster in the lead, we ripped my wrists apart, sending fabric remnants flying.

Levi and I lunged at each other. He grabbed at my hair and I kicked, catching his shin and twisting my leg to shift his ankle and unbalance him. But he grabbed me, brought me down with him. We hit the coffee table, which toppled, sending pottery and detritus flying. We rolled once, twice, until he was on top of me, hands pinning my arms.

"You could have had me," he said, lips hovering near mine, my bile threatening to rise.

"I want no part of you, asshole."

I aimed a knee between his legs, but he blocked. The move caused him to shift his weight just enough for me to scissor my legs, bring myself to the top. I crawled away, but he grabbed my ankle. The monster kicked back, smashing fingers under boots, and reveled in his scream.

I climbed to my knees, pain radiating in a dozen places, and then to my feet, my cheek throbbing with pain with each movement.

Levi had done the same, but he'd picked up a piece of the broken chair. I hoped to god Lulu hadn't bought aspen.

He speared it toward me. I kicked, heard his wrist snap. The stake dropped, and he leaned down to grab it again when a roar filled the air, shaking the windows.

Too late, I thought, and I could feel the magic roaring toward us from the hallway. He was coming.

"*The wolf,*" I said, in a voice not quite my own.

Levi, face bloodied, leered at me. "Filthy bitch," he spat, and with speed I'd never seen before, he darted to a window I belatedly realized was open. And then he was gone.

The loft door burst open, and I snapped my gaze to it.

Wolf, the monster said again, and retreated to heal.

Connor's hair was mussed, his shirt torn, but he was whole. And he was furious.

"It was Levi," I said, cradling my shoulder. "Clive's brother. He went out the window."

Connor ran to it, looked outside. "Gone," he said and cursed viciously. Then he turned back to me, eyes hard and cold and blue, but anger faded to relief. He strode toward me, put his hands on my arms. And then he went rigid with anger I could actually feel percolating in the air.

"He hit you."

I nodded.

"I don't care if he's too damaged to have kept his conscience. He is a dead man."

"Between you, me, my parents, and the AAM, you're probably right. I think I broke his wrist, maybe his nose."

"Good," he said, then looked me over. "Come sit down. I can feel your pain from here." He led me to the sofa, and I used his arm to lever myself down to it.

"What else hurts?"

"I'm sore, but mostly my shoulder. I landed on it again. That's the worst of it. Are you okay?"

"Scrapes," he said, and worry filled his eyes. "I don't know how he got past us. Then he sent two friends to play with me, and I couldn't get up here fast enough."

"Friends from the AAM?"

"Yeah. I recognized them from the Grove."

"Assholes," I muttered. "Are they down?"

"Down, but not dead. I left them to check on you. They may have gotten away."

"Doesn't matter," I said, shaking my head and leaning into him, nearly crying from the relief of it, but there'd been too much near crying these last few days. "We're okay."

"I'm sorry," he said again.

"Don't be. He didn't get past you."

Connor pulled back. "He was in here. Either he was invisible, or he got past me."

"Neither, and both," I said, and Connor's brow furrowed. "He was in the loft, waiting for me. He used glamour. He's got quite a bit of skill—can convince people they're seeing exactly what they expect to see."

"Like an empty apartment."

"Like that," I agreed. "Con, he didn't mention Miranda. He took credit for you, for Blake. But not for her." I didn't mention that she'd reported me to the AAM. I'd take that up with her directly.

He was quiet for a moment. "She did it to herself, or had someone do it. To blame vampires? To get the Pack's sympathies? Mine?"

"Possibly all of the above."

He swore bitterly. "She put heat on you."

"It doesn't matter. You know the truth, and you'll tell your family. That's enough for me."

He pressed a kiss to my forehead, then rose. Wordlessly, he went to the kitchen, opened drawers until he found a bank of clean tea towels, filled one with ice from the freezer.

While he worked, a black cat slunk out of the hallway, padded toward the couch, sat down in front of it, and looked at me.

"You were supposed to be guarding the place," I told her.

She just blinked.

"Did you know he was in here? Did you let him in here? Unlock the door in hopes he'd give you treats?" I shifted and accidentally tweaked my shoulder, winced at the pain.

To my great surprise, she padded toward me, bumped her head against my leg.

Connor came back, ice pack in hand, and looked down at the cat. "Well. That's a change of mood."

"She's touching me voluntarily," I whispered, afraid to move and send her scampering. "She must be relieved I'm alive to feed her."

"She's not the only one," he said and sat beside me. Carefully, delicately, he pressed the towel to my cheekbone while the cat trotted off to her water bowl.

"Levi's damaged," I said. "Seriously deranged. He believed we were going to have some kind of romantic love affair, and you got in the way. And he seriously hates shifters."

"Yeah, I got that from the notes. Fuck me, Elisa."

"Okay," I said, nodding. "But we'll have to clean up first."

He laughed, pressed the gentlest kiss to my temple. Then turned his head to look at the damage done. The broken chair, the overturned table, the slashed wall. "She is going to have a fit."

"Lulu or the cat?"

"Yes. We should make vampires wear fucking bear bells."

"I—what?"

"Bear bells, so the vampires make noise when they move around." He used two fingers to mimic little walking legs. "That way, the glamour wouldn't work."

"The bears don't wear the bells," I said, lips curving. "People wear bells so the bears know they're coming."

"Oh," he said. "I guess I got that backward."

No guessing about it; he'd said it to make me laugh.

"I let the monster fight him."

His brows lifted with pleasure, with interest. "Did you?"

I nodded. "We've been . . . trying to work together."

Saying that aloud helped settle something inside me, and I wasn't sure if the ease was from me, or from it.

"Wise of both of you," Connor said. "And advantageous." He

leaned in, pressed a soft kiss to my lips. "Just make sure you stay in charge."

"Am and will," I said, and I looked toward the windows. "He probably wouldn't go back to the hotel. Not now. Let's go talk to Clive. We have things to discuss."

We took turns cleaning up the loft and cleaning up in the bathroom, and sending messages.

Connor sent a warning to the Pack, in case Levi found his way there again. He also sent a message to Alexei, to keep him updated. I did the same for Lulu, then sent a message to my parents, told them we'd come by the House when we could, but to stay on high alert until Levi was found. I asked they relay the update to Nicole personally. I also had the inkling of an idea, and asked my parents to talk to Johnson, the guard who'd been injured when Clive had come to Cadogan House. He might be able to give us a little window.

I called Theo en route to the Portman Grand.

"Levi confessed to killing Blake and attacking Connor," I told him. "Two of Clive's vampires helped him."

There was a moment of stunned silence. "And how do you know this?"

"He was waiting for me in the loft. He can hide himself with glamour."

"Jesus, Lis. Are you all right?"

"Banged up, but I'll heal." I was getting sick of saying that. "We're going to the Portman Grand. I want to have some words with Clive."

"You think he knew?"

"That Levi killed Blake? Probably not. But that his brother is a threat? Yeah, I think he did know."

"I'll meet you at the hotel," he said. "Don't do anything rash, Lis. And don't make more trouble for yourself."

"Oh, the trouble won't be for me," I assured him. "But I'll be the one to end this."

Theo beat us to the hotel; we found him waiting in the lobby, surveying the luxury. "Posh," he said when we reached him. The Portman Grand was one of the finest hotels in Chicago and probably the most expensive. Marble and wood and gold, with towering ceilings and the cool, quiet, rarefied air of luxury.

"Vampires," Connor and I said together.

"That word covers a lot of ground," Theo noted.

"Same for 'shifters,'" I said. "If you need to talk about fighting or carousing or anything involving motorcycles. Do you know which rooms they're in?" I asked Theo.

"Clive's in thirty-two eleven. Levi has the room next door. Staff confirmed Levi left three hours ago, hasn't been back. His room's been cleaned since then."

So we'd been right about that. He was running, but not back to the hotel. Not back to his brother.

"Did Gwen talk to Clive?"

"Briefly," Theo said. "Asked where Levi was, got no answer. Said he was wanted for questioning in Blake's death, in Connor's attack. Still got no answer."

"What was her sense?" Connor asked.

"That he was surprised by the allegations, but not the violence." He looked back at the door, put on what I thought of as his "grown-up" face. "We don't have warrants," he said. "We can ask questions, and they can refuse."

I started to argue, but Theo held up a hand.

"Trespassing won't get his brother off the streets, and fighting with the AAM isn't going to help your case."

"I'm angry that you're right."

"You should be used to that by now. Gwen's working with the state's attorney, and we'll get Levi. We'll get the ones who helped him, and if Clive knew about it, we'll get him, too. I'm asking for a little trust, which I know probably feels unfair. But I'm asking for it anyway."

I nodded, and he looked at Connor. "You going to be able to maintain?"

"As much as I need to," Connor said. Which I knew wasn't agreement, but a reminder that he'd do exactly what he believed he needed to do. Nothing more, nothing less.

I got a response from Cadogan House as we rode up to the thirty-second floor, then walked to the room Theo had identified. Since this was my mission, I pounded a fist on the door.

It opened a moment later, and I didn't waste any time. "Clive. Now."

The female vamp who answered looked me up, down again, gave Theo and Connor the same treatment. Then settled that arrogant gaze on my face again. "Are you here to surrender?"

"No. We're here to discuss his brother's attack on me." I held up my wrists, the bruises now vibrant.

Something flared in her eyes. Knowledge, I thought. And a little bit of fear. "A moment," she said and closed the door in our faces.

"She knows something," Connor murmured.

"She absolutely does," I agreed. "Maybe she was the target of his friendship before me."

The door opened again. "You may enter if you hand over your weapons."

I snorted. "I'm not handing over my blade, and Theo is authorized to carry his weapon on duty. We're searching for Levi, and if we find him first, Clive might not like it. He has five seconds to decide whether to talk to us." I smiled politely. "Five. Four. Three."

The woman's lip curled, but she stood aside. "Enter."

"Good choice," I said quietly as we passed her. "And I'd start thinking very seriously about a career change."

We walked inside to find a large and well-appointed suite that smelled of lemons and cinnamon and the coppery tang of blood. That sparked my hunger, and the monster's interest, but I pushed it down. I'd refuel when this was done.

Vampires were arranged behind Clive, all of them in tailored black. Clive looked me over, took in the bruises. "It appears you've been fighting again. How unsurprising."

"I was attacked in my home by your brother. Levi lay in wait inside my apartment, used his glamour to make us believe he wasn't there. He's been stalking me." I offered the copies of the notes Theo had thought to bring.

Clive's expression didn't change; he probably believed he'd hidden his reaction completely. But it was the lack of apparent surprise that did him in. And the nervous glances exchanged by the vampires behind him.

"These weren't signed by him," he said and handed them back.

I ignored that. "He fled after attacking me. Your brother is disturbed." That did it, putting a flash of molten anger in his eyes.

"This is obviously a ruse intended to draw attention from your dangerous behavior."

I snorted a laugh. "He was lying in wait for me, bound and threatened me, and I'm the one engaging in dangerous behavior?" I tilted my head. "I'm curious, Clive. Did you know he was violent when you sent him to my door? Did you encourage him to communicate with me? To watch me?" My own anger rose, dancing along with the monster's Great Offense that he didn't believe me. "To try to kill me in my own apartment because he's manufactured an imaginary relationship with me?"

"Whatever you're raving about, you undoubtedly brought it upon yourself. If you'd sworn the oaths you were supposed to swear, had moved into a House, it wouldn't have happened."

But I could see in his eyes that he knew exactly who his brother was, *what* his brother could do.

"He's tried this before, hasn't he?" I asked quietly. "Maybe gotten too attached to someone. Hurt someone even though he didn't mean to do it. Other imaginary relationships?"

"Clive," whispered the vampire to his left. "If she's telling the truth—"

"She never tells the truth," Clive said, shifting the narrative. "My brother's issues are his own." But one of the vampires moved quickly into a hallway. Probably to confirm the report, or to get to Nicole before we did.

I glanced at Theo. "It's interesting, don't you think, that the so-called Compliance Bureau wants to punish me for saving a life, but when one of their own stalks and attacks me, and tries to kill the crown prince, the rules just don't apply."

"You have no proof."

I held out my wrists again.

"The CPD has evidence," Theo said. "They're investigating."

Clive snorted. But fear had begun to furrow his brows. "Bias," he spat. "Of course their investigation would be biased toward a Sullivan and a Keene. You get away with everything."

"We do?" Connor asked and looked at me. "Did you know that? Because I didn't, and I'd have raised much more hell if I'd known."

"Same," I said. "If you choose to believe your brother didn't just attack me, where is he?" I glanced around, counted. "Because he seems to be the only member of the Bureau who's not here. Well, him and the other two Bureau members who attacked Connor outside my apartment."

Clive's jaw tightened. "If you don't have a warrant, get out."

"Okay," I said, gave Theo and Connor a nod. "Let's go. We'll find Levi ourselves, and what happens, happens."

"Touch him, and you'll pay."

I snorted. "How? By making me give up my freedom? You already proposed that deal."

"Recall you only have"—Clive paused to actually check his watch—"twenty-four hours before your freedom is forfeit."

"You unmitigated asshole," Connor said, stepping forward. Connor's rage was barely checked, his urge to protect nearly pushing him beyond reason.

I put a hand on his chest, felt him vibrating with fury, and his eyes flashed to me. No longer entirely human, they shifted in the light from blue to gold like a wolf in moonlight.

I wished for a moment Connor and I had the same telepathic connection as my parents, could silently communicate in a room of enemies. So I let him see the truth in my eyes. After a moment of tension and magic, he stepped back.

I turned my gaze back to Clive, offered a thin smile. "As to the forty-eight hours," I said. "You may be confused about our terms. My father agreed I wouldn't leave Chicago. And I only agreed I would *meet* you in forty-eight hours. I didn't commit to doing anything specifically when I got to that meeting."

Red began to creep up Clive's neck, color his cheeks. "Bitch," he spat, the word venomous.

"I'll admit it's a very technical argument, but vampire deals run that way." I smiled. "And since I've just voluntarily come to your hotel room, and I'm communicating with you and your"—I cast a glance to the other AAM vampires, who now had uncertainty in their eyes—"*team*, I've fulfilled my agreement to meet you, if a little earlier than we'd planned. So, long story short, I've met the terms of our contract and have no other obligations to you."

Clive lunged. Two of his vampires grabbed his arms.

Behind me, Connor growled. "Please," he said softly. "Please make a move so I can finish you here and now."

"You have to be careful when negotiating," I told Clive. "Can't be ruled by your emotions, or you'll make mistakes. I learned that one from my father. And before you spout off," I said when he opened his mouth again, "recall that your brother has killed a member of the AAM."

The other vampires were moving nervously now.

"I imagine Nicole takes a pretty dim view of that, and the *Canon* probably describes very specific penalties. Unlike the Bureau, which hasn't even been codified, has it? It's just an idea. A proposal, and one that can be ended at Nicole's whim."

"I will destroy you."

"You won't, actually. I'm not sure if I mentioned this, but the roadblocks you put up between us and Nicole are toppling as we speak. She's going to know about the lines you've crossed, and the lines your brother completely obliterated. And I'm pretty sure any regulatory violation I committed by saving Carlie is going to be a mere drop in a very large bucket.

"So here's what's going to happen," I said. "You can tell me where your brother is, and the CPD can pick him up and deliver him to Nicole and tell her what's gone on here, and see how she wants to handle it. Or you can lie and delay and, like I said, maybe we find him first. It's up to you."

"I wish he'd never heard of Cadogan House," Clive said, freeing his arms and standing straight again.

"We all wish that for you, Clive. Where is he?"

"I don't fucking know where he is." He straightened his sleeves, grasping for dignity. "He's supposed to be here."

I could feel the truth of that, and I nodded. "Okay, then."

There were footsteps behind us. Gwen stood in the doorway, cops arrayed behind her. She stepped forward, holding up her screen in one hand, badge in the other. "Detective Gwen Robinson," she said. "I have duly authorized warrants for the arrest of Clive, for the arrest of Levi, to question you, and to search any rooms reserved or paid for by the AAM."

"I did nothing," Clive said, attempting to lunge again. But cops moved in, replacing the vampires who'd held him.

"Oh, I guess I forgot to mention," I said. "You assaulted a guard at Cadogan House, and he's going to press charges. Rules matter, after all."

He was cursing when I glanced at Gwen. "Have fun in here."

"Oh, we will," she said with a thin smile. "It's going to be a fun night."

TWENTY

That was neatly done," Theo said, when we made it down to the lobby again.

"I'll be honest—it felt good. Really good. But it's not over." I rolled my shoulder, trying to spin out some of the residual ache. "I know the CPD won't be able to hold Clive long. And while he'll probably back off investigating me because of his brother, Levi is still out there and the AAM proper thinks I broke the rules. I've still got to fix that."

"How?" Theo asked, concern lacing his voice.

"I'm not entirely sure. I want to talk to my parents."

"I'll take you," Connor said.

"I'm going to go back up and help the CPD," Theo said. "Stay in touch."

I nodded my agreement and, when he'd disappeared behind gilded elevator doors, looked up at Connor. "Can we refuel first? I fought and lost some blood—"

"And argued with assholes," Connor added.

"And argued with assholes, and I could use some coffee. And a muffin. And possibly a scone or seven."

"You assured me you didn't have your mother's appetite."

I smiled. "My mother would have ordered three of each and growled if you got too close to the bag. If you don't enjoy the adventure of a hungry vampire, I can leave you home next time."

He laughed. "At least you admit your being hungry is an adventure."

"Vampiric hunger is a strategic choice." I narrowed my gaze. "Much like you flashing your shifter eyes in a room full of vampires."

"Amusing, wasn't it?"

"And you say I'm a troublemaker."

"We're both troublemakers in our way."

"Probably." I stopped, looked up at him. "I don't care how we do it. But we're taking them all down."

"Oh, yeah," Connor said, with a deadly smile that had nothing of humor in it. "We absolutely are."

Two bottles of blood and a cup of coffee. That was all I had room for. I'd be hungry for food soon enough, but the predatory contentment, and jolt of caffeine, was worth it.

We drove to Cadogan House, parked on the street, were waved inside by guards.

"Any sign of him?" I asked.

"None," said one of the guards. "It's been quiet, and we're hoping it will stay that way."

We nodded, walked toward the House. If the sword spoke to the monster tonight, it made no reaction. Too tired to be seduced by magic after its battle. *Our* battle.

"I always thought of this place as your castle," Connor said, gazing up at the stone façade. "Rapunzel in her tower."

I chuckled. "I always thought of the Keene house as your castle." It was a Queen Anne–style house, complete with turret and balcony. "And you were, I don't know, beauty and the beast?"

His laugh was a low rumble as he opened the door and the receptionist nodded politely. "They're in your father's office."

"Thanks," I said, and we walked across the foyer.

"Why are you nervous?" he asked.

"The monster sometimes gets edgy here because of my mother's sword. But it's quiet so far."

He squeezed my hand, and we stepped into the office, found my mom and dad in the sitting area. They both jumped to their feet when we entered, came toward me with concern in their eyes.

"I'm fine," I said, holding up a hand. "We're both okay. A little bruised, but okay."

"Mr. and Ms. Sullivan," Connor said.

My mother snorted. "You've never called me that in your entire life. No point in starting now. Sit," she said, gesturing us back to the chairs. "Let's take a break and talk. You need to rest; you still look pale."

"Vampire," I pointed out.

The noise my mother made told me she didn't appreciate the joke.

"Do you need anything to drink? To eat?" my father asked.

Connor looked at me. "No, thank you," I said. "We're good."

We sat down, and I gave my parents a moment to look me over, assure themselves that I was fine.

"Clive is now in the custody of the CPD," I said, "thanks to Johnson." I gave them the rest of the update.

"I'd like to get my hands on Levi, that miserable little monster," my mother said. "Not just for hurting you—although that's more than enough. Lying in wait is a coward's game."

"I'm fine," I assured her. "Held my own, just like Connor."

She nodded, exhaled.

"I checked our records for the human name you gave me," my father said. "Greg Voss, as Levi was then known, applied to join Cadogan House twice. Both times before your mother joined the House. I haven't seen a photograph of Levi, and didn't make the connection."

"Of course you didn't," I said. "Why would you? Cadogan House rejected him."

My father nodded, but there was still guilt in his eyes that I wanted to wash away. Violence so rarely affected only the victim; its effects spread like ripples in a damnable pond.

"I reviewed my notes. Voss had been adamant Cadogan was the right House for him," Dad said, "went on and on about its qualifications. How he'd selected it from all the others. How he deserved it. But there was nothing about the skills, the passion, the ethic he'd bring to the House. I had a bad feeling about him, and asked the guards to search his history. They found a sealed juvenile file, but we weren't able to obtain the details. We presumed it involved violence, given the size of the file."

"It would be in character," I said, cold sweat beading when I recalled the hot flash of his anger.

Connor reached out, squeezed my hand. I squeezed back, collected myself. "So you rejected him?" I asked.

Dad nodded. "He applied again the next time we were open for submission, was denied again. Didn't try a third time."

"How did he take the rejection?" Connor asked.

My father reached out for a tablet on the coffee table. "Not well." He swiped it, then offered the tablet to me.

He'd pulled up a list of communications, each dated about a week after the other and running for nearly four months after the last rejection.

"He sent you letters," I murmured and opened one at random. With Connor reading over my shoulder, I found the same tone of faux intimacy in the notes he'd sent me. The excitement. Opened another, then another, and found the same escalation, from bafflement to fury to declarations of war. The mania was obvious, and so was the pattern. More evidence we'd use to keep him from hurting anyone else—if we could find him before that happened.

"This is the entire set of communications?" I asked.

Dad nodded. "There was silence after those. I assumed he'd

moved on. Joined another House, affiliated with a Rogue community. Apparently not."

"Those were reasonable assumptions," I said, and I handed back the tablet. "Can you send these to Theo and Petra? They'll need to review and send them to the CPD."

"Maybe there's something in the letters we can use to pinpoint his location," Connor said. "To find him, to stop him."

Dad nodded. "Do you think his stalking has something to do with the House?"

"I suspect that's how he learned about me —following House news—but it evolved into something else. He said in his first note he was glad I'd decided not to go back to Paris; he mentioned Paris in the loft, too. I get the sense that kickstarted this new stage."

That seemed to loosen something in the set of my father's shoulders. "All right."

"What about Nicole?" I asked.

"Luc found her, as suspected, deep in meetings and with no idea what was happening here. She can't leave New York until tomorrow—apparently there's alleged financial fraud, and federal investigators are involved. But when she's reached a stopping point, she's coming here to deal with these issues."

"What does 'deal with' mean?" Connor asked, moving incrementally closer to me, as if his nearness was a shield.

Dad looked at me. "The Bureau botched its handling, and she'll deal with them directly along with members of her own guard. But she's also insistent rules be equally applied in this, shall we say, new era. She wants to speak with you directly."

"Interrogate?" Connor asked.

My father kept his gaze on me, strong and steady. "She hasn't called it that. We've requested the meeting take place here, which is at least a minimal advantage. She agreed."

"When?" I asked.

"Tomorrow. Midnight."

Damn it. I'd guessed this was a possibility given Clive's temporary arrest, but I thought I'd have more time to prepare for it. Well, it couldn't be helped. I'd have to figure out a way through it. And, if possible, a way to use it to my advantage.

I sighed, looked at my parents. "Is the AAM truly better than the Greenwich Presidium?"

"Yes," my parents said together, and looked at each other in a way that spoke of shared experiences. Shared fears and triumphs in the years before I'd been born.

"That's it, then," I said. "We'll deal with this tomorrow. In the meantime, can I use the library?"

"Of course," my father said with some surprise, then his gaze settled on Connor. "While you're there, I'd like to speak with Connor."

They looked at each other for a moment, two strong men, both important to me.

"Up to him," I said.

Connor nodded, the deal made.

And my curiosity firing.

It was the largest room in the House. Two stories of books, including the wrought iron balcony that ringed the upper floor. There were massive skylights, library tables on gleaming floors, and of course, the vampire librarian, who'd snuck me detective mysteries when I was younger. They'd come in every few weeks, a numbered series about an eleven-year-old detective with a pet finch, glasses, and a little leather satchel. I saved my allowance for a month to buy a matching bag and wore it until the straps wore through.

I wasn't sure what I was looking for here. But if I was going to face down Nicole directly, I knew I was going to need good, convincing arguments. Legal arguments. And vampire law was stored here. The *Canon* filled dozens of volumes that took up dozens of shelves, but I started with the *Revised Canon of North American Vampires: Desk Reference*, which felt heavy enough to contain most of the important rules. I carried it to a table, took a seat, and began scanning the table of contents.

Most of those contents were mind-numbingly boring: the rights and obligations of Houses; the accounting methods Houses were obliged to use; AAM committee structure. I skipped ahead to the criminal provisions, found the rule that I presumed the AAM was trying to use against me, even though no one had specifically mentioned it. Maybe not a big surprise, given we now knew details weren't Clive's strong suit.

The provision read, "The making of vampires is prohibited to any and all vampires who are not Masters." That seemed, unfortunately, clear enough. I wasn't a Master or a formal Rogue, so I was prohibited from making vampires. It seemed impossible that I was the only unaffiliated vampire who'd done so. Again, I was the example to be made.

I flipped forward a few pages to the list of penalties for vampires who engaged in prohibited acts. They were . . . remarkably specific. The guillotine and something called "iron pinning" had been taken out during the *Canon*'s revision when the AAM had been created. Staking, seclusion, and House repudiation remained in play, and there were options for vampires to appeal decisions they thought were unfair.

I was perusing those sections, which were filled with words like "appellee" and "respondent," when I found something. Vampire crimes could be resolved through trials, just like in the human world. Or, according to one line at the very bottom of the list, vampires could instead choose something called the "Rule of Satisfaction." Two vampires physically fighting to resolve a dispute; the person who won the fight, won the argument.

I'd read enough Jane Austen to recognize a duel when I saw one. So Uncle Malik and Alexei had been onto something.

I sat back, crossed my arms. I was no legal scholar, but it looked like if I'd violated the rule, either I had to rely on Nicole to decide not to enforce it—which would be great if I could come up with some leverage—or I had to shimmy my way out of the punishment.

Still, dueling was old-fashioned, and I wasn't a *Canon* scholar. So I wrote down the language and moved through the stacks until I found the man I needed.

The Librarian stood in midrow, peering at boxes that held print copies of old magazines. He was on the shorter side, with pale skin and dark wavy hair and hands on his lean hips.

Slowly, he shifted his gaze and gave me the Official Librarian Death Stare.

"I don't have any food or a beverage," I said. "I only have a question." I wiggled the paper.

His lips twitched. "Good to see you, too, Elisa. Doing a little research on the AAM?"

"Something like that. I have a question about interpretation of the *Canon*. But I need discretion."

His brows lifted, disappeared into dark wavy hair. "Will it hurt Cadogan House?"

"Not at all."

"What's your question?"

I handed him the paper. He took it and read, lips pursed. "I see your handwriting hasn't improved."

"I don't write many letters."

He humphed, then looked up at me. "You're wondering about Satisfaction."

"I am. Is it still in use? Is it still something I can request?"

Frowning, but eyes alight with curiosity, he walked back to the *Canon*, selected a volume, then pulled out a little shelf extension and opened the book on it.

"I didn't know they did that," I said.

"Because you'd have used them for snack holders," he said, turning pages until he found the one he wanted. Then he studied it with furrowed brow.

"As you may know, not all of the *Canon* was revised when the AAM took power," he said. "The Rule of Satisfaction is one of the sections that wasn't." He flipped forward a few more pages. "There's no commentary, so I can't speculate as to the modern intention. If this was a human legislature, we could review the debate transcripts. But vampires don't keep those." And he seemed exceedingly displeased by that failure.

He considered for a moment, staring blankly at the spines in front of him while tapping fingers on the open volume. "They didn't change the rule when they could have. You have a reasonable argument that, even though it's old-fashioned, they made a choice to keep it on the books, so the Rule still exists and can be used by vampires." He shifted his gaze to me. "But that doesn't mean the AAM will buy it."

Fortunately, I only needed Nicole to buy it. And I knew how to negotiate.

TWENTY-ONE

I reviewed a few more books that might give me additional ammunition and, just in case, to check if sanctuary from any other Sup group was an option. Short answer: It wasn't, as far as I could tell.

Maybe I could just live at Taco Hole. It was neutral ground, and I could build up my pain tolerance.

Connor messaged when his conversation with my dad was done, so I made my way back downstairs, found him waiting on the portico, the cool breeze ruffling his hair. It was chillier now than it had been when we'd gone inside.

"How was your meeting?"

Connor just looked at me, expression bland. "If he'd wanted you to know, brat, he'd have told you."

"That bad?"

"Good or bad is none of your business. What did you find in the library?"

"A bit of *Canon* law that might help us. Maybe."

"You sound very confident."

"Yeah. I have to think it through. Let me mull it over a little, then I'll give you the details, okay?"

His stare went even blander. "You're asking me to trust you while you conceal information from me."

"It's different when I do it for reasons I don't have the brain power to articulate right now. Something, something double standard?"

He rolled his eyes. "Fine. You have twenty-four hours."

"You're hilarious." I leaned into him as we walked down the sidewalk. "Let's go back to your place. I'm exhausted."

"And hungry."

"Only a little," I admitted. But didn't object when he grabbed a deep-dish pizza from an all-night joint on the way home.

He dropped it onto the counter when we reached the town house, and the shifter and not-quite-sorceress circled like animals.

"Thanks," Alexei said, then dumped a slice on a plate. I watched in horror as he horizontally dissected the pizza, then placed each layer separately around the plate.

"What in the name of all that is good and delicious are you doing?" Lulu stared at him in horror. She was right. It was very upsetting.

He chewed, swallowed. "I'm eating pizza."

"None of us think that's what this is." She looked up at us. "Right?"

"He doesn't like his food to touch," Connor said, apparently unbothered. He should have been bothered.

"It's pizza. And it's deep dish. Of course it's going to touch. That's the point."

"Not the way he eats it." Connor glanced at me, lips curled in amusement. "Are you so fastidious, brat, that you can't let a man eat a pizza the way he wants? What kind of world would that be?"

"Pizza autocracy," Alexei said, and cut through a wedge of cheese, bit in.

"A sane one," I said, dishing up my own slice. "I've seen a lot of crazy things today, but that might be the weirdest."

While we ate, Connor and I told them about our very dramatic evening.

Lulu looked me over, nodded. "You seem whole for now." But there was worry in the set of her brows.

"I'm as good as I can be." I looked at Alexei. "While we're interrogating you, did you find anything blackmail-worthy?"

"Nothing," he said, shaking his head. "If Clive has any skeletons in his closet, they're well hidden."

"It's logical the AAM would be careful," I said, "especially when staffing something called the 'Compliance Bureau.'"

"What about Jonathan Black?" Connor asked.

I shouldn't have been surprised that he'd asked Alexei to take a look, so I kept it to myself.

"You said you weren't sure if he was a friend. Given his interest in you, I think that's a question we need to answer now."

"I didn't say a thing," I said and held up my hands for peace.

"What did you learn?" Connor asked.

"He has connections to certain criminal ventures of the supernatural variety."

"Dark magic?"

"Among other things. I didn't get many details; the names of his clients are completely hush-hush. He's very discreet. But there's no dispute he reps criminals."

I'd say that kept him out of the "ally" category, regardless of his request. I'd definitely be careful the next time we interacted. "Anything about him that definitively relates to this?"

"Not that I could find." Alexei looked at me, apology in his eyes. "I'm sorry."

"No apology necessary. If you had more time, I'm sure you could find something. But the clock is very much against us."

"So what's the plan?" Lulu asked.

"She's playing vampire lawyer," Connor said, sipping his drink.

"Still mulling it over," I said. "But I think I'm going to need a place to meet them again. Even if I'm right about my legal theory,

I'm going to have to address it in person." And since my father had already offered it up as a meeting spot to Nicole, Cadogan House seemed like the logical possibility. "Lulu said something about using Levi as a lure. I think we can make that happen, or at least try for it." But I checked the time. "We need to talk to the Ombuds, to Gwen, but it's too close to dawn for me to drive."

"Not a problem," Connor said and gestured to the artscreen. "You can chat with them that way."

I contacted the OMB, and we let Connor futz with the electronics.

My screen buzzed. I pulled it out, thinking it was confirmation from Theo or a reminder to feed the starter again, but found something else entirely.

> You lied to me. You will regret it.
> —Your enemy

"I'm sorry to report Levi and I aren't friends anymore," I said and showed everyone the note. And realized, with great relief, that he'd made a very big mistake.

"He didn't anonymize the message," I said and grinned up at Connor. "He got sloppy and forgot to encrypt it, or whatever tech-scrambly thing they do. There's a legitimate US number attached. That means I can respond. And we can lure him out."

I sent the message to Theo for analysis. The group call took a little more time to coordinate, but with a scant half hour until dawn, everyone was available via screen.

Gwen in a very dull-looking CPD conference room. Roger, Theo, Petra at the OMB office. My parents at Cadogan House. Me, Alexei, Lulu, and Connor at the town house.

"Gorgeous room," my mother said, getting the ball rolling. "Your home is beautiful, Connor."

"Thank you," he said and looked to me.

"Thanks to everyone for joining in," I said, ignoring him and looking at their boxed images on-screen. "This is a weird, supernatural *Brady Bunch* view, but it's appreciated. Long story short, Levi remains on the loose, and Nicole Heart is coming to Chicago to deal with Clive and question me. So we've got a stalker and a bureaucrat." And hopefully no Testing.

"You look like you've got an idea," Gwen said approvingly and crossed her arms. "Let's hear it."

"I have a sandwich of an idea," I said, "made up of the information and ideas that everyone else has contributed. So thank you for that."

"Leave it to your daughter to use a food metaphor," my father said to my mother.

Theo smiled. "And taking responsibility for your problems doesn't mean you have to solve them alone."

"It's appreciated. Let's start with you—I assume Levi hasn't been located?"

Theo got Roger's nod, reported. "No. He wasn't at the hotel, and it appears some of his personal effects are missing. Some clothes, some shoes."

"He's on the run," Connor said.

"Most likely," Roger said. "We've also identified the two AAM vampires who assisted him—Klaus and Sonder. They're gone, too."

"What did Clive have to say about that?" I wondered.

"Still in denial," Theo said. "Gwen and I talked to him, and he's still talking about false accusations and perfidy by Chicago's vampires." He rolled his eyes.

Gwen took the reins. "We searched the hotel, including the Bureau's suites. We found nothing that links Levi's stalking activities to the Bureau. But we did find a set of bloody clothes in the closet in Levi's room."

"Blake?" I asked.

She nodded. "Housekeeping had cleaned the space, but we found traces of his blood in the sink, shower. That's still being tested."

"It will be Blake's," I said. "It would have been very messy work."

"Another reason to use the Pedway," Petra said. "So you don't attract attention while you're literally covered in blood."

"We didn't find a sword," Gwen continued, "probably because he's taken that with him. But given his sloppiness, there's a good chance we'll find traces on that, too. When we get him. Which we will."

"What about the letters Levi sent to Cadogan House?" my father asked. "Do they help?"

"Not yet," Theo said. "There were some references to Chicago—including a friend who'd lived here once, who we thought might have offered him a place to stay. But the friend moved to Philly ten years ago, and his apartment is now home to a very nice human family. We didn't have any more leads until he sent you that very sloppy message."

"That's our ticket," I agreed. "I think we pick a time and place, and we lure Levi out. Maybe send him a fake newsletter saying Connor and I will be there for some kind of event. Something that will make him think he can get to both of us at once."

My mother frowned. "He may be too smart to fall for that."

"Not if we add one more element," I said. "Not if we tell him we'll be at Cadogan House."

There were sounds and nods of agreement. "He'll want to come back here," Dad said. "He can close old wounds."

"That's my thinking."

"And we'll be there to wrap him up," Gwen said.

"How does this help with the AAM?" my father asked.

"We know the AAM only selectively enforces the prohibition on making new vampires. When I talk to Nicole, I can offer him up in exchange for her dropping the issue." I leaned forward. "He's killed another vampire, attacked a human, stolen a car, hit a shifter. He's doing damage throughout the city, attracting human attention. She'll want him wrapped up. And that might be enough to have her drop her claims against me—especially if I offer not to press charges."

"It's a good argument," my father said. "I don't know if she'll agree, and it presumes you can get Levi to Cadogan House, but it's a start."

"Clive isn't going to like that at all," my mother said. "Assuming he's been released by then, he might see his brother's arrest as your fault, regardless of what the AAM does."

"I think there's a pretty good risk of that. But I also think, if we can get Clive to Cadogan House and he sees his brother, maybe he'll have a reckoning."

"That's a gamble," my father said.

"I know. And that leads me to my next option." I gathered my courage, looked at Connor. "As Alexei suggested: a duel."

"No," Connor and my father said simultaneously.

I held up a hand. "At least hear me out before you start with the pronouncements. If we can get the pieces in place, it's a way to wrap up everything at once. To put Levi behind bars, and deal with Clive."

I laid it out for them: my *Canon* hunt, the Rule of Satisfaction, and the likelihood Clive was going to be a problem we had to solve, regardless of what the AAM did.

"And if they hurt you?" Mom asked.

"I have no intention of getting dead," I said. "I get to pick the weapon, and I'm very good with a katana. I'd rather fight for my life than be forced into seclusion by the AAM. Or worse," I added, willing her to understand the real choice. "You'd do the same thing in my place."

As if resigned, she sighed, looked at my father. "Thoughts?"

"The Rule of Satisfaction hasn't been used in a long time. But based on what we know of him, Clive may welcome the opportunity to best you. And rules can be put into place—limitations on the scope of the duel—that would reduce the risk."

Clive would never agree to limitations, but I didn't need to voice that here.

"I want the rest of the AAM out of my city."

We all looked at Gwen, at the ferocity in her eyes. "I'm just getting to know many of you, and you seem to be good, honorable people." She made a point of looking at me, which I appreciated. "They aren't. I want Heart's agreement to move them back to Atlanta as soon as Levi is in custody. We'll let the attorneys worry about prosecution."

"We'll do what we can," my father said. "I'll talk to the guards, and we'll arrange for additional, but unseen, eyes and ears on the grounds. Nicole will arrive shortly after dusk. She plans to speak with Clive and the others before your discussion."

"Which is at midnight," I said. "So we should try to get Levi here by one a.m. at the latest." I looked at Petra. "Think you could mock up something we could send back to him?"

"Oh, I'm sure I could."

I nodded. "When he takes the bait, which he will, we'll need everyone ready to grab him. And be prepared—he has unique glamour," I said, and told them about it. "That's how he got into the loft. So don't be surprised if he seems to appear from nowhere."

"Appreciate the warning," Gwen said. "We'll tell any uniforms assigned. There's danger here," she added, shifting her gaze to my father. "This plan comes to a peaceful resolution—for you, for Cadogan House, for Hyde Park, for Chicago—only if the vampires all act reasonably. And they haven't shown much reason or logic so far."

"We'll be as ready as we can," he said.

I looked back at the group. "Any questions?"

"Watch your back before then," my father said. "Levi's out there somewhere, and will be especially attentive after you drop your bait."

"Same goes," I said. "You're all friends and family, and you could all be targets. So please be careful."

"I don't know about everyone else," Petra said, "but I'm definitely feeling the love."

"Clever girl," Connor said, when Lulu was tucked into the town house's guest room and we sat in front of the fire in the master. "But if you get hurt, you will have hell to pay."

"From you and Dad both," I said. "Do you think Petra's note will work?"

It was an impressive bit of design—a faux newsletter designed to look like a gossip sheet for Chicago socialites—that said Connor and I had been seen around Chicago together and were reportedly going to an "important" party at Cadogan House tomorrow night with several dozen other guests.

"I do. And I think he's most likely to try for you on the way in or out."

I nodded. "Dad's going to leave the gate open, set the lights so it looks like there's a party outside. Levi will like the shadows, I think. Sneaking in and among the people." I sighed. "Unless he realizes it's a ruse, and we lose our chance at him."

One way or the other, we'd see tomorrow night. Because dawn approached, and sleep beckoned.

I toed off boots and jeans, decided sleeping in my T-shirt was good enough, and climbed onto the sumptuous mattress.

Connor undressed and climbed into bed in boxer briefs that—glory to the world—left very little to the imagination.

"Come here," he said, and I slid into the crook of his shoulder.

He wrapped his arms around me, sighed heavily. "I've wanted this for hours. Just this. Peace and quiet and you."

"It's not bad," I agreed. "Pretty damn good, actually."

"Are you worried?"

"Yes," I said. "Are you?"

He paused thoughtfully. "No. I'm anticipating, and I'm ready for a fight. I'm ready to resolve two issues that are hurting you, hurting us. But I'm not worried about the result. Because one way or the other, they won't get their hands on you."

He kissed my temple. "Sleep. The rest is for tomorrow." His voice dropped to a whisper. "But I'm glad you're here, with me, in my house, in my bed."

As light fell across the city, I fell into sleep, safe in his arms.

TWENTY-TWO

Something hit me in the face, and I jumped awake, brushed at the wings of the dragon I was sure had come to gnaw my bones.

And found a sports bra in my hand.

Blinking, I looked up, found Connor in the doorway in shorts, running shoes, and nothing else. "Come on. We're going for a run."

I pulled the hair from my face. "Why would we do that?"

He walked to the window, opened the heavy blackout drapes so moonlight shone through. "Because it's fun?"

"You and I have very different ideas of fun."

He grinned. "No, Lis. I think we've proven that's not true."

He had me there. And several other ways.

"This will be good for you. You can run off the nerves, and you'll be ready for what comes next."

Right. I checked the clock. Sixish hours to go.

"Have they found Levi?" I asked.

"Nothing yet," he said. "They're looking."

I plucked up my screen, checked my messages. "Nicole has arrived. We're confirmed for midnight. No messages from Levi."

"He may not send one."

"Maybe not," I said. "But maybe I should poke the bear." I

typed a draft, showed it to Connor. "A response to his last message."

"'You can't be my enemy if I don't care about you. Life goes on and I'm with a real man.'" He handed the screen back. "Immature and guaranteed to piss him off."

"Enough to have him come for both of us tonight?"

"Possibly."

"That's all I need," I said and sent it.

"If he comes at you, how's the shoulder?"

I rolled it. "Only twingey."

Connor nodded his approval. "If you're a good vampire, there's a spinach smoothie waiting at the end of our run."

I narrowed my eyes as I took him in from the gorgeous planes of his face to the planes of his abdomen. "Is that how you look like that? Spinach smoothies?"

He lifted a brow, put his hands on his hips, tapped the diagonal muscles at the edge of his hips. "Like this?" he asked, but there was no modesty in the tone.

"I figured it was just magic."

He snorted. "Magic doesn't hurt. But no, it's work. You train plenty; so do I. So let's get to it. Be down in five."

"Who's the bossy one now?"

"The prince, of course." Then winked before closing the door again.

"*Be down in five,*" I mimicked and threw my legs over the side of the bed.

"I heard that," he called out.

Damned shifter hearing.

Because he was right, and I did need to burn off some energy, I got dressed, pulled my hair into a ponytail, and met him in the kitchen.

He glanced up, gaze taking in the sports bra and running

shorts I'd donned, and the skin left bare against the late summer heat. "On second thought," he said, voice gravelly, "maybe we should make other plans."

"Your plan was just fine," I said.

He looked me over again. "It definitely has its upside."

"Mm-hmm. Why you stalling? Are you nervous about running against a vampire with super strength and super speed?"

He snorted. "Bring it, dead girl."

Can and will, I thought, and smiled.

"Two legs or four?" he asked.

"Two," I said.

"In that case . . ." He pushed off, ran down the hallway toward the front door.

"Damn it," I said and followed him.

We were both snort-laughing by the time we got to the door and were through it, made it down the steps and to the sidewalk. The air smelled of rain, but the sidewalks were still dry. It hadn't come yet, but it would. The storm would break, and carry away the last of summer, the dregs of heat and dust, and escort in the chill of fall.

We reached the street and both paused for a sobering moment, to check for magic and enemies, to see if they'd found the town house, found us. But the night was quiet, the few sounds made by humans. Most were inside, waiting for the rain to fall.

But not us. Not when the night was here for the taking, and we had freedom left to spend.

"Go," I said and took off in front of him.

I heard him curse and push off behind me, catch up in seconds. We both ran hard, not yet full-out, but enough to challenge each other. Down one dark street, turning the corner, and sprinting down the dark sidewalk, laughing even as we breathed harder, pushed harder. He began to outpace me—his damned legs were longer, and he was literally built for running, at least in wolf form—so I accelerated, and nearly beat him to the entrance of a small park at the end of the street.

Nearly.

He slapped the wooden sign first, then looked back at me, grinned in victory.

Chest heaving, I grinned back. Both of us had hands on our hips, bodies gleaming with exertion under the rising moon.

There was joy, utter and sheer joy, in his eyes. "You don't just run. You love running," I said.

"Shifter," he said and ran a hand through his hair. "Running is life. Running is Pack. It's prey and escape and companionship. There's very little shifters love more."

I arched an eyebrow.

"Well, obviously we also love *that*. Immensely." He looked around at the park. Mums bloomed on the pathway; frogs croaked in the darkness nearby. "I run here from NAC headquarters. It's a longer route than from the town house, but it's quiet, peaceful."

A frog let out an enormous croak.

"Mostly quiet and peaceful," he amended, and looked back at me, smiled.

"Why not run as a shifter?"

"Because humans tend not to like seeing a wolf run past their windows. They think we're going to eat their corgis."

I looked at him, considered. "How many times have you had to shift naked in front of animal control?"

He grinned. "Twice before I learned my lesson."

He'd wanted to run to help me settle my nerves. But not just that, I realized. If all failed tonight, if we were hurt or separated, we'd still have had this moment together.

"Thank you."

Connor nodded, brushed a finger along my cheek. "You're welcome." Then he rolled his shoulders, stretched his arms. "Back to the town house?"

"I've got a little more in me," I said, and the monster pinged me with interest. I glanced at Connor. "You want to race the monster?"

That he looked at me with competitive interest, not fear or terror, made me fall a little deeper. "Really?"

I felt its earnest agreement. "Yup. It thinks it can take you."

He snorted, all cockiness.

This time, I beat him to the door.

I turned back, breath huffing, and grinned victoriously.

He climbed one step, which put us nearly eye to eye. "You're fast. The monster is fast. But I'd have beaten you on four legs." He kissed me, quick and hard. "Spinach time."

It took me a minute to comprehend the offer. Smoothies. "That's not the way you woo a girl into your house, into your bed," I said, and we walked inside.

Connor froze halfway across the foyer, looked back at me, gaze narrowed. "I thought you were asleep when I said that."

"I know." I grinned and walked past him. "Vampire hearing's pretty good, too."

"Freaking vampires," he said and followed me into the kitchen.

He opened the refrigerator, but closed it quickly. And then looked at me. "I know this isn't what you want to hear tonight, but I have bad news."

"In the refrigerator? What is it?"

"The sourdough starter . . . is dead."

I blinked at him. "What?"

He put a hand over his heart and looked up at the ceiling, gaze vacant and thoughtful. "It died an honorable death, and we mourn its loss."

I narrowed my eyes. "Damn it, Connor. Did Alexei eat the starter?"

He pulled out the empty jar, held it up. "I suspect he did."

Honestly, directing shifters not to eat my homemade bread prep work wasn't something I'd thought I'd ever have to say. "Is he nursing the mother of all stomachaches?"

As if on cue, Alexei padded into the kitchen, this time in gym shorts. He nodded at us, pulled a gallon of milk from the refrigerator, and disappeared again.

"Probably," Connor concluded.

I looked back at him. "Shifters eat a lot."

Connor's look was bone-dry. "You eat people."

"Only in a manner of speaking." I let my grin go wicked. "And only if they ask nicely."

He moved forward, caught me with an arm around the waist. "Oh, I'll ask nicely."

I smiled. "Thanks for making me laugh."

"Feeling better?"

"I'm . . . ready," I decided. "Ready to end both very uncomfortable chapters of my life." I looked back at him. "There will be more than this. Probably worse than this."

"My cousin's friends tried to kill you."

"Good point. Go get dressed."

Lulu appeared in the doorway of the master bedroom after I'd showered, and wasn't wearing her paint-spattered clothes.

"You aren't working tonight?"

"Not tonight. Alexei thought it would be better if I stayed here, just in case the AAM tries some kind of double cross."

"Right. Super smart."

"So what are you wearing?" she asked, and there was actual

suspicion in her eyes, and it felt so gloriously normal—so us—that I nearly cried.

I pulled out the military-style black jacket I'd hung in the master bedroom closet. "I was thinking about this."

"That could work," she said and sat down on the bed. "Fancy in here."

"They like their creature comforts," I said, pulling leggings from the pile of clothes I'd brought back from the loft. I looked up at her. "And how are you?"

She lifted a shoulder. "Better, I guess. I think Mateo was kind of self-centered."

"Based on what you told me, I'd say definitely." I sat down beside her. "You are, of course, invited to tonight's nonsense if you don't want to stay here. You could hang in the Cadogan House library."

"Too much magic," she said. "I'm good here. He's got every option on that wall screen, so I'll binge my way out of grief."

"Want me to steal some art from the House for you to critique?"

"No," she said with a laugh, "but thanks for the offer." She leveled her gaze. "You aren't going to do anything ridiculous tonight, are you?"

"You mean other than possibly dueling a vampire? Of course not. That would be silly."

She shook her head. "Reason forty-two why I hate supernatural drama. It's always life or death with these people."

"Only the fundamentally unreasonable ones," I said. "Which Clive plainly is. Unfortunately, they've made family problems everyone's problems, and I'm on cleanup duty." I put an arm around her shoulders. "I'll be fine."

"You can't guarantee that."

"No," I agreed. "I can't guarantee anything. None of us can. But I'm in the best position to stop this, so I'm going to try my damnedest."

She put her head on my shoulder. "Sometimes I wish you were a lazy-ass slacker."

I acknowledged the little knot of fear in my gut. "Sometimes I do, too."

I went downstairs wearing black—jacket to leggings to boots—accented by the bright red of my katana scabbard. And got a wolf whistle for my trouble.

"You clean up good," Connor said, snatching me toward him with a hand at my waist. He kissed me solidly, left me more than a little breathless.

"You're in a good mood," I said. He wasn't dressed for combat, but then shifters rarely were.

"I'm feeling optimistic."

The monster lifted its metaphorical head. And instead of trying to wrestle control from me, asked me a question.

please?

I considered. Clive and the others already thought I was damaged or different, so fighting with exceptional skill wasn't going to change that. With one caveat. *Can you keep my eyes from changing?*

Silence, then: *will try*

If you can prevent that, I told it, *I'll invite you out when the time is right.*

There was thrill in its answer, and delicious warmth as it settled into bone and muscle. No friction between us, just ease and readiness for action. It had wiped away the lingering nerves, the jitteriness of adrenaline, leaving only calm behind.

I closed my eyes, breathed in deeply, exhaled hugely.

"I should be the only one who makes you sound like that."

I glanced at Connor, grinned. "We're going to fight together. The monster and me. In public."

"Good."

"It's just—I'm worried about my eyes."

"Still green now. I'll signal you if they change." He stepped to me and tipped up my face, kissed me well and properly. "You'll be careful."

"Yes. But if it comes down to me and Clive and a katana, I take him on my own."

"Of course. And I'll have your back. Let's send this asshole home."

It was my entire agenda.

Connor and I met Petra, Gwen, and Theo outside Cadogan House shortly before midnight. We'd parked in front of the House; they'd parked a few blocks away, to keep our vehicles from being too noticeable.

My father had spared no expense making Cadogan look exactly like Petra had promised: soft music flowed from speakers on the lawn, and the grounds were lit for a gathering, with path lights and torches burning.

"It really does look like a party," Gwen said. "It's beautiful."

"You're welcome to a tour when this is all done. Your people in position?"

"And in contact," Gwen said with a nod. "They've got a wagon waiting for transport. Any contact from Levi?"

I shook my head, but knew in my gut he would come. He may have already been close.

"Clive?" I asked Gwen.

"Released at dusk into the custody of the AAM. According to witnesses, he remains very, very angry at you and had a very heated discussion with Ms. Heart outside the building. And I may have accidentally told him you were having a kind of victory party tonight."

"Excellent thinking," I said with a smile. The angrier he was, the more mistakes he'd make.

"And since they both know about it and could be nearby," Gwen said, "let's get inside."

We walked down the path to the front of the House, were greeted in the foyer by Luc and Lindsey, who'd returned from New York. He looked every bit the cowboy, from the jeans and boots—an exception to the Cadogan black dress code—to the tousled dark brown hair.

I made the introductions.

"Detective," Luc said, stepping forward with a handshake. "Good to meet you."

"Same here," she said and gave Lindsey a nod.

"We're going to take you downstairs into the guards' room. You'll have full access to the security feeds down there. Kelly, our guard captain, can tie you in to your unit comms."

"Good enough," Gwen said and glanced back at us. "Good luck."

"And to you."

"Be careful," Theo said, squeezing my hand before he and Petra followed them.

I blew out a breath, tried to calm my nerves. I knew I'd be fine once things were underway. It was the waiting that was hardest. The anticipation of what was to come.

"She won't hurt you," Connor said, and I looked back at him, nodded.

"I know. But I don't know her. I don't know what she'll say, or what she'll want, or what she'll demand of me. That's what makes me nervous."

"Alaska," Connor said, wrapping me in his arms. "If all else fails, we'll go to Alaska. They'll never find us there."

I snorted. "They'll never find *me* there. I'm an urban girl, and that's as sub-suburban as you can get. I want a coffeehouse on every corner."

He humphed, kissed me.

"Be smart. Be good. I'll be here, whatever the outcome."

"Same," I said, and brushed my fingers against his. It was time to end this.

TWENTY-THREE

Nicole Heart waited in my father's office. My father made the introductions, but I hardly heard a word he said.

Then he left us alone. We stood in the middle of his office, facing each other.

She was beautiful. She was a tall woman, with dark skin and a curvy figure. Her hair was closely cropped, emphasizing her dark eyes and thick lashes, her round cheekbones, generous mouth. She wore an ivory suit today in a fabric that skimmed her curves. And the power she'd been afforded skimmed all of her and put a faint tingle in the air.

"We haven't met," she said, her words soft, her tone lightly accented. "But I know of your work."

"Same," I said.

"Why do you think I'm here, Ms. Sullivan?"

"Because you believe I've broken *Canon* by turning a human despite her imminent death."

"Do you admit you've broken *Canon*?"

"I make no admission, other than changing Carlie."

"Only the barest distinction between those," she said with a small smile, clasping her hands in front of her.

"I was taught by my father."

Whether she considered that a threat or explanation, she didn't show it. She made a noncommittal sound. "Given the time that has already been allocated to this issue, let's get to the meat of it, shall we? You breached our law. That is plain. Although there were difficulties, Clive offered his terms, and they stand. Name the House that will Commend you and confirm you will submit to Testing."

"No."

"Then you will be taken to Atlanta and placed in seclusion until you can agree."

"No, I won't."

She watched me, predator assessing prey. "The manner of your making—the identity of your parents—does not give you license to act as you choose. Rules matter."

Now she sounded like Clive, although she was much more collected. "They do matter. But let's be honest, Ms. Heart. Rules are made up."

Her gaze snapped back to mine.

"Every rule," I said. "Just words decided by someone in power. But when you get to the core of it, it's not the words that matter. It's how they live in the world. The AAM's rule, this rule about making vampires, is old and it's cruel. It's inflexible."

"Rules aren't meant to be flexible. They're meant to be rules."

"You allow Rogues to make vampires."

"They do not command media attention."

That was a new one. "I do not command it. It is given to me, unwillingly. Regardless, I told no one about Carlie, nor is the media aware she was changed. But, now that you've mentioned it, if you persist in selectively enforcing the rules against me—if you persist in punishing me for saving a human against a monster—I'd be happy to involve the press. I believe they'd find I have a very interesting story to tell."

"Threats are beneath you."

"Threats are what I have. As you've pointed out, my name is

my burden and my leverage. You try to use it to make an example of me. I will use it to defend myself."

She watched me for a moment, those dark eyes cool and measuring. She still hadn't moved from her position a few feet away, hadn't so much as shifted her clasped hands. It took power, concentration, to exercise that kind of control.

So, naturally, I wanted to see if I could upset it. "You've wanted to have me tested for a very long time."

The satisfaction of seeing that mere flinch, the dilation of pupils, was a warm and comforting glow.

"There remain questions regarding the manner of your making."

The similarity of what she said and what I'd heard so many years ago sent a chill down my spine. No matter the outcome of this meeting, she was not my ally.

"No," I said. "There don't. No one has inquired about the manner of my making since the AAM's failed efforts to test me as a child. Efforts that were rejected."

"Ms. Sullivan, I am responsible for the safety of thousands of vampires. For helping them achieve a safe and productive immortality. You are an unknown. That makes you a threat."

"To you."

This time, her jaw worked, another chip in the glorious façade.

I held up a hand. "I'll save you the trouble of responding to that, and I'll tell you the same thing I told Clive. I have no interest in vampiric policies. I'm not even a member of my father's own House; if I had been, I'm fairly certain you wouldn't even have attempted this particular mission. I do not plan to build a vampire army, or to make any additional vampires. I do not want to be a Master. I worked for the Ombuds' office until one of your vampires accused me of a murder I did not commit. I enjoyed that work, and wish I was still doing it." The truth of that struck me in the gut.

"In short, Ms. Heart, I am not my father. I am not my mother. I am not a superhero or a secret weapon or an atrocity, or whatever other threats you and your vampires might have imagined. I'm just a vampire trying to do the right thing."

"A very pretty speech that solves nothing."

"I am not a problem to solve." I nearly threw up my hands, had to work to maintain my control. "If you were me, what would you have done?"

"I would have obeyed the law."

I looked at her for a long time. "Then I pity you for that."

My screen buzzed, and I pulled it out, found a message from Theo. LEVI SPOTTED ON FOOT TWO BLOCKS NORTH.

He was early, so it was negotiation time.

I put the screen back in my pocket. "I've made the AAM an offer. Leave Chicago with assurances you won't pursue this further, and I won't explain to the media why you're attempting to punish me."

"Rejected."

My smile was thin. "In that case, I'll also be explaining to the media that you've employed a dangerous vampire and his brother, who I'm fairly certain had full knowledge of his condition, for years. That you sent Levi to Chicago, where he attacked me, violated a human, and committed murder, and yet you have no idea where he is. I'll also be forced to ask why you're so focused on punishing me for breaking rules, but allowing them to break rules with impunity." I cocked my head at her, a move I'd seen my father make a thousand times before. "Is it animosity against Chicago, by chance?"

She was quiet for a very long time. And when her hands clenched tighter, knuckles whitening with it, I knew I had her.

"As long as you remember that you have no interest in my position, or in Masterdom, the AAM will agree to conclude this matter. Should those circumstances change . . . we will reevaluate."

It was my turn to watch her, to read the emotion in her eyes.

"Agreed," I said, "as I've no interest in either. And I will even make a show of good faith."

I walked to the office door, opened it, and found my father waiting.

We exchanged a nod. As I strode to the front door, I heard my father speaking with Nicole.

"Come with me," he said. "I believe you'll want to see this."

The air was chilly and dry, rustling the trees and flickering the torchlights. I tucked into my ear the tiny communication bud Lindsey offered on my way out the door, met Connor on the sidewalk.

He glanced back at the House.

"Resolved," I said quietly and tucked my arm into his. "Let's pretend to be lovey-dovey and take a walk." I led him to the path that ran along the edge of the property, not far from the wall Levi would have to scale to get through.

"Do recall your parents can hear you," came my mother's voice through the bud.

"Times when telepathy would be handy," I murmured, and leaned into Connor, two lovers taking a stroll through a garden on a beautiful late summer night.

"Location?" he whispered, pressing a kiss to my hair to cover the question.

"We're heat-tracking," Lindsey said. "We've got him outside the eastern wall, about twenty yards to your left. We can't get too close; we don't want to spook him."

Connor neatly switched positions to put him closer to the wall. I growled, but he put an arm over my shoulders. "I won't apologize for that."

"Your funeral," I murmured. "I don't need a shield."

"Mmm-hmm," Connor intoned. "It's a gorgeous night." He

raised his voice so Levi could hear. "I'm glad I have you all to myself. Your parents' House really is impressive."

"Moving toward you," Lindsey said. "He's on the wall."

"The stars are beautiful tonight," I said, lifting my eyes to the top of the wall. I couldn't see anything. But now that I'd experienced it, I could feel the soft vibration of Levi's glamour.

Connor's lips were at my ear. "Can you see him?"

I shook my head, just as the warning echoed through.

"He's on the ground!" came Lindsey's shout. "Moving toward you."

She finished the sentence just as a scream split the air. I thought, at first, it was a wounded animal. But floodlights poured visibility across the Cadogan grounds, putting trees and shrubs and benches in sharp relief.

And the vampire who ran toward us, handgun lifted. Levi looked worse in the harsh lights, as if he hadn't slept in days.

Connor and I split apart, both of us drawing weapons.

"Levi," I said, as he blinked in shock and surprise. "It's done. Put down the gun." Positions echoed through the earbud as guards and officers moved in, moved around and behind him.

"It's not done," he said, hand shaking. "And I've got silver fucking bullets now."

I was in front of Connor before he could object, shoving him backward as guards moved closer, but not close enough.

"Your fight is with me," I said. "Not Connor. Drop the gun."

"You protect him!" Levi cried out, his anguish obvious. "Even now. A fucking wolf."

"My fucking wolf," I said, putting a hand on my chest, a week's worth of fear and fury building, exploding. "You don't even know me. None of you know me—not a single member of the AAM has any idea who I am."

He lunged toward me, gun lifted. My roundhouse kick had the

gun flying, and Gwen jogged forward, badge raised and glowing in the moonlight like Excalibur.

"Chicago Police Department," she called out, as officers put him on his belly on the grass. "Levi, you are under arrest for the murder of the vampire known as Blake," Gwen said. "I understand your Master would like to have a word with you before you're put on a plane for extradition to Atlanta. And now, a word from our sponsors."

I grinned as a deputy stepped forward with zip ties. "You have the right to remain silent," he called out, and announced the rest of Levi's rights and responsibilities as the other CPD officers moved in, tightening their circle.

"That was almost disappointingly easy," I heard Petra murmur.

Famous last words.

There was chaos in my ear as people began to scream, to issue warnings. And then I watched Clive come running toward us.

"Nicole let him in," someone said. I think Theo.

"Get the hell away from him!" Clive pushed through the vampires to his brother, still on the ground and now sobbing into the grass.

"You hurt him," Clive said. He went to his knees as Nicole walked toward us beneath the floodlights, two more vampires behind her. Had she wanted Clive to see this? To witness it?

Vampires, I thought ruefully.

"He's not hurt," I said. "Just disappointed he couldn't shoot Connor with a silver fucking bullet." I was still pissed, apparently.

I walked toward them, leaned down toward Clive. "You knew," I said and was certain I was correct. "You knew he was broken and dangerous, and you let him keep his freedom. *You* broke the rules."

Rage all but boiled in his eyes now, spat from his lips. "You don't know anything. Everything was handed to you."

"No," I said. "It was not." If only he knew how hard my parents had worked to ensure I took nothing of my privilege for granted.

"You break any rules you want," he said. "Cadogan House constantly ignores the rules, and they are never punished. If he'd gotten in, he'd have been fixed. He'd have been better."

And there it was.

"Your brother needs help, Clive. But Cadogan House isn't the solution. It never was. And punishing me won't help Levi."

"But it will help me," he said. "I invoke the Rule of Satisfaction!"

Oh, the glorious irony, I thought silently, that I'd been denied my chance to fight him, and he'd called me out.

"Stand down," Nicole said. "Stand down, Clive. You have no basis to demand Satisfaction. The AAM's business here is concluded."

"No!" Clive said, throwing out an arm as if throwing off her authority. "I have personal reasons. She does as she pleases and it will stop."

"Clive—" she said again, the word a threat, but it was my turn. "I accept."

The words echoed across the lawn, so there was no doubt of my intentions. I felt magic blossom behind me, knew Connor and my parents didn't like it. But this was my fight.

Nicole's brows lifted. "It is unnecessary. Our business is done."

"My business with Clive is not done," I said, shifting my gaze to him as the same slow, maniacal smile I'd seen on Levi's face spread across his. "He has accused me of murder, of being a rule breaker. I've read the Rule of Satisfaction, too," I said, and enjoyed the shock in his face, probably that I knew anything of the *Canon*.

"I elect to fight with blades," I said, then looked at Nicole. "Does the AAM object?"

Nicole looked at me, then at Clive, and considered. The moment stretched so long crickets literally began to chirp in the intervening silence. I suspected her internal debate was simple: Would this fight rid her of one problem or create yet another?

After a moment, she nodded. "The AAM has no objection. The demand for Satisfaction may proceed."

I moved back and held out a hand, assuming someone would press a katana into it, and felt Connor's fingers brush against mine as he handed me my scabbard. "We protect each other," he whispered. "Go get him."

Clive unsheathed his sword.

"I will destroy you," he said. "I will fight for everyone who follows the rules and still gets fucked in the end."

"Life isn't fair, Clive. Welcome to immortality." I unsheathed my sword, light catching and sliding across the blade. "I'll fight for Levi," I stated, "because he didn't need rules. He needed help. I'll fight for Connor, who he attacked. I'll fight for Blake, who he killed. And I'll fight for Carlie, for every time I defend her life to you and those like you." I leered at him, disrespect dripping from my tone. "It was still worth it. It will always be worth it."

Clive screamed, and as I knew he would, lunged forward, blade outstretched.

Keep the eyes hidden, I told the monster, *and we'll fight him together.*

That had a thrill moving through me.

He swiped and we successfully blocked, but the blow ricocheted through my shoulder. If the monster could feel the pain, it ignored it, pushed back and swung again, pulling my dagger with my free hand. Clive swung again, and we used both blades to block this one, then push it back toward him. He grunted, reset, came forward again.

Some vampires fought like lovers—seduction with a blade.

Some fought like dancers, blade and body sinuous and smooth. Clive fought like a hammer—useful as a blunt instrument, but not much finesse. He had strength enough to issue blow after blow, but with the monster behind me, we were all but tireless.

He lunged forward and we flipped backward, then came up with a spinning dagger slice that cut a stripe across his shins. He cursed, struck downward. We jumped over the blade, hit the ground and rolled, and came up with sword and dagger crossed.

"Try again," I said, in that half voice that wasn't quite mine.

He looked confused, but wasted no time in jumping forward. This time he feinted left with the blade, but used a side kick that hit my left flank and pushed the air from my lungs. I jumped back, sucked in a breath, heard Connor growling beside me with growing impatience.

My fight, I thought. *My rules.* But he had a point. So I took the advance, using the katana to block while I stabbed at Clive with the dagger, catching his arm this time, then spinning away before he could strike back.

"For a favorite child of the AAM," I taunted, "you aren't especially good at fighting, Clive. Is that why you stood by and watched last time?"

"*Traitor,*" he muttered.

"Hmm. That sounds like something Levi would say."

"You aren't fit to speak his name," Clive roared, and he struck again, the blow forceful enough to send the dagger to the ground, hidden now in dewy grass.

"Brat," Connor murmured behind me. A warning that his patience was near its end.

"You never let me have any fun," I murmured and brought my blade down. Clive blocked it, and I saw his muscles quiver with the reverb of sword against sword.

He stared at me through locked blades, teeth gritted against the combined force of me and the monster he didn't know existed.

"You smell like wolf," he said. "Do you think that makes you special? Whoring yourself to a shifter?"

"None of us are special, Clive. We're all just vampires."

"You don't really believe that."

I stepped back, let my blade fall. This point, if no other, had to be made. "I absolutely believe that."

Thinking I'd conceded, he stepped forward. I spun around him, kicked the back of his knee. Too surprised to catch himself, Clive hit the ground, sword skittering away. What hadn't worked on Levi, ironically, worked on his brother. About damned time.

And then the tip of my katana was at his neck.

Clive went still—supernaturally still—but his eyes shifted, rose along the blade until they met mine.

"Yield," I said, lips curled in predatory victory.

His eyes went wide, then narrowed. "Are you too scared to kill me?"

"You are an idiot," I said quietly. "I'm not going to kill you. Not when I've got you on the ground." I leaned down, just a little. "I beat you. And that's more than enough for me."

He opened his mouth for more invective, and I pressed the blade harder, just enough to have a line of crimson appearing at his throat.

I could see it in his eyes. He may not have wanted to die, but he didn't want to yield, either. Didn't want to admit defeat, suffer the humiliation of it.

"Yield," I said again, utterly calm. His eyes wheeled, looking for escape, considering options.

"Last chance," I said.

"Fine," he threw out, like a verbal strike. "I fucking yield. But the AAM isn't done with you."

"Oh, it's done," Nicole said, stepping forward. "And it's done with you, as well."

I stepped back, sword still pointed, while Nicole and her vampires rushed forward. They lifted Clive to his feet.

Then she moved closer, the scent of peaches and tingle of magic lifting in the air. And she looked at me in silence for what felt like a very long time.

"I am not entirely sure what you are, Ms. Sullivan," she said quietly, so that only I could hear. "But you have acted honorably, even when others have not. I find that is a good test of character. To be absolutely clear," she called out, pinning Clive with a glare, "this matter has been concluded, and the AAM has no further questions of Elisa Sullivan respecting the making of the human known as Carlie Stone."

"Damn right you don't!"

We all froze. I knew that voice. I knew that tone. I looked back, and found Carlie on the edge of the crowd.

There actually *was* a party on the House's lawn. But it wasn't strangers or friends of the House. It was Roger Yuen. My parents. Uncle Malik. To my surprise, Gabriel Keene and four more shifters. And, to my utter shock, Ronan, and four more vampires who I guessed were from his coven.

They'd come here . . . for me? To side with me, and stand by me, because they believed I'd done right, or that the result made up for my rule breaking.

My throat tightened with emotion, and I was perilously close to tears.

"We're done," I managed to say to Nicole, then left her behind, strode toward Carlie.

She'd . . . blossomed. There was no other word for it. Vampirism had a way of honing features down to their most beautiful renderings, and she was no exception. Pale skin, long dark hair, and a wide smile that was instantly endearing. Every feature enhanced just enough to make it difficult to look away.

I hope she considered becoming a stronger version of herself at least some payment for the pain she'd have suffered during the transition.

"Hi," I said, feeling suddenly awkward. But her smile was brilliant.

"Hi!" Without hesitation, she wrapped me in a hug, squeezed tightly. "How are you?"

"I'm good," I said with a bubbling laugh. "How are you?"

"I'm fine," she said when she stepped back, mouth pursed in a pout. "But I didn't even get to unsheathe this thing." She pointed to the dagger at her belt. "And I've been training."

"Good! How's that going?"

"With your vamp genetics, pretty damn good." Her grin was wide and cheerful, and it tugged at my heart. She was so open, so willing to be vulnerable. That, I thought, made her exceptionally brave.

"Thank you for coming all this way," I said, and the most important question occurred to me. "Why are you here?"

"To support you, just in case the AAM got handsy. In, you know, an assholey way. Ronan got a call."

I glanced at Ronan, tall and dark skinned, with wide eyes and a thoughtful face. "A call?"

He gestured to Theo. "He seems like a very good friend," Ronan said.

"He is." I looked back at him. "And so are you."

His eyes widened.

"I was an ass, and you came anyway. So I'd say that makes you a very good friend."

His lips twitched. "I believe we both had some preconceived notions that led us both to say some regrettable things." He held out a hand. "Truce?"

I thought of Jonathan Black's deal, the insincerity of it. And the actual friendship this man offered.

"No," I said. "Friendship." He smiled as we shook on it. "I've got business to attend to. But if you're staying in town, you should come see Connor's town house. It's beautiful, and there's plenty of room for guests."

For my next act, I would make more animosity disappear.

"You asked them to come," I said, when I'd reached Theo and Connor. Theo looked back at me, a little smile tugging at one corner of his mouth.

"He did?" Connor asked, with a glint of appreciation in his eyes.

"Yeah. To stand up for me."

"Since the truth is out and I couldn't do this before . . ." Theo wrapped his arms around me, lifting me off my feet in a ferocious hug. "We missed you at the office this week."

"That was entirely your doing," I pointed out.

"Actually, it was my doing."

We turned back, found Roger Yuen walking toward us.

"You missed the action, boss," Theo said, putting me down again.

Roger smiled. "Nah, Gwen let me monitor from the CPD van, just in case you wanted more assistance. But I had the sense you'd want to handle this one on your own."

"I did. But thanks for keeping an eye out."

"You're welcome." He paused, added, "I considered it a job interview, actually."

Everyone looked at me. "A job interview?" I asked.

"For a full-time position with the OMB. You showed bravery, creativity, and when it came to the wire, decency. I'll apologize once again for putting you on leave. It's the cost, unfortunately, of transparency."

"I know. I don't like it, but I know. The job?" I prompted.

"Full-time," he said again. "You'd be an Assistant Ombudsman."

I watched him for a moment. "With an actual badge?"

His lips curled. "With an actual badge."

"And Theo is my partner."

Roger looked at Theo, who nodded. "Done," Roger said.

My final demand involved a rumor. Whispers in the darkest corners of the Internet, but never seen in real life. "I want a Leo's Coffee titanium card."

Theo snorted. "Free coffee for the lifetime of the holder? Total myth. And even if it weren't, you're immortal. There's no way they'd agree to that."

I'd taken a chance for exactly those reasons, with the hope of negotiating down to Leo's Coffee in the break room.

But Roger smiled with a knowing cant that said he had skills we hadn't even considered. "Also done."

"*It's real,*" Theo quietly said, wonder and hope in his voice. "*The titanium card is real.*"

"Big day for you," Roger said, squeezing Theo's arm. Then he held out a hand to me. "Welcome aboard, Ombud Sullivan."

We shook on it, and the deal was done.

Theo leaned toward me. "I want in on that card."

I snorted. "Dude, you do your own negotiating. My card, my coffee."

"Not a good way to begin a partnership," he said with amusement, then looked at Connor. "We good?"

"We were always good," Connor said, squeezing Theo's shoulder. "Doesn't mean I won't be an ass if she's in trouble."

"Same goes."

They shared one of those manly backslapping hugs that looked more painful than friendly, but whatever. My boys were friends again.

My parents were last; they'd waited for me away from the crowd. I looked at my father, who curved his fingers into a little heart.

Sweet and mortifying, both at the same time.

"Come here," he said, and opened his arms.

I obeyed, and worked very hard not to cry. Even as an adult, that look of love—all-encompassing and all-forgiving—made me weepy.

"You made your own path," he said. "It's not the path we would have chosen, but we're very proud of you."

"Thanks, Dad."

"As for your handling of the AAM . . ." There was deep satisfaction in his chuckle. "You are very much my daughter."

My mother snorted. "As if there was any doubt."

He shifted, looked at Connor. "I won't tell you to take care of her, because I know she can take care of herself. But you'll help her. You'll care for each other."

"We will," Connor said.

EPILOGUE

The next evening, there was one bit of work that needed to be resolved.

I went to the NAC building, was told Miranda was in the garage, and walked toward it, but then I stood outside the closed door for a moment and thought.

We protect each other.

That had become our creed, a kind of operating principle for our relationship. And now it was time for me to do my part, to protect what I could.

I opened the door, found her alone and working at one of the counters that lined the wall.

Now that I'd decided my course, I didn't waste any time. "We need to talk."

She looked up, dismissed me, looked away. "What do you want?"

"I want nothing from you. But you owe Connor a favor. I intend to see he collects."

She snorted. "I give exactly what I'm obliged to give. Loyalty to the Pack. Period."

"Do you?" I asked, cocking my head at her. "That's not what I've heard."

She stood up. "If you have something to say, then say it and get out."

"You're impatient, Miranda. That's part of your problem. The other part? Levi remembered you."

"Who the fuck is Levi?"

"He's a vampire. He's the member of the Compliance Bureau who took your call the night you ratted out your prince to a group of vampires."

For the first time in our acquaintance, she actually looked concerned about something I'd said. "I don't know what you're talking about."

"You do. You told him I turned Carlie."

She was quiet for a moment, probably rethinking her moves, her steps, then narrowed her eyes at me. "You have nothing. I hear he's as crazy as they come."

"He's disturbed," I agreed. "But his memory is intact. And I bet you used your own screen to call him, Miranda. The Ombudsman has Levi's screen now, and they're working on getting his records."

Her mouth firmed into a hard line, and her eyes narrowed into fulminating slits. "So what if I told. You broke the rules. You deserve to get punished."

"Maybe. But I wasn't the only one involved. I saved Carlie from the Pack. I saved Carlie *because* of the Pack. You reported me—and therefore the Pack—to the AAM. You nearly cost the prince his life. That's not very loyal."

She snorted, all bravado now, and not very convincing. "What do you know about loyalty? You don't even have a House."

"I don't need a House. I'm loyal to people who are worthy of my trust, which does not include you. Doesn't Gabriel need to know you aren't trustworthy? That you turned on the Pack? On his son?"

All the color drained from her face. She knew what I had now, and what I intended to do with it. Or what I wanted her to believe I intended . . .

She turned her arm, showed me the wound she still hadn't shifted to heal.

"Oh, I know you were cut. But Levi didn't do it."

"Then it was some other vampire."

"No, it wasn't." I tilted my head, made a point of looking at the laceration. "I'd bet, if we have a doctor examine it, they'll be able to tell us the angle of the wound. Prove that you're the one who used the knife on yourself."

She fumed in silence for a full minute. "What do you want? Money?"

"No." I thought of the salary I'd just agreed to.

"Then what?"

"Loyalty to Connor. He'll be Apex one day. We all know it. So stop working against him, and start supporting him. And if you don't, I'll have to tell everyone what I know. And what you did."

Miranda looked at me for a long, quiet moment. "I don't like you. And I don't like you with Connor. He's not even *immortal*."

Those four words were sharp as a slap, a reminder of a very important difference between shifters and vampires. A reminder that, no matter how great our love, his life would be far shorter than mine. And I might live an eternity without him.

I winced and watched the flare of knowledge in her eyes. And knew I'd given her new ammunition to use against me.

She cocked a hip against the counter, confidence renewed. "I also don't like that you get away with shit because of who you are. But the Pack is my family. So fine. I'll support him."

I wasn't sure I believed her. But that had to be enough for now.

"Good," I said. "You do anything that undermines his claim to the Pack, his rise to Apex, and every shifter in the country will know what you did. You'll have nowhere to run. Nowhere to hide."

She took a step forward. "You fuck the Pack, and you'll have nowhere to run. Nowhere to hide."

"Understood," I said.

A stiff nod, and she turned away. We weren't going to be friends, Miranda and me. But I didn't need to be friends with her. I just needed her to do her part.

I left her to her work and went back outside, found Connor waiting by the SUV, eyebrow quirked. "Business?" he asked.

It was only because of the question that I finally sensed the magic we'd spilled into the air. Two strong women in strategic combat.

"Business," I said.

For a moment, I considered repeating the fear she'd managed to dig free, the thorn she'd so neatly uncovered, that I'd been ignoring since I'd returned to Chicago.

Connor was mortal. I was not.

But I wasn't ready. I wasn't capable of considering that weakness right now. So that particular trauma would have to wait.

"All done here," I said. "Let's go to your town house. I thought I could spend the night—just the two of us. Assuming that espresso machine has been installed."

His eyes flashed gold, and then his body was against mine, his mouth on mine, inciting and teasing as he slid his hands into my hair. He was strong, beautiful, and already powerfully aroused. Darkness a cloak around us, he deepened the kiss, throat grumbling with pleasure.

"As delicious as this is," I murmured, my own breath ragged, "getting arrested for public indecency isn't how I'd like to spend the evening."

His teeth found my earlobe, tugged. "The Pack won't report me. And even if they did, it would be worth every damned second."

I had absolutely no doubt, and felt like I was riding a wave of magic, of infatuation.

No, that wasn't fair. This wasn't either of those things. It was simpler and more complex.

It was love.

Connor kept staring at me with that look on his face. The look of victory—and anticipation.

"What?" I asked, feeling defensive.

"Is there anything else you'd like to say?"

I narrowed my eyes; Connor just beamed. "Do you want to say it at the same time?" he asked.

"I don't know what you're talking about," I said. "And even if I did, I wouldn't agree to that deal because I'd end up putting myself out there and you'd say you like graphic novels or pickles or carburetors or something."

"That's quite a list," he said, lips twitching. "And I think an attack on my character."

"Well deserved," I said dryly, but kept looking at him, kept smiling at him. Kept marveling that we'd gotten here. And could see the same wonderment in his eyes.

He brushed a lock of hair from my face, tucked it behind my ear. And looked at me as if I was a miracle.

"I love you," I said, and felt tears shimmer again, but pushed them relentlessly back.

"I love you, too. And pickles, apparently."

I rolled my eyes. "Predictable."

"No, I'm not. And you certainly aren't. And I love you in spite of it." He leaned down, pressed his forehead to mine. "Who would have thought, brat?"

"Not me, puppy. Not me."

He traced a finger along my shoulder. "Let's go home. I have plans for you."

I was entirely on board.

Read on for an excerpt from the first
Chicagoland Vampires Novel,

SOME GIRLS BITE

Available now

ONE
The Change

At first, I wondered if it was karmic punishment. I'd sneered at the fancy vampires, and as some kind of cosmic retribution, I'd been made one. Vampire. Predator. Initiate into one of the oldest of the twelve vampire Houses in the United States.

And I wasn't just *one* of them.

I was one of the best.

But I'm getting ahead of myself. Let me begin by telling you how I became a vampire, a story that starts weeks before my twenty-eighth birthday, the night I completed the transition. The night I awoke in the back of a limousine, three days after I'd been attacked walking across the University of Chicago campus.

I didn't remember all the details of the attack. But I remembered enough to be thrilled to be alive. To be shocked to be alive.

In the back of the limousine, I squeezed my eyes shut and tried to unpack the memory of the attack. I'd heard footsteps, the sound muffled by dewy grass, before he grabbed me. I'd screamed and kicked, tried to fight my way out, but he pushed me down. He was preternaturally strong—supernaturally strong—and he bit my neck with a predatory ferocity that left little doubt about who he was. What he was.

Vampire.

But while he tore into skin and muscle, he didn't drink; he didn't have time. Without warning, he'd stopped and jumped away, running between buildings at the edge of the main quad.

My attacker temporarily vanquished, I'd raised a hand to the crux of my neck and shoulder, felt the sticky warmth. My vision was dimming, but I could see the wine-colored stain across my fingers clearly enough.

Then there was movement around me. Two men.

The men my attacker had been afraid of.

The first of them had sounded anxious. "He was fast. You'll need to hurry, Liege."

The second had been unerringly confident. "I'll get it done."

He pulled me up to my knees, and knelt behind me, a supportive arm around my waist. He wore cologne—soapy and clean.

I tried to move, to give some struggle, but I was fading.

"Be still."

"She's lovely."

"Yes," he agreed. He suckled the wound at my neck. I twitched again, and he stroked my hair. "Be still."

I recalled very little of the next three days, of the genetic restructuring that transformed me into a vampire. Even now, I only carry a handful of memories. Deep-seated, dull pain—shocks of it that bowed my body. Numbing cold. Darkness. A pair of intensely green eyes.

In the limo, I felt for the scars that should have marred my neck and shoulders. The vampire that attacked me hadn't taken a clean bite—he'd torn at the skin at my neck like a starved animal. But the skin was smooth. No scars. No bumps. No bandages. I pulled my hand away and stared at the clean pale skin—and the short nails, perfectly painted cherry red.

The blood was gone—and I'd been manicured.

Staving off a wash of dizziness, I sat up. I was wearing different clothes. I'd been in jeans and a T-shirt. Now I wore a black cock-tail dress, a sheath that fell to just below my knees, and three-inch-high black heels.

That made me a twenty-seven-year-old attack victim, clean and absurdly scar-free, wearing a cocktail dress that wasn't mine. I knew, then and there, that they'd made me one of them.

The Chicagoland Vampires.

It had started eight months ago with a letter, a kind of vampire manifesto first published in the *Sun-Times* and *Trib*, then picked up by papers across the country. It was a coming out, an an-nouncement to the world of their existence. Some humans be-lieved it a hoax, at least until the press conference that followed, in which three of them displayed their fangs. Human panic led to four days of riots in the Windy City and a run on water and canned goods sparked by public fear of a vampire apocalypse. The feds finally stepped in, ordering Congressional investigations, the hearings obsessively filmed and televised in order to pluck out every detail of the vampires' existence. And even though they'd been the ones to step forward, the vamps were tight-lipped about those details—the fang bearing, blood drinking, and night walk-ing the only facts the public could be sure about.

Eight months later, some humans were still afraid. Others were obsessed. With the lifestyle, with the lure of immortality, with the vampires themselves. In particular, with Celina Desaulniers, the glamorous Windy City she-vamp who'd apparently orchestrated the coming-out, and who'd made her debut during the first day of the Congressional hearings.

Celina was tall and slim and sable-haired, and that day she wore a black suit snug enough to give the illusion that it had been poured onto her body. Looks aside, she was obviously smart and savvy, and she knew how to twist humans around her fingers. To wit: The senior senator from Idaho had asked her what she planned to do now that vampires had come out of the closet.

She'd famously replied in dulcet tones, "I'll be making the most of the dark."

The twenty-year Congressional veteran had smiled with such dopey-eyed lust that a picture of him made the front page of the *New York Times*.

No such reaction from me. I'd rolled my eyes and flipped off the television.

I'd made fun of them, of her, of their pretensions.

And in return, they'd made me like them.

Wasn't karma a bitch?

Now they were sending me back home, but returning me differently. Notwithstanding the changes my body had endured, they'd glammed me up, cleaned me of blood, stripped me of clothing, and repackaged me in their image.

They killed me. They healed me. They changed me.

The tiny seed, that kernel of distrust of the ones who'd made me, rooted.

I was still dizzy when the limousine stopped in front of the Wicker Park brownstone I shared with my roommate, Mallory. I wasn't sleepy, but groggy, mired in a haze across my consciousness that felt thick enough to wade through. Drugs, maybe, or a residual effect of the transition from human to vampire.

Mallory stood on the stoop, her shoulder-length ice blue hair shining beneath the bare bulb of the overhead light. She looked anxious, but seemed to be expecting me. She wore flannel pajamas patterned with sock monkeys. I realized it was late.

The limousine door opened, and I looked toward the house and then into the face of a man in a black uniform and cap who'd peeked into the backseat.

"Ma'am?" He held out a hand expectantly.

My fingers in his palm, I stepped onto the asphalt, my ankles wobbly in the stilettos. I rarely wore heels, jeans being my preferred uniform. Grad school didn't require much else.

I heard a door shut. Seconds later, a hand gripped my elbow. My gaze traveled down the pale, slender arm to the bespectacled face it belonged to. She smiled at me, the woman who held my arm, the woman who must have emerged from the limo's front seat.

"Hello, dear. We're home now. I'll help you inside, and we'll get you settled."

Grogginess making me acquiescent, and not really having a good reason to argue anyway, I nodded to the woman, who looked to be in her late fifties. She had a short, sensible bob of steel gray hair and wore a tidy suit on her trim figure, carrying herself with a professional confidence. As we progressed down the sidewalk, Mallory moved cautiously down the first step, then the second, toward us.

"Merit?"

The woman patted my back. "She'll be fine, dear. She's just a little dizzy. I'm Helen. You must be Mallory?"

Mallory nodded, but kept her gaze on me.

"Lovely home. Can we go inside?"

Mallory nodded again and traveled back up the steps. I began to follow, but the woman's grip on my arm stopped me. "You go by Merit, dear? Although that's your last name?"

I nodded at her.

She smiled patiently. "The newly risen utilize only a single name. Merit, if that's what you go by, would be yours. Only the Masters of each House are allowed to retain their last names. That's just one of the rules you'll need to remember." She leaned in conspiratorially. "And it's considered déclassé to break the rules."

Her soft admonition sparked something in my mind, like the beam of a flashlight in the dark. I blinked at her. "Some would consider changing a person without their consent déclassé, Helen."

The smile Helen fixed on her face didn't quite reach her eyes. "You were made a vampire in order to save your life, Merit. Consent is irrelevant." She glanced at Mallory. "She could probably use a glass of water. I'll give you two a moment."

Mallory nodded, and Helen, who carried an ancient-looking leather satchel, moved past her into the brownstone. I walked up the remaining stairs on my own, but stopped when I reached Mallory. Her blue eyes swam with tears, a frown curving her cupid's bow mouth. She was extraordinarily, classically pretty, which was the reason she'd given for tinting her hair with packets of blue Kool-Aid. She claimed it was a way for her to distinguish herself. It was unusual, sure, but it wasn't a bad look for an ad executive, for a woman defined by her creativity.

"You're—" She shook her head, then started again. "It's been three days. I didn't know where you were. I called your parents when you didn't come home. Your dad said he'd handle it. He told me not to call the police. He said someone had called him, told him you'd been attacked but were okay. That you were healing. They told your dad they'd bring you home when you were ready. I got a call a few minutes ago. They said you were on your way home." She pulled me into a fierce hug. "I'm gonna beat the shit out of you for not calling."

Mal pulled back, gave me a head-to-toe evaluation. "They said—you'd been changed."

I nodded, tears threatening to spill over.

"So you're a vampire?" she asked.

"I think. I just woke up or . . . I don't know."

"Do you feel any different?"

"I feel . . . slow."

Mallory nodded with confidence. "Effects of the change, probably. They say that happens. Things will settle." Mallory would know; unlike me, she followed all the vamp-related news. She offered a weak smile. "Hey, you're still Merit, right?"

Weirdly, I felt a prickle in the air emanating from my best friend and roommate. A tingle of something electric. But still sleepy, dizzy, I dismissed it.

"I'm still me," I told her.

And I hoped that was true.

The brownstone had been owned by Mallory's great-aunt until her death four years ago. Mallory, who lost her parents in a car accident when she was young, inherited the house and everything in it, from the chintzy rugs that covered the hardwood floors, to the antique furniture, to the oil paintings of flower vases. It wasn't chic, but it was home, and it smelled like it—lemon-scented wood polish, cookies, dusty coziness. It smelled the same as it had three days ago, but I realized that the scent was deeper. Richer.

Improved vampire senses, maybe?

When we entered the living room, Helen was sitting at the edge of our gingham-patterned sofa, her legs crossed at the ankles. A glass of water sat on the coffee table in front of her.

"Come in, ladies. Have a seat." She smiled and patted the couch. Mallory and I exchanged a glance and sat down. I took the seat next to Helen. Mallory sat on the matching love seat that faced the couch. Helen handed me the glass of water.

I brought it to my lips, but paused before sipping. "I can—eat and drink things other than blood?"

Helen's laugh tinkled. "Of course, dear. You can eat whatever you'd like. But you'll need blood for its nutritional value." She leaned toward me, touched my bare knee with the tips of her fingers. "And I daresay you'll enjoy it!" She said the words like she was imparting a delicious secret, sharing scandalous gossip about her next-door neighbor.

I sipped, discovered that water still tasted like water. I put the glass back on the table.

Helen tapped her hands against her knees, then favored us both with a bright smile. "Well, let's get to it, shall we?" She reached into the satchel at her feet and pulled out a dictionary-sized leather-bound book. The deep burgundy cover was inscribed in embossed gold letters—*Canon of the North American Houses, Desk Reference*. "This is everything you need to know about joining Cadogan House. It's not the full *Canon*, obviously, as the series is voluminous, but this will cover the basics."

"Cadogan House?" Mallory asked. "Seriously?"

I blinked at Mallory, then Helen. "What's Cadogan House?"

Helen looked at me over the top of her horn-rimmed glasses. "That's the House that you'll be Commended into. One of Chicago's three vampire Houses—Navarre, Cadogan, Grey. Only the Master of each House has the privilege of turning new vampires. You were turned by Cadogan's Master—"

"Ethan Sullivan," Mallory finished.

Helen nodded approvingly. "That's right."

I lifted brows at Mallory.

"Internet," she said. "You'd be amazed."

Photo by Dana Damewood Photography

Chloe Neill is the *New York Times* and *USA Today* bestselling author of the Captain Kit Brightling, Heirs of Chicagoland, Chicagoland Vampires, Devil's Isle, and Dark Elite novels. She was born and raised in the South, but now makes her home in the Midwest, where she lives with her gamer husband and their bosses/dogs, Baxter and Scout. Chloe is a voracious reader and obsessive Maker of Things; the crafting rotation currently involves baking and quilting. She believes she is exceedingly witty; her husband has been known to disagree.

Ready to find
your next great read?

Let us help.

Visit prh.com/nextread

Penguin
Random
House